"Harvey, considered to be the 'it girl' of Southern fiction, introduces the first novel in the Peachtree Bluff Series this spring. Child, this book is everything! We're hoping to see this soapy read on the Hallmark Channel."

—Jamey Giddens, *Daytime Confidential*

"Full of heart, emotion, and Southern charm . . ."

—*PopSugar*

"If you're looking for a new series to get lost into, this story of three sisters and their mother will have you flying through the pages."

—*Glitter Guide*

the secret *to* southern charm

ALSO FROM KRISTY WOODSON HARVEY
AND GALLERY BOOKS

Slightly South of Simple

the secret
to southern
charm

A NOVEL

Kristy Woodson Harvey

G

GALLERY BOOKS

New York   London   Toronto   Sydney   New Delhi

G

Gallery Books
An Imprint of Simon & Schuster, Inc.
1230 Avenue of the Americas
New York, NY 10020

First Gallery Books hardcover edition April 2018

GALLERY BOOKS and colophon are registered trademarks
of Simon & Schuster, Inc.

For information about special discounts for bulk purchases,
please contact Simon & Schuster Special Sales at 1-866-506-1949
or business@simonandschuster.com.

The Simon & Schuster Speakers Bureau can bring authors to your live event.
For more information or to book an event, contact the Simon & Schuster Speakers
Bureau at 1-866-248-3049 or visit our website at www.simonspeakers.com.

Interior design by Davina Mock-Maniscalco

Manufactured in the United States of America

10   9   8   7   6   5   4   3   2   1

Library of Congress Cataloging-in-Publication Data

Names: Woodson Harvey, Kristy, author.
Title: The secret to southern charm : a novel / Kristy Woodson Harvey.
Description: First Gallery Books trade paperback edition. | New York :
    Gallery Books, 2018. | Series: The Peachtree Bluff series ; 2 |
    Identifiers: LCCN 2017058399 (print) | LCCN 2018001545 (ebook) | ISBN
    9781501158117 (ebook) | ISBN 9781501158100 (paperback) | ISBN
    9781501195242 (hardcover)
Subjects: LCSH: Domestic fiction. | BISAC: FICTION / Contemporary Women. |
    FICTION / Family Life. | FICTION / Romance / Contemporary.
Classification: LCC PS3623.O6785 (ebook) | LCC PS3623.O6785 S43 2018 (print)
    | DDC 813/.6—dc23
LC record available at https://lccn.loc.gov/2017058399

ISBN 978-1-5011-9524-2
ISBN 978-1-5011-5810-0 (pbk)
ISBN 978-1-5011-5811-7 (ebook)

To my mother-in-law, Dottie Williams Harvey,

who loves a good story as much as I do

Praise for Kristy Woodson Harvey

"A major new voice in Southern fiction."

—Elin Hilderbrand, *New York Times* bestselling author

"Harvey pulls the reader into the hearts and souls of her characters."

—Heather Gudenkauf, *New York Times* bestselling author

"Southern fiction at its best. . . . Beautifully written."

—Eileen Goudge, *New York Times* bestselling author

"Sweet as sweet tea on the outside and strong as steel on the inside. . . . Kristy Harvey is a natural."

—Ann Garvin, author of *On Maggie's Watch* and *The Dog Year*

Praise for *Slightly South of Simple*

"Kristy Woodson Harvey really knows how to tell a southern tale. Every single time her stories unwind gently, like a soft wind in Georgia, then that wind catches you off guard and throws you into her characters' tumultuous lives. *Slightly South of Simple* is the same. One gracious, old home inherited from Grandma, one mother who has so many secrets if the walls talked they would pour out like lemonade on a hot summer day, and three headstrong sisters, all working their way through the chaotic mess and joy of life, together. I loved it."

—Cathy Lamb, *New York Times* bestselling author

"Kristy Woodson Harvey cuts to the heart of what it means to be a born-and-bred Southerner, complete with the unique responsibilities, secrets and privileges that conveys. Discover four women who are at once different yet utterly the same, and a town that you won't ever want to leave. Interior design, family secrets, life on the coast . . . it's easy to see why everyone is buzzing about *Slightly South of Simple*."

—Cassandra King, author of *The Sunday Wife*
and *The Same Sweet Girls*

"Heartfelt and warm, *Slightly South of Simple* deftly explores the familial ties that bind us—and those that have the power to break us. Kristy Woodson Harvey's cast of characters—and the charming beach town of Peachtree Bluff—will crawl into your soul and stay there."

—Colleen Oakley, author of *Close Enough to Touch*

"Fans of Nancy Thayer and Patti Callahan Henry will devour this story of the first of three sisters, the men in their lives, and the mother who bonds them all."

—*Booklist*

"Harvey's devotion to realistic character development pays off by the end of the novel, which provides clear resolutions to some plots and leaves other hanging in a way that practically begs for a sequel . . . *Slightly South of Simple* is so warm, inviting and real . . ."

—*Bookpage*

"My prediction is that writers come and writers go, but Kristy Woodson Harvey is here to stay. The warmth, wit, and wisdom of this novel pave her way into the exclusive sisterhood of southern writers."

—*Huffington Post*

"With a charming, coastal Southern setting, *Slightly South of Simple* is a heartfelt story about the universal themes of love, loss, forgiveness and family. I'm thrilled to hear that this book is part of a series and look forward to getting to know this cast of strong Southern women even better."

—*Deep South Magazine*

home

sloane

Time had lost its meaning. I only realized it was night because the water outside my bedroom window at my mother's home in Peachtree Bluff, Georgia, wasn't blue anymore. It was black and shining like fresh-paved asphalt. But inside, in my room, on my TV, it wasn't night. It was Saturday morning, the third precious birthday of my son Adam, Jr., or AJ, as we called him. My strong, national hero of a husband, in his off-duty khaki shorts and collared shirt, was holding our other son, six-month-old Taylor, in one arm. I was behind the camera cooing, "Smile for Daddy one more time. Can you smile for Daddy?" Taylor smiled. Who wouldn't smile for the handsome man holding him?

It was almost funny to see that six-foot-three soldier with his big, sculpted arms and huge hands made for protecting holding that tiny baby. But Adam wasn't just a strong and loyal soldier. He was my husband. He was my boys' father. He was my home.

His arms were the only place I had truly felt safe, special, and loved. His smile was the one that changed my life, had convinced me to marry, to have children, to put myself out there and love this big. His heart was the one that, after a decade of feeling so terrorized by my father's death, had made me feel safe again. Adam had changed absolutely everything.

His dark hair, peppered with gray, was buzzed short. His kind brown eyes twinkled at me through the camera as he said, "Three, Sloane. Can you believe he's three?"

We were in front of our town house on post in North Carolina. Adam liked the idea of us being in a town home, of having other families close by. He didn't say it, but he liked the idea of other families being close by because he wouldn't always be around. It was inevitable. He felt like we were safe here when he was away.

The video panned over our house, a sweet Carolina blue with a front porch on a street, like all the streets on post, named after a World War II battle campaign. My mother had decorated the generic four-bedroom interior, converting one of the bedrooms into a playroom and sparing no expense on the open-floor-plan living room, dining room, and kitchen downstairs. It was almost embarrassingly beautiful.

We shared a driveway with my friend Maryanne and her husband, Tom, who was a part of Adam's unit, and their four kids. Tom called, "Hey, Sarge!" and gave Adam a double thumbs-up. We were all still basking in the glow of Adam's promotion to sergeant first class. There were a lot of perks that came with the job.

But hands down the perk that meant the most to Adam

was the respect, the feeling of a job well done. Junior enlisted soldiers would come to him, asking for advice, wanting his opinion. He always said he was raising men, and he didn't just mean his sons. Those boys were his now, even though he wasn't much older than some of them. It was his job to protect them, to instill in them morals, values, and a sense of pride in their country and in themselves.

Adam was an imposing man, a strong leader, but he also had a kind heart. Maybe the Army didn't care about that. But I had to think his empathetic nature was a factor in his promotion.

We loved living there, surrounded by other military families, the only ones who could truly understand the life we had chosen.

Four of our favorite couples and their small children were scattered around our postage-stamp front yard, each of them, from the largest officer to Maryanne's newborn baby, wearing a Mickey Mouse party hat. AJ was attempting to ride his new mini scooter through the grass, the red Keds and white Jon Jon with the red fire truck Mom had sent him for his birthday seeming more than a little out of place amidst the other children in their shorts and T-shirts.

My husband had protested the outfit, but I had simply kissed him and said, "Oh, sweetheart, he's only little once. Let me have this."

Adam had pulled me to him then, kissed me longer, and said, teasingly, "If you get the girly outfits, I get buying him a BB gun for his sixth birthday."

This was a common joke between us. I was, ironically, very anti-gun. He was a soldier, a card-carrying member of the NRA, a proud Second Amendment supporter. We would never agree on this. We would never agree, in fact, on a number of things. But that's what made us work.

Back on the screen we were all singing, "Happy birthday, dear AJ! Happy birthday to you!"

We cheered as it took him not one, not two, but three tries to blow out the three candles on his cake.

"Third time's the charm?" Adam asked me, looking into the camera.

We both laughed, sharing that private moment, my favorite man in all the world holding one of our sons, his arm around the other.

Adam smiled into the camera, that special smile he reserved just for me, a secret we would never let the rest of the world in on. I hit pause on my sticky remote. Sticky from what I couldn't say. Popsicle? Go-gurt?

I pulled the two down comforters I had wrapped around me up closer to my chin, trying to soothe the perceptible chill that ran through me as my mind pulled out of that world, where Adam was here and we were happy, and back into the present, the real world where life was bleak, empty, and so cold it felt like the depths of the arctic instead of a seventy-eight-degree night in Georgia.

My bed was covered with letters Adam had written me over the years, the ones I carried in a leather portfolio my mom had gotten me when I was accepted into art school. Whenever I traveled, it was the first thing that went into my suitcase. This trip to Peachtree had been no exception. A few of the letters fluttered when I disturbed the comforter.

I glanced over at the nightstand to see my dinner untouched on its tray. My mom was trying, bless her heart. I almost smiled because nothing ever changed, not really. I did the same thing with my sons now, putting the broccoli on their plates even if I knew they wouldn't take a single bite.

The mere thought of eating turned my stomach, made bile rise up the back of my throat. I couldn't remember the last time I had even gotten out of this bed or had a sip of water. I certainly hadn't bathed in far too long. How long had it been since I heard Adam was MIA? Two days, a week, a month? It terrified me. Who had been taking care of my children? Even if I couldn't eat, I would bathe tomorrow. I would face my boys. But this was something I thought every day.

I looked back at the TV, studying Adam's smiling face, so joyful and alive. He was my home. He was my everything. I sank even deeper into the covers, and the sobs, so powerful they seemed like they were in danger of stealing the very life from me, overtook me as I realized it: I may never be home again.

TWO

red sky at night

ansley

The sun had nearly set when I sank into the plush cushion of the outdoor sofa on my front porch in Peachtree Bluff. Despite my exhaustion, anxiety, and sorrow, there was something about this porch and this particular sunset, a burning red and hot orange, that always soothed my mind.

My grandson Taylor's fever from the day before seemed to have finally broken, and I hoped beyond hope that AJ, snuggled safely in my bed instead of his own, wouldn't be woken again by nightmares.

I looked down at the piles of sand on the front porch, the clumps that had fallen out when AJ decided to strip off his bathing suit and run naked through the sprinklers. That little rascal. I smiled. That was the thing about children. All day, the stinkers can drive you nuts, but the minute they're asleep, you want to gaze at them, drink them in, suppress the urge to wake them for one more cuddle, one more giggle, one more moment in time.

"Do you think I should wake Taylor to give him more Tylenol before I go to bed?" I asked my mom. The thought made me cringe. There would be bribing, bargaining, and selling my soul. Taylor would whine and wriggle until I thought I would lose my mind and promise candy, a trip to the toy store, a pony—anything to make this stop. Then he would finally let me shoot the Tylenol in his mouth, take a sip of water, and reach out for the Popsicle I would have ready to take the edge off the taste. I didn't want to do it. But I loved those grandbabies more than life.

I looked beside me at Mom, awaiting her sage answer, and almost laughed. She could have been on a greeting card, dressed as she was in a floral, zip-front housecoat, her hair tightly wrapped in the curlers she would sleep in, her pink satin bedroom slippers hugging her slender feet. Although the frequent Botox and touch-up sessions from her dermatologist in Florida would have indicated otherwise, Mom had been a fixture on this wide front porch, which originally belonged to her parents, for more than eighty years.

I had replaced my grandmother's matching rockers with cozy teak chairs and a couch, small white Saarinen end tables, and a teak dining table and chairs on the opposite end. It was the best porch in the world, and I never wanted to leave. Maybe this was why my grandmother had left the house to me in her will. She knew how much I adored this home, that I was the only one capable of loving it as much as she did.

"Darling," Mom said, pulling one of the sea-blue Serena and Lily herringbone throws off the back of the sofa and wrapping it around her shoulders, "if the child's fever spikes in the night, he will wake up. Good heavens, what do you think the pioneers did?"

I laughed, sinking back into one of the new Dalmatian-print throw pillows I had just gotten. They accentuated this sweeping white clapboard home, situated on the water a block from downtown, with the black shutters I had added after much ado—and digging up a photo from the late 1800s that proved to the historical association that there had once been shutters on the house and, as such, if I could copy them exactly, I could replace them.

I could hear Emerson's and Caroline's voices wafting down from the uncovered, upstairs porch with its six outdoor loungers perfect for sunbathing. My friend and handyman Hippie Hal had added a platform for yoga at the end of the porch, outside the bay window of my bedroom, the largest of the five in the main house.

I shook my head. "I don't know, Mom. I would have made a very poor pioneer."

She looked at me seriously. "That you would, darling."

In contrast to my mother, I was still wearing the tailored tan-and-white-striped shirtdress I'd had on since I showered from my day at the beach with my rambunctious grandsons. Caroline had picked out this dress for me, and I absolutely loved it. It hit right at the knee and was cinched at the waist. It reminded me of an updated 1950s housewife frock, which, with the cooking, cleaning, and child rearing, I basically was—minus the husband, of course.

I wished I could be a little more like my mother, comfortable enough to be on my front porch in my bathrobe. But the tourists walking by from downtown deterred me. Had I said that to my mother, she would have replied, "It's your damn front porch. If you want to sit out here stark naked, you should."

I pulled the cork out of the open bottle of rosé and poured "just a splash," as Mom would say, into each of our oversized Riedel wineglasses. Her splash was more like a third of the bottle, but who was I to judge? The woman was old enough to make her own decisions. And she would.

I took a sip, trying to dull the pain that, while Emerson and Caroline were up there sharing the secrets of sisters, Sloane, my little wounded bird, was entrenched in the darkness of her room, in the pitch black of her new reality. I took a deep breath and felt a sob welling up within me, but I suppressed it.

I looked into my mother's blue eyes, the same eyes I saw each time I looked at my own face in the mirror, and I could feel her strength, the strength I had always borrowed during the toughest moments of my life.

These past few months with my girls back in Peachtree Bluff had been one of those hard times, one of those periods in their lives when, though I wanted to save them, protect them, shelter them, I couldn't. Yet again, the universe had delivered challenges for my grown daughters whom I had loved and wanted so much, those children whom I had sacrificed for, crossed that line between right and wrong quite a few times for.

I could not erase the fact that Caroline's husband, James, had cheated on her with a supermodel or that her son had been born in the midst of that, and I could not bring Sloane's husband, who was missing in action in Iraq, home.

Quite a few times I had thought that at least Emerson, my youngest, was OK. But I sensed something was slightly askew with her, too. Maybe it was that, though she was filming her biggest movie to date, she hadn't quite found the acting success she had dreamed of. Maybe it was that she hadn't found the true love she dreamed of—or maybe, I had to consider, that was only my wish for her.

The reality was that I couldn't even handle my own love life, much less hers. So I sat on the front porch, beside my mother, the person who made me feel perhaps the most complicated emotions of all, the one who, though I knew she loved me unconditionally, never felt the way about me that I do about my girls, never felt the need to change it or fix it.

She took a sip of her wine, and while she looked out over the water, the sunset making it nearly the same shade as her dark rosé, I looked at her. I wondered what was happening in her mind, what complicated firing of synapses was taking place to make her a little different these days.

But breaking me out of my thoughts, she said, "Red sky at night, sailor's delight."

It's something she had said to me countless times throughout my life, but this time I felt slow tears rolling down my cheeks. Adam loved to fish, and this red sky would have meant that, in the morning, offshore conditions would be perfect.

It was an ordinary phrase, yet for my daughter, nothing was ordinary, nothing was right. Sloane's entire life had been turned upside down in one moment. I thought, unfairly, cruelly, that this was Adam's fault. He had always wanted to be more than a husband and a father. Why couldn't that be enough for him? Why couldn't he have a normal job, with regular hours that let him get back home to his young family?

Mom squeezed the top of my arm but didn't say a word. What was there to say?

"What do I do?" I whispered.

She shook her head. "You can't fix this for her, Ansley."

I shrugged. "I know that, but I can't even get her out of bed." I paused and took a deep breath. I didn't want to say it out loud. But I had to. "It has been almost three weeks, Mom. I'm afraid if she doesn't get out of that bed now, she never will."

I had spent countless hours Googling depression, calling doctor friends, and buying books that, due to my status as grandmother-turned-primary-caregiver for two toddlers, had sat practically untouched on my bedside table. But the reality remained. I had already learned about depression in the worst way, which might also be the best way: firsthand experience. I knew what it was like to find out your husband was dead, that you were the only one left to fight for your family. But Sloane wasn't there. Not yet. She needed help. But how could I help someone who didn't want it?

Caroline, Emerson, and I had been entertaining Sloane's boys constantly, trying to distract them from the fact that the only time they saw their mother was when they crawled into bed with her. She would smile at them blankly, without even seeing them, and stare back at the TV screen where home videos of her and Adam with the boys were playing on a continuous loop, night and day. We were doing the best we could, but they wanted their mother. Taylor cried for her five or six times a day, and it broke my heart. AJ was acting out. Throwing toys and tantrums over nothing, pinching Taylor. We were doing all we could for them, but I felt fairly certain these boys had lost their father. They couldn't lose their mother, too.

My mom shook her head again. "I'm proud of you," she said. "I'm proud of how you've stepped up."

Though she had said nothing that could possibly help me in this impossible situation, as she took my hand, I felt calmer. It was, as it always had been, my mother who gave me this incredible strength and inner peace, my mother who lent me fortitude when I needed it most. It was then that I realized it. Sometimes, being a mother isn't about having to fix it. Sometimes, the best thing a mother can be is there at all.

THREE

the light

sloane

June 16, 2010

Dear Sloane,

I will be home in ten days. Ten days until I get to hold you and kiss you and make you my wife, ten days until we get to stand in front of our family and friends and say how much we love each other, how we fell in love in this most unusual way that we will both cherish for the rest of our lives. I don't know how you've done all this while I was away, planned this entire wedding for me, for us. I am so grateful to you, my beautiful girl. And I am the luckiest man alive that I get to spend the rest of my life proving it to you.

All my love,

Adam

june 16, 2017

"GET UP." I VAGUELY heard Caroline's voice breaking through my dream, where Adam and I were driving down the road, singing to the radio on the way to our favorite hotel in the North Carolina mountains, a small bed-and-breakfast in downtown Blowing Rock that had a fireplace in every room and amazingly reasonable off-season rates. His parents knew how much we loved it and every Christmas, they gave us a gift certificate for two nights at the hotel—and two nights of their expert childcare services. It was my favorite gift. "You've been wallowing in here for thirty-four days," Caroline said. "And you kind of stink."

Ah, yes, Caroline. Always the tactful one.

I opened one eye, and it all came flooding back to me. Adam wasn't in the car beside me. Adam wasn't in the North Carolina mountains. Adam was gone. Adam was lost somewhere in the Middle East, somewhere I couldn't find him. My heart began to race with panic.

My sister threw open the curtains, and I thought I might go blind from the harsh brightness. How had I ever relished the feel of the sun on my skin or lain in it to warm my body? I wanted to tell Caroline to close the curtains. Then it hit me. Was Adam in the sun? Was he being scorched alive by the very thing that was supposed to give him life?

It had been thirty-four days since those uniformed men came to tell me my Adam was Missing in Action, my mind filled only with terror and dread, worst-case scenarios that pinged day and night like a loose ball on a racquetball court. The death didn't scare me; the torture did. The starvation, the pain, the indignity. For years, ever since the night we met only three weeks before his deployment, I imagined I could feel Adam, that my heart was connected to his the way the moon is connected to the tide. That connection controlled our world.

Looking back on those thirty-four days, I don't remember my sons' laughter. I don't remember them snuggling in bed with me. I don't remember my sisters taking turns sleeping with me, my mother feeding me, my grandmother singing to me. It is as though my mind is a bloody crime scene that has been wiped meticulously clean. The only thing I can recall from all those days is my memories of the past, my videos of the happy times, my letters from Adam.

Day thirty-four and still, every time my bedroom door opened, I felt a jolting panic that someone was going to tell me he was gone. My mom had come in just before Caroline and paused my video, which terrified me at first, but I was too weak and exhausted to protest. "Darling," she said, "time to get up. The boys are having a very hard time without you. If we need to get you to a doctor or on some sort of medication, we can and we will. But you have to get out of bed."

I thought of my children. I felt like I was crumbling from the inside out. I loved them. I needed them. They needed me. But I was so numb, my heart a desolate desert where nothing could live, nothing could grow. My children were better off without me.

When I didn't say anything, Mom left. But now Caroline was

here, playing bad cop to Mom's good cop. It was a pretty proven strategy, but it wasn't going to work on me. It was clear they had decided today was the day for the intervention. But I wasn't ready to be intervened upon, so it didn't much matter. Caroline lay down beside me in bed but abruptly got up and moved to the chair—she had forgotten how badly I stunk. If you stink too badly for even your sister to lie beside you, that's a problem.

She crossed her arms. "Sloane, you are neglecting your children, and quite frankly, you're neglecting me." I think she was trying to be funny, but I was past the point of finding anything funny. "Your kids need you, Sloane. They're miserable and angry and they don't understand what's happening. It's your job to be there for them."

I was used to Caroline's insults, her judgment, and her harshness. I braced myself for what she would say next. So when she took a deep breath, softened, composed herself, and said, "Sweetie, I want to read you this essay Vivi wrote for school," it was actually worse. If she had yelled at me or told me I was being selfish, I could have taken it. But her sympathy meant I was even worse off than I had thought. Changing her tactic from forceful to soft meant something was shifting between us. I didn't like that.

"It's titled 'My Hero.'" She cleared her throat, and I knew this essay was about her uncle Adam, her hero. I wasn't sure I could take it. But I knew how she felt. He was my hero, too.

So it caught me off guard when Caroline read, "My Aunt Sloane is my hero. Her husband, my Uncle Adam, is a sergeant first class in the Army, which means he fights hard for our country and goes on special missions that no one else can do. When he is gone fighting, my Aunt Sloane goes on special missions too. She takes care of my cousins AJ and Taylor all by herself. She even homeschools them. They are really smart. AJ can already read, and even little Taylor knows his alphabet. She cooks all their meals and sings lots of songs and she always remembers to buy me a birthday present even when she's really busy. She calls my mom every day to make sure we are OK, so we always remember how much she loves us. My Aunt Sloane prays hard to God every day to keep my Uncle Adam safe.

"That's how I know he is OK, even though he is Missing in Action in Iraq because his helicopter crashed and he was captured by insurgents. Everyone is worried, but I know he is OK because my Aunt Sloane knows he is OK because she prays about Uncle Adam every day. She prays hard and she works hard and she loves her family and is the best mom. That's why my Aunt Sloane is my hero."

I'm not sure when I started crying, but I felt something shift in me when Caroline read my eleven-year-old niece's words that I knew her Uncle Adam was OK because I prayed for him every day. Was that true? Did I know? I wasn't sure of anything anymore.

"It's amazing, isn't it?" Caroline said.

I nodded. I wanted to say something. I wanted to thank her or tell her to hug Vivi for me, but my mouth wouldn't work. So instead I let her feed me a little chicken soup. I didn't want it, but I didn't want to feel this way anymore either. That was progress, I thought.

"I would kiss you," Caroline said, "but you smell worse than the crab pots on the dock."

As Caroline was feeding me, AJ burst through the door, my mom on his heels, with so much energy that I felt even more tired. "Mommy, Mommy," he said urgently. "Mommy! I've got to ask you a question," he said, peering up into my face from the floor below. Caroline smiled at him, a laugh in her throat.

"Is Daddy dead?"

I froze, the few bites of soup I'd eaten growing heavy in my stomach.

"Oh, honey," Mom said, taking his shoulders gently and saying, "Let's go play while Mommy finishes lunch."

"Is he, Mommy? Because Billy down the street says Daddy is dead."

I felt something stir inside me, something that felt a little like fight, a little like hope. "No," I eked out, my voice sounding rough and rusty, like a screened door that hasn't been opened in far too long. "No, sweet boy. Of course Daddy isn't dead." It was then that I realized I believed it. I believed my husband was alive.

"Oh, good," AJ said, his voice laden with relief. "Because he's going to get me a BB gun for my sixth birthday."

Mom and Caroline chuckled, and I almost smiled. Almost. The simplicity of children, the wonder of it all, was one of the great joys of life. I had forgotten that.

It wasn't until after they had left, until after I hit play again, that I realized Mom had set up an easel in the corner of the room with a single canvas, a paintbrush, some paint, and a small palette. But I didn't paint anymore. And she certainly wasn't going to get me to paint now.

I looked back at the screen where Adam was talking, videoing me as I gave AJ his first bath. Then I looked back at the easel. There was something about it that seemed inviting, that tugged me toward it.

I tried to sit up. My eyes got starry and everything went black. I persevered, though, putting one foot on the ground and then the other. I held onto the wall as everything went black again. With my past flashing on the screen beside me, I picked up that brush.

I don't know how long I sat there, but when I looked at what I'd created, I felt a little better. It was an abstract piece of blacks and grays with hints of silver.

As I examined my work, something inside me felt a little lighter, a little less closed off, as if maybe the world as I knew it wasn't ending. Maybe.

My little sister Emerson came through the doorway quietly. She was the tall one, the most beautiful one, the nearly famous one. Even still, Caroline and I both felt the need to protect her. There was such an innocence to her, even at twenty-six. We couldn't help but want to shelter her.

She stood beside me, studying the painting, and said, "It's sad. But it's beautiful."

"Thanks," I whispered, realizing there was paint all over me. I set the brush down on the palette. Emerson took my hand and said, "Come on, sweetie. Let me get you into the bath."

Was this what my life had come to? People had to bathe me

now? I thought of my grandmother downstairs, who had come to live with us, whom my mom was taking care of. My grandmother. Caroline and her two kids. Emerson. My own two kids.

It had started out as so much fun, all of us in the same house, playing and laughing. That was me then. The me I was now couldn't imagine ever smiling again. Ever laughing again. Ever . . . Adam, oh Adam. Where was he? What was happening to him? Would I ever know?

It was September 11 all over again, knowing my dad was in that tower, knowing it had fallen, not knowing if he was alive but feeling certain I would never see him again. I had believed I knew what my mom went through in the wake of my dad's death. I felt like I understood her, that losing your father had to be equivalent to losing the love of your life. But I hadn't, not really. Not until now. I remember overhearing my mom telling her friends it still haunted her that she couldn't remember telling my dad good-bye, that she couldn't remember if she had kissed him before he left that day, that between packing lunches, making sure Emerson had her costume for her play, signing my permission slip, and telling Caroline she had on too much makeup, she couldn't remember if she told him she loved him.

At the time, I had thought that was silly. He was dead. We would never see him again. Who cared if she had kissed him good-bye? But now I understood. All I could think about was what I said the last time I had talked to Adam, what I wished I had done differently. It wasn't a good feeling.

I heard the water running, and I let Emerson help me to the bathroom. I couldn't believe how devoid of energy I felt, as if every ounce of the person I had been was running out of me like the bathwater down the drain. As Emerson helped me with my shirt, I realized I wouldn't have been able to do this without her. I glanced at the mirror and didn't recognize myself. My face was gray and drawn, making my brown eyes hollow. I'd been worried about losing the last ten pounds of baby weight. Now my skin was taut over my ribs and belly.

I lowered myself into the tub, allowing the water to cover my face. I opened my eyes under the water and watched the bubbles coming out of my nose, the light from the chandelier above me wiggling and distorted. For a moment, I considered not coming back up for air. I could let the water take me away, where I wouldn't have to feel or think or fear anymore. I could just leave. Quietly, without a struggle.

As my lungs grew hot, I heard an echoed, faraway "Mommy."

If I didn't take that next breath, my children would be all alone. I lifted my head out of the water, gasping for air. Taylor, my twenty-month-old, laughed at the sight of me. "Mommy!" he said again with glee. "Mommy, Mommy, Mommy!"

He leaned his face over the tub and planted a sticky kiss on my cheek, wrapping his warm arms around my wet neck. I remembered Vivi's essay. I remembered I was someone's hero. I had promised Adam, had vowed to him, that when he was away, I would be here, raising our babies and continuing our life. It was my job as a military wife to make good on that promise. This was my role, the one I had chosen. Or maybe it had chosen me. It was hard to tell now.

I closed my eyes and saw my painting again. I felt its strength. I thought of Vivi again, of her belief in me.

I believed in Adam. It was going to be OK.

It would be easier to retreat back into my cocoon of memories, my home videos, my letters, my sorrow. But Caroline was right. Mom was right. Emerson was right. I had my boys to live for. I had to carry on.

Instead of succumbing to the dark, if I was ever going to come out of this, I had no choice but to look for the light.

My son's blue eyes were a perfect start.

FOUR

transitional

ansley

When I opened the door to the store that morning, the first thing I did was rush to my store-manager-turned-design-assistant, Leah, and hug her. Her strawberry-blond hair was pulled up in a tight ponytail, and she was wearing an emerald-green silk blouse, the exact color of her eyes. The dusting of freckles across her nose had become more prominent this summer.

I looked around. Everything seemed pretty much the same despite my almost total absence over the past month. The living room display set up at the front of the shop, the tables of accessories, the shelves of books and candles. The only thing better than the inside was the gorgeous view out the window of the waterfront. And I never took for granted that work was a two-block walk from home. It was the best commute I knew of.

She laughed. "What was that for?"

I shook my head. "What was it not for? You have run my entire life for more than a month, Leah. There aren't enough thank-yous."

She waved me away like it was nothing, and before I could say anything else, she asked, "Any thoughts on those ceilings at the Turner house?"

But it wasn't nothing. That she had taken over like this said a lot about her future at the store, her future with me—and made me realize that I needed to give her a raise.

The Turners had just bought the house at the end of my street. It was surrounded by water on three sides and, built in the mid-1700s, was one of the oldest white clapboard houses in town. That, of course, posed a few design challenges. But if there was anything I loved, it was a challenge. Admittedly, I had a few more than I wanted coming at me these days, but I could handle one more if it meant figuring out how to make seven-and-a-half-foot ceilings seem taller and make tiny rooms feel more spacious.

I nodded. "I've been going back and forth, but I think we need to rip them out like we did in the kitchen. Let's stain the exposed rafters to give them a beam-like feel and lacquer the shiplap between them. It will give them a few more inches of height." I paused. "And will add so much character."

She smiled. "I love that, and we are so on the same page. I was thinking about going a little bit transitional, adding some modern flair."

This was why I loved Leah. She got me. "Yes!" I said excitedly. "It's never going to be a grand home, no matter what we do, so I say we mix key antiques with new upholstery and some unexpected accessories."

Leah nodded and handed me the mood board she'd been working on. "Faye loves gold, so what about these?"

The Barbara Cosgrove jar lamps with gold stripes and gold shades would be a perfect, fun touch on the pair of antique demilune commodes we were using underneath a pair of windows in the living room.

"Let's mix natural fiber rugs with those great antique Persian ones they have."

Leah nodded and made a note. "The ones with the blues, right? The greens aren't going to work."

"Exactly," I said, walking toward the back of the store to check out the boxes waiting there for me. This was the best thing about having a store. You got presents every day.

"Oh, and Leah," I called. "I want one of us to be there every day during construction. We need to make sure the original floors, moldings, window casings, and those amazing pocket doors are properly restored."

She nodded, standing beside me now. "Do you want them burned back to the original?"

I thought for a second. "Only in the rooms with the egg and dart."

The bell on the door tinkled, and my mouth started watering before I even turned around.

"As I live and breathe, if it isn't Ansley Murphy in her store."

I turned to smile at Kyle, with his tanned limbs, sun-kissed hair, and perfectly chiseled jawline. To be clear, I was drooling over the coffee he was delivering. I'd leave the drooling over Kyle to the younger generation. "Can you even believe it?" I asked.

Kyle was beside me now. I turned, and he kissed me on the cheek. "Our girl looks a little better," he said.

I smiled. "She's a mess, but she's out of bed." I shrugged. "I'll take it."

He handed me my cup. "What is it?" I asked.

"I felt like you needed comfort and stability, so I went back to your old favorite: skinny vanilla soy latte."

I was a little hurt when he didn't add, "But you don't need the skinny," like he usually did.

"I know Sloane loves chocolate milk," Kyle continued, "so I made her some with a bit of ashwagandha to relieve her stress. It's amazing if I do say so myself."

I held my breath as I asked, "Did she drink it?"

He smiled and nodded, satisfied. "Leah," he said as she panted over. "Iced coconut chai latte for you, my friend."

"Thanks, Kyle," she said breathlessly. She took a sip. "It's so good."

Kyle turned back to me and winked. He knew what he did to these poor girls. To my knowledge, he hadn't been romantically connected to anyone in at least six months. That seemed unusual for him.

The door tinkled again and, to my surprise, it was Kimmy, Peachtree Bluff's resident produce girl. I hadn't seen her in a couple of weeks, and she looked different. Her previously spiky half-blue hair was longer and all black again. It was softer, cute. Cuffs with diamonds traveled up her ears, and a tiny diamond stud twinkled in her nose. "Oh, good," Kyle said. "You're here."

I looked from one to the other, trying to assess what they were up to.

"We're making you dinner tomorrow night," Kimmy said.

I put my hand to my heart. "What?"

Kyle nodded. "Yes. Chef Kimmy and I are making dinner for all the Murphy women."

"And the two tiny men," Kimmy added.

"You don't have to do that," I said, flattered.

"Of course we do," Kimmy said.

"We love you, Ansley," Kyle agreed. "Now that Sloane is out of bed, let's give her a reason to stay out. Let's celebrate a little."

"You sweet, darling children. I accept your very kind offer."

Kimmy grabbed a cup out of the insulated Coke crate–turned–coffee carrier that was hanging by a leather guitar strap around Kyle's neck. She tapped her cup to mine. "It wasn't an offer," she said. "We were doing it whether you liked it or not."

It was one of those times that made me remember why I lived in Peachtree Bluff, why this town meant so much to me. These small kindnesses might not have seemed like much. But at times like these, small kindnesses were actually everything.

WHEN I GOT BACK home that afternoon, Mom and Caroline were chatting on the white linen living room couch while Caroline fed Preston a bottle. The house seemed quiet. Too quiet.

"Where is everyone?" I asked.

"Emerson convinced Sloane to take the boys out in the wagon," Caroline said, adjusting the swaddle blanket on her shoulder that covered part of the sleeveless white blouse she had paired with perfectly fitted black shorts. It was simple, but on Caroline, impossibly chic. "Vivi is riding her bike with them."

My eyes widened. I was impressed. "That's major."

Mom exhaled and put a hand up to the opera-length pearls that hung over a simple pink, long-sleeved shift. Looking at the two of them side by side, it was easy to see where Caroline got her style. "Y'all need to stop babying her. If you keep doing everything for her, you're just going to make her worse."

Caroline smiled down at Preston as she said, "I feel so sorry for her. Even I'm having a hard time doling out the tough love."

I sat down in one of the club chairs across from Mom and Caroline. "I think we're even more sympathetic because we've all lived what she's living, not being sure if someone you love more than life is dead."

"Oh, I don't think she thinks he's dead," Mom said.

"Well, she knows he's in a horrible situation."

"Right," Mom said. "She's in a horrible situation, he's in a horrible situation, and you're all complicit in letting her wallow in it."

Caroline sat Preston up on her lap, leaning his chin into her hand, and patted his back to coax out a burp. "No, we're not," she said. "Not anymore."

"And it worked, didn't it?" Mom asked.

This conversation was making me uncomfortable and a little bit angry. Sure, Mom hadn't let me come home or helped me in any way after my husband, Carter, died. And, yes, it turned out OK. But that didn't mean that's what I needed to do with Sloane. I loved my mother and I respected her, but freezing me out like that when I needed someone to lean on had nearly killed me. I wasn't going to put my daughter through that.

"Kimmy and Kyle are making dinner for us tomorrow night," I said, changing the subject as the door slammed.

"They are?" Emerson asked. "That's so nice."

Sloane trailed in behind her, Taylor on her hip. His head was resting on her shoulder, and I could almost feel his bliss at having his mother back. Sloane was so thin that her little shorts were hanging off her hips. Her light brown hair was ratty and pulled back into a slouchy ponytail. The circles under her doe eyes had circles. Usually Sloane had rosy cheeks, clear skin, and that sort of natural, effortless beauty reserved for Neutrogena commercials. Now, she was so pale and sallow, her normally full cheeks sunken in. I hardly recognized her. I wished I could hold her and make it better like she was doing for Taylor.

"I want some more of that chocolate milk," Sloane said, exhausted.

"If you want chocolate milk, then you shall have chocolate milk."

I could hear Vivi and AJ laughing and yelling out on the lawn.

"Is this dinner a family thing?" Emerson asked. She leaned casually against the wall, her leggings and tank accentuating her lithe body. She was eating well again, off that dreadful juice cleanse she had been on when she got to Peachtree Bluff, but her legs and arms still looked too thin to me. And she was a bit pale, too, which was odd, considering she was getting plenty of June sunshine.

I cocked my head to the side. "Well, no. I suppose not. Did you want to invite some friends?"

She took a sip out of the water bottle in her hand as she strode across the room and said, "No friends. I just thought I'd ask Mark."

She was gone before we could ask her any questions, that smart girl.

"Well, that's new," I said.

"Not as new as you might think," Caroline said. "You know, Mom, you should really get better control over your household."

Mom laughed heartily. I looked at Sloane, hoping for a smile, but her face was as stone cold as ever.

"I've always liked Mark," Mom said. "And it's time for Emerson to settle down."

"Let's not get ahead of ourselves, Mom," I said. "It's just dinner."

"Dinner with the entire family," Sloane pointed out, sharing a look with her sister.

That was true. I liked Mark, and I loved the idea of Emerson settling down. I didn't disapprove of her laser focus on her career, but I wanted her to have other things, too. I wanted her to have more.

"Mommy, I sirsty," Taylor said.

"I can get him something to drink," Caroline said, though she was still burping Preston.

"It's OK," Sloane said, walking toward the kitchen.

"See, coddling," Mom said.

I rolled my eyes. I couldn't do this with her. Not today.

"Hey, Mom," Caroline said. "I'm going to put Preston down for his nap. Do you mind listening for him? I'm going to take Grammy out to lunch." Caroline winked at Mom, and she winked back. Those two were always up to something. I wished Mom could be a tiny bit better at disguising the fact that Caroline was her favorite.

"That's fine," I said, my mind still on Sloane. "I'm going to go make some tea," I said, getting up and heading to the kitchen. It was terribly transparent, but if I wanted to help my daughter, then that was my prerogative.

As I reached my arms out to take Taylor from Sloane—as exhausted as I had been, I missed the boys like crazy while I was at work—I glanced out the window at the house next door that once belonged to Mr. Solomon, my crazy neighbor whom I had fought with for years over the fence that separated our yards. Happily, we made up in the weeks before his death, thanks to Caroline, of all people. Now it sat empty and alone, almost sullen, as if it were reaching out to me.

It wasn't as large or grand as this house, but it had a charm that had always drawn me in. I wondered for the millionth time who would scoop it up when it went on the market and how I would convince the buyers to let me decorate it. And, for a split second, Jack, the first boy I had ever told how much I loved that house, crossed my mind. But he was gone, I remembered. And so were those sunny, carefree summer days.

FIVE

enlisted

sloane

June 18, 2013

Dear Sloane,

I can't express how painful it was to leave you and AJ today. There's a huge hole in my heart, a piece of me missing without the two of you. I felt like I couldn't breathe as I walked away from you, and now, as I sit here, awake in the middle of the night, writing to you, I feel that pain again. Thank you for being the mother and woman you are, for taking care of our son when I can't, for loving both of us in the way you do. Already counting down the days until you are both in my arms again.

All my love,
Adam

THERE'S NOTHING LIKE WATCHING your husband board a plane to the Middle East to make you realize that you have absolutely no idea how to be a mother. The first three weeks with AJ had been tough, sure, but Mom had been there the first week and Adam had been so hands-on the second two that I hadn't truly realized how difficult it would be. Mom was in New York because it was grandparents' day at Vivi's school. Caroline was having such a tough time, her life revolving around hormone injections and IVF, that I felt almost guilty breathing in the sweet-smelling, perfectly pink head of my brand-new baby boy. Emerson was in LA, Grammy was in Florida, my mother-in-law had just had a knee replacement, and my best and only real friend on post in North Carolina had just been stationed in California.

That night with AJ had been the worst one by far. He wanted to feed every hour and a half and screamed in between. My nipples were raw and bleeding, and I was pretty sure I had a UTI, but my doctor didn't want me to take an antibiotic. Every square inch of my house was filled with some sort of baby apparatus, and the trash cans were filled with dirty diapers that I hadn't yet found the time or energy to take out. AJ was screaming, and to keep from throwing him out the window, I did the unthinkable, the thing my pediatrician had harped on like it was life or death: I turned on the TV. I was sure social services would sense I had broken the primary rule of parenting and arrive at my door any minute. But almost instantly, AJ quit crying.

I was so tired I couldn't even feel the overwhelming mom

guilt. I lay down on the floor right beside his bouncy seat and closed my eyes. If I couldn't nap, just for a few minutes, I was sure I would die.

I was roused from my sleep by the feeling that someone was watching me. When I drowsily opened my eyes, I saw a protruding, pregnant belly—and then I saw the woman it belonged to. I screamed and lunged for AJ, who looked at me curiously.

All she said was, "First baby, huh?"

I didn't respond. I looked up at her face, her mousy brown hair cut to her chin, a Cindy Crawford mole above her lip. She wasn't wearing any makeup and had on a simple hot-pink cotton maternity dress that tied in the back. She wasn't beautiful, but she was cute—probably not a murderer or kidnapper. But better safe than sorry.

"Sorry," she said. "I'm Maryanne. I'm your new neighbor. Your back door was standing open, and I just wanted to make sure you were OK."

My breathing slowed, and I felt my pulse return to normal. "Oh gosh," I said, finally waking up enough to figure out what was happening. I looked around, mortified. "I'm so embarrassed. Please forgive the mess. I promise I'm not usually like this."

She held out her hand, and I let her pull me up.

"You don't have to apologize to me, honey. I feel your pain." She pointed to her belly. "This is number two. Tom was deployed when number one was three months old, and I thought I would die then. I can't imagine if he had left when he was as little as your guy."

Anger, sadness, fear, and self-pity welled up in me all at once, and I burst into tears.

Maryanne hugged me, which only made me cry harder.

"Listen, sister," she said, "you're going to make it. It's going to be fine. I'm going to teach you how to do this without losing your ever-loving mind."

I nodded, wiping my eyes. Maryanne looked around, and I felt self-conscious again about my mess. But she said, "Wow. This place is incredible."

I appraised the room as well, noticing for the first time in a while the custom-made couch, stylish art, mirrored gold end tables, and antique dining table with the beautiful oyster-shell chandelier over top. Admittedly, that was a little odd, but my mom had thought being stationed in North Carolina meant we would be living on the coast. I loved it anyway. It reminded me of home.

"My mom's a decorator," I said, apologetically.

"You don't say," Maryanne replied.

From that moment on, we were best friends. We were Army wives. We were in this together. Maryanne taught me that mothering on your own meant getting on a schedule and sticking to it no matter what. It meant Stroller Strides with the other moms on post at 9 a.m.; a trip into town every day, even if it was just to Starbucks; taking advantage of one nap to clean the house and the other to relax. "You're a single mother now, Sloane," she said. "You have to preserve yourself at all costs. It doesn't matter if the laundry gets done, and no one is coming home to eat a five-star dinner."

In the name of self-preservation, Maryanne and I enlisted two other wives to start a supper club. Once a week, each of us prepared dinner for the entire clan. It wasn't fancy and our houses weren't always spic and span, but it gave us adult time, and most importantly, camaraderie, the thing that we needed to survive almost as much as our husbands did. Those women became my sanity.

Now, all I could think about was them. How could I have done this to my best girlfriends? While they were on post fighting the fight, worrying about me, I was selfishly hiding away in my bed, letting others take care of my children. I felt like a sellout. I couldn't face them.

I couldn't count the number of missed calls I had. Maybe my friends weren't calling only to check on me; maybe their husbands were with Adam. I don't know how I hadn't thought of it before. I felt so selfish. These were my friends, the women who saved me, who taught me how to be an Army wife. I sat down at the end of my bed. I had actually made it up that morning. It wasn't much and it took most of my energy, but it was a start. I glanced at my painting in the corner of the bedroom. I knew I would give it to Maryanne. It was just her style. I searched for her contact and pushed *Call.*

"Oh, thank God," Maryanne said, all in one breath. "We were all so afraid that something had happened to you."

"I'm sorry," I said. "I really am. I couldn't face anyone. I basically lost five weeks of my life." I paused, my lower lip quivering. With tears in my throat I said, "I'm so sorry, Maryanne. I don't even know if Tom's OK."

When Major Austin, the rear detachment commander, had come to tell me the news, I hadn't been in the frame of mind to ask. He had said, "Sloane, Adam is DUSTWUN, but we have every reason to believe he is alive. I know I don't have to tell you this, but finding him is our top priority."

My blood had run cold when he had said "DUSTWUN." Duty Status Whereabouts Unknown. It meant he could have been captured. He could simply be missing. He could be AWOL. If I knew my husband, he wouldn't want to die in the line of duty, but if that's what he was called to do, he would. Being killed in the line of duty would have been preferable, in fact, to anyone insinuating he was a deserter.

That's when I said, "You find out who has him, Major. Because you know just as well as I do that Adam would never, ever under any circumstances desert his men." It was my only moment of strength in all of this. Army wives don't often take a stand with their husband's higher-ups. It isn't our role. But I said, "Major Austin, I don't want anyone speculating that my husband was in any way at fault here."

He cleared his throat. "I promise you I'll do everything I can, Sloane."

I knew this would have caused a media frenzy. Soldiers didn't go missing all that often these days. This would be big news. Speculation that my husband was AWOL was more than I could bear.

Now, I heard the shake in Maryanne's voice when she said, "Adam, Tom, Brian, Luke, Jeremy, and Thad were all in the helicopter when it went down west of Mosul."

Maryanne paused and cleared her throat. I could sense she was trying to gather herself. "So now we have to pray that they're still alive."

My heart sank, but, just like those first days with AJ on post, I didn't feel quite so alone. I had the fewest children of these wives. And the most family. Things could be far, far worse. Despite my devastation for my friend, knowing we were all in this together bolstered my spirit.

"How are your kids?"

She sighed. "The only one who really knows anything is out of the ordinary is Tommy. He asks me every day if they've found Daddy."

"Oh, Maryanne."

"What about AJ?"

I cleared my throat to keep my voice from cracking. "He asked me if Daddy was dead."

I looked out the window at the boats passing by, at the children swimming. It seemed so odd that life could go on and the world could continue to turn when our husbands were in such peril.

"And what did you tell him?" she asked. I could practically see her sitting on her old brown sofa in the town house beside mine. I could see her bare feet, the piles of laundry she was most certainly folding, and could hear the children running all around her.

"I told him of course Daddy isn't dead." I could tell by the silence on the other end of the phone that Maryanne didn't agree with what I had done. But, for the life of me, I couldn't

41

understand why. I was so convinced our husbands would come home to us that I couldn't imagine another outcome.

"We're going to get them back, Maryanne. I know we will."

I thought of her, on post, with her four children. And of my other friends whose husbands were missing, too. "They're stronger together," I said, feeling my spirits rise, knowing it as clearly as my own children's faces. "They'll take care of each other, Maryanne. They'll make it home."

It wasn't only our husbands who were stronger together. We Army wives were, too. If anyone could survive this, if any group of women was prepared to stand strong and see their husbands home, it was us. For the first time since I'd heard the news, I could imagine the day when Adam would be back in my arms.

I heard voices down the hall, slowly walked to the doorway, and peered out to see Emerson with Taylor on her hip, Grammy crouched down on the floor with AJ, and Mom putting a load of laundry in the washing machine.

It was going to be tough, and there would be hard days. But my fellow wives were just like the women down the hall from me. We were family. We could weather any storm that came our way.

———

A FEW HOURS AFTER my call with Maryanne, I could feel anxiety and panic well up in me again. Were my sons missing out by growing up with a father who was gone half the time? How long would he be gone now before they found him? Months? Years?

I looked around my room, straightened the throw pillows on the bed, and restacked the papers—or more aptly, unopened bills—on my desk. I needed to pay them, especially the credit card bill, but I couldn't face them yet. I opened my computer.

An email from my favorite kids' store pinged onto the screen. Forty percent off. Well, that was a great deal. The boys needed some new shorts, didn't they? Sure, I was buried underneath a mound of credit card debt that not even my husband knew about, that I could probably never pay off. But that didn't mean my children should suffer, did it? Weren't they suffering enough right now? And, I mean, 40 percent off even the sale prices? They were practically giving the stuff away.

I zoomed through the site, adding items to my cart. Shorts and T-shirts, fleeces for the fall, a couple of cute toboggans— and all for less than fifty bucks. What a deal! I felt a little zip of electricity that was almost soothing. Some people ate; some people drank. Of all the unhealthy things I could do, this was far from the worst. It wasn't like I was damaging my health.

I held my breath as the order processed, crossing my fingers that my card wouldn't be declined. I had no idea what the balance was, but I knew it had to be almost maxed out.

Approved! Success. This was why I online shopped. A declined card at a real store was too humiliating.

The guilt would come later, as would the agonizing feeling that Adam would be so disappointed if he found out our emergency credit card was nearly maxed out all the time and I was accruing massive amounts of interest charges by paying the minimum every month. But Adam wasn't here. I was. And if this was what I needed to get through this rough patch—like all those other rough patches—then so be it. Plus, my dad put aside money for the three of us so we never had to worry. Mom was bound to give me my share soon, and I could pay the whole thing off no problem, with plenty left over.

There were a couple of times I had thought about asking Mom about the money. But, even though I had lived in New York for the first fifteen years of my life, I still considered myself a Southern girl. And a Southern girl would never do such a thing. It would be not only rude to put my mom on the spot, but also tacky to talk about money.

With my feelings temporarily assuaged, I did the one thing I had been dreading since the moment those uniformed men showed up on our front lawn. I called my mother-in-law. I was sure my in-laws must have felt completely abandoned by me. But I hadn't been able to face them, because as horrible as this was for me, it had to have been even worse for them. Adam was the love of my life, the father of my children. But he was their son, their pride and joy, their entire reason for existence.

As the phone rang, I prayed she wouldn't answer. But on the third ring, she did. And as soon as I heard her say, "Sloane," in that sweet Southern voice of hers, the one that lulled and rolled melodiously, I burst into tears.

"I'm just so sorry," I said. "I'm the worst daughter-in-law."

"Oh, honey," she said. "No. Of course you're not. I've talked to your mother every few days, and I know how terrible it has been for you."

I wiped my eyes and tried to focus on breathing. She

needed me to be strong. "But it's even worse for you," I said. "I know it is. And I couldn't even bother to pick up the phone."

"Sweetheart," Linda said, "it's OK. We have much, much bigger fish to fry right now." Then she began to cry too. Somehow, her tears made me feel stronger.

"Linda," I said calmly, "listen, I know Adam is OK. I feel it in the very depths of my soul. He's alive and he's going to come home safe."

Linda paused. "But Sloane, I think we have to at least consider—"

I cut her off. "No, Linda. I don't think you're hearing me. He's my *husband*. I'm positive he's going to come home. I'm not hopeful. No wishful thinking. I am *sure*."

I was proud of how confident I sounded.

"Well, then," she stammered, "I certainly hope you're right, sweetheart. And I wish I had your faith."

I bit my lip and looked out over the water. Being surrounded by things this beautiful made it hard not to have faith or believe that everything was going to be OK.

"I'll bring the boys to Athens soon." I looked down at my left arm, noticing how frail I was. It was shocking how much a body could deteriorate in one short month. I felt a cold shiver run down my spine. If this had happened to me inside my air-conditioned room, in my comfortable bed, with people trying to help me along the way, how much worse had it been for Adam?

"That would be wonderful, Sloane. As soon as you're feeling up to it, please do."

I nodded even though she couldn't see me. "And, Sloane, if you need a break, Don and I are happy to take them for a few days. You know how we adore those boys."

"Thanks, Linda. I love you so much, and I'm praying that the next time I'm talking to you we've gotten the good news."

She cleared her throat and said, "Me too, sweetheart. Me too." She paused and added, "Sloane, you take care of yourself, OK?"

"I will," I said. "I promise."

"Love you, and please send our love to the boys."

As I hit *End,* I felt so much better that I had called her. And I could tell from the sound of her voice that she felt better, too.

SIX

an excellent start

ansley

I couldn't decorate my grandmother's house when I first brought the girls to Peachtree Bluff after my husband died. It was ridiculous, to say the least. I was a decorator, for heaven's sake. An out-of-practice one, perhaps, but our whole lives were hinging on my ability to get my groove back, to return to paint colors and fabric swatches, floor stains and throw pillows. Yet, I couldn't bring myself to tear up the hideous harvest-gold shag carpet in the living room. We lived with chipped laminate countertops for far longer than I'd like to admit.

It wasn't because I didn't have an idea for the house—I had millions. It was simply that, to me, decorating meant creating a home and a family, and decorating a home that wasn't ours in New York meant accepting that Carter was never coming back. If I didn't ask him which accessories he liked best for his man cave, then it wasn't his home. If it wasn't his home, then he was really dead. So I scrubbed that ugly tile, vacuumed that hideous carpet that was worn down to nothing in the high-traffic areas, and told myself I wasn't redecorating the house because I couldn't afford it.

That was partly true, but I'd managed to squeeze enough out of the Victim Compensation Fund money we had gotten—after I had paid off Carter's debts—to at least take care of some of the essentials in a new design scheme.

Caroline whined and complained that she couldn't possibly have anyone over to this disgusting house. Granted, Caroline would have whined and complained no matter what. She hated me, hated Peachtree Bluff, hated her new life. Emerson whined occasionally that she really wanted a pink room and hers was a putrid green. But it was Sloane who pulled me out of it, Sloane who, in her quiet way, made me face what I'd been feeling all along.

"Mom," she had said quietly to me one day, a bag in her hand.

I remember I was standing by the sink, hand-washing dishes because, predictably, the dishwasher that hadn't been re-placed since the '70s had finally conked out and—you guessed it—I couldn't bring myself to replace it. She handed me the bag. Inside was a beautiful painting, one that I knew right away she had done. Sloane had been an artist her entire life, and even when she was little, her paintings were distinguishable from everyone else's.

"I was thinking that when you redo your room, you could put this painting in there." She smiled encouragingly. She understood, in her childlike way, what I was going through. So I said, "You know, Sloane, I think you're right. It's time to move on, isn't it?"

She shrugged. "Redecorating the house isn't forgetting Daddy, Mom. It's just making it so we can live here. I mean, you know, really live."

She was always wise, that girl. She was the quietest, but also the most intuitive of my daughters. She understood what drove people. I put my arm around her and said, "How about we redo it together, Sloane?"

She nodded and, just like that, I had a partner in crime, someone to run decisions by and help make choices that would shape the life we were moving toward. It was incredibly difficult moving on without Carter, but Sloane was right. She knew our new life was different, but that didn't mean it had to be bad. I knew it intellectually; I just hadn't figured out a way to put it into practice emotionally. Ripping up that carpet the next day with Sloane, Emerson, and Caroline was an excellent start.

If only helping Sloane now could be as easy as ripping up that carpet, we'd be all set.

I was sitting on a stool at the kitchen island, looking at my phone, when Caroline walked in. Preston and Mom were both napping, Vivi was at a friend's house, and Caroline's husband, James, who had gone back to New York for a couple of days for work, would be here any minute. Kimmy and Kyle would be here in two hours to start setting up our dinner.

"What are you doing?" Caroline asked.

"Worrying," I said. "What else?"

She wrapped her arm around my shoulder. "I know," she said. "I'm sorry. Anything in particular or just the usual?"

I sighed and got up, turning on the tap to fill the teapot. "I just got off the phone with Linda."

"Oh." Caroline opened the cabinet beside me and pulled out two mugs. "You sit down. I'll make the tea."

I did as she said. "She's worried about Sloane." As Caroline filled two strainers with loose-leaf tea, an herbal, calming blend that Kyle had concocted as an experiment, I added, "She thinks Sloane's delusional."

Caroline looked confused. "What do you mean?"

I shrugged. "She said Sloane is convinced Adam is going to come home." I paused. "She said she didn't know whether she should call and that she wanted Sloane to have hope. But Sloane was so insistent about his coming home safe that it worried her."

Caroline poured the steaming water into two oversized brown-and-white-striped Henri Bendel mugs. "But that's just how Sloane is. She's positive. She's hopeful. She's the Pollyanna of the family."

I nodded, hoping she was right.

"I have some news that might cheer you up," she said.

I looked at her doubtfully as Emerson came through the doorway. I could just make out the line of her neon bikini underneath the pareo she had tied around her neck.

"I was looking up Hippie Hal's phone number for one of the neighbors, and when I Googled him I found out today is his birthday."

That was nice, but why this might cheer me up, I wasn't sure. "I invited Hal to dinner tonight so that we could surprise him and celebrate. Kimmy is going to pick up a cake across the street on her way here."

"Oh, fun," Emerson said. "I love Hal."

"That's great, sweetheart," I agreed.

"You OK, Mom?" Emmy asked.

"Yeah. I'm excited for you," I said. "I'm excited about Mark." Something about Emerson had seemed lighter lately, like a fog had lifted. Now that I knew she was inviting Mark, her high school sweetheart, to dinner, I had to wonder if he was the reason for the change.

She smiled sweetly. "I am too. I mean, I've been sort of putting him off, but I'm here now. And we can worry about the future in the future."

"Exactly," Caroline said.

I heard Caroline's gasp and followed her gaze to the driveway. The black Mercedes convertible James had bought for her when she got her license pulled up. I watched as her face fell, and it was clear that she had just remembered what her husband had put her through, that he had cheated, and that everything was different. I took her hand and squeezed it as he walked through the back door.

"There's my girl," he said, sauntering in, pulling Caroline to him and kissing her. He had come straight from work, in his suit, to see her. It made me happy.

There was no denying I had always had my doubts about James. With his dark, coiffed hair and suits that were too fitted for my liking, his obsessive gym-going and charming dimples, I was afraid he was too charismatic to be a faithful husband. I hadn't been wrong on that end. But in some ways, I had misjudged James, too. There was no doubt that, despite his total lack in judgment, he truly loved my daughter. He was fighting for her every way he knew how. "Hi, ladies," he said to Emerson and me.

"I'm going to get the kids settled in at James's house," Caroline said. James had bought the house down the street so he could stay in Peachtree Bluff and try to convince Caroline he wasn't an awful person. It could be a long visit.

Emerson raised her eyebrow at me. "Never a dull moment at the Murphys'."

I nodded. Wasn't that the truth? In the driveway, James put his arm around Caroline, and she smiled up at him. I couldn't help but think of my first love. Jack had come back to Peachtree Bluff and fought for me, despite my misgivings, like James was fighting for Caroline now. I was so close to having a second chance at happily ever after, a second chance at true love. For the first time since Carter died sixteen years earlier, I felt like maybe true love could happen to a woman more than once.

And then I let him go, told him it wasn't the right time for us. Now he was gone. I didn't even know if he was still in Peachtree Bluff, if the fifty-eight-foot Huckins I had helped fully restore for him, the one he had named *Miss Ansley* for me was at the dock. I couldn't bear to look.

I told myself I couldn't be with him because of Sloane and Caroline and Emerson and my mother, because of how busy I was. I told myself if we were together, the secrets we had shared were in danger of coming back to light.

But as I watched James and Caroline make their way into the three-bedroom guesthouse on the back of my property, I couldn't help but wonder if it wasn't something more, if there wasn't a bigger reason I couldn't open up to Jack, a reason that I hadn't yet admitted. Even to myself.

SEVEN

history

sloane

February 24, 2010

Dear Sloane,

No matter how old you grow, how gray your hair, how wrinkled your face, when I close my eyes, I will always see you the way I did that very first day. Those bright eyes, that oversized UGA sweatshirt, your hair swept up off your neck. I couldn't imagine anyone more beautiful. I know you worry sometimes when I'm away about the rumors and other women and what happens when soldiers are gone. I'd be lying if I said some of the rumors weren't true. But since that day, Sloane, for me, there is only you. There is always only you.

All my love,

Adam

THE DAY I MET Adam was the best day of my life. I know you're supposed to say that about your children's births. Or maybe your wedding day. But, without that first day, the first time I laid eyes on him, I wouldn't have had any of that.

After my dad died, I decided, firmly, that I would never love anyone that much again, because when you love that much, there is so very much to lose. I wouldn't, couldn't do it again.

I dated, of course. I had boyfriends, but I always kept them at arm's length, cracked the door enough to interest them but never opened it all the way.

Adam says, for him, it was love at first sight. For me, it was just another day standing in line at the post office. It seems fitting, actually, that we would meet at the post office. I had no idea then that letters would become one of the most critical parts of our love story.

It was December 17, a freezing cold afternoon in Athens, and my last exam was the next day. I couldn't wait to get home to Peachtree Bluff, back to my mom and my sisters. I had recently broken up with my boyfriend, partly because it was never going to go anywhere anyway and partly because I couldn't think of a good Christmas gift for him. That was, at the time, my opinion about true and everlasting love.

The post office that day reminded me of a subway stop—minus the public urination and homeless people. It was crowded and loud. Some people were cheerful and joyous; some were crabby and ill. Many were talking on their cell phones; most were coughing. Everyone believed his or her package—and its destination—was most important.

I had noticed the man standing in front of me with a passing interest. I assumed he was in the military based on his haircut, but his jeans and button-down with rolled-up sleeves didn't give anything away. He seemed well bred and supremely confident.

Adam turned to me and smiled, and my heart did this thing. This scary thing. This thing I hated. It raced, and my stomach flip-flopped. I could feel my cheeks tinting the slightest bit red—probably not full-on maroon like my poor mother's would have been, but a little red. It made me want to run.

"Anything liquid, fragile, or perishable?" he asked.

I laughed in spite of myself. He had the cutest dimples, and I'd never understood what a "chiseled jawline" was until that moment.

"I'm sorry," he said. "That was the best thing I could come up with. It was really lame."

I laughed again. "It's better than what I was thinking."

He raised his eyebrows questioningly.

"Mailing yourself home for Christmas?"

He grimaced. "That really is bad." We both laughed.

I peered around him toward the front of the line. "We don't seem to be moving, do we?"

He shook his head. The lady at the counter must have had thirty packages. But, whereas a few minutes ago I was annoyed, now I was sort of excited. The longer she fretted over priority versus regular, the longer I got to stare at that face.

"I tell you what," he said. "I'm not in the business of doing this, but I have a good buddy who works for the postal service. What if I take you to lunch, and I'll get him to mail our packages?"

Our. It was our first *our.* My internal warning bells dinged. This was a total stranger. Whom I met in line at the post office. He could be a serial killer, a rapist, a litterer. I had a vision of myself locked in a trunk, trying to kick out the taillight like I saw on *Oprah.* But he had such an honest face. And such beautiful hazel eyes. And I could picture my lips on his lips more than I could picture myself being stuffed into his trunk.

"This is an extremely important and very special pair of bedroom shoes for my grandmother," I said. "But if you're sure you're up to the task . . ."

My new friend put his hand on my back and led me out the door, which, of course, he held open. "I'm Adam," he said.

"Sloane."

Over lunch I learned that, as I had suspected, Adam was in the Army. "I'm spending Christmas with my family before I head back to Iraq in a couple weeks," he had said.

I was confused and a little scared by how much I hated the idea of his being overseas. I needed to walk away from this one. Not only did I feel dangerously aware of the potential for love here, but I also knew if I did develop feelings for him, I would have to spend the rest of my life worried. That was the opposite of what I was going for. I didn't want to spend months at a time alone. I didn't want to worry. I didn't want to feel. I was about to tell Adam I needed to go, that I had an exam.

But then I pictured him in his Army uniform, the brass buttons over his taut chest. And the rest, as they say, is history.

I couldn't help but wonder, as we all sat down to dinner at the outdoor teak dining table that night, if Emerson wasn't making a little history of her own, bringing Mark to dinner with our entire family—minus Adam.

I had put on a maxi dress that was way too big now, and Caroline had fixed my hair so it wasn't stringy or in my face. I had never been big on makeup, but I had to admit that the little bit of highlighter and blush Emerson had swiped on my cheeks had made a huge difference. "When you look better, you feel better," she had said. I didn't agree with that, but I didn't protest, partly because it was easier not to and partly because I didn't want her to be embarrassed of her big sister at her first family dinner with Mark.

He was so cute and clean cut, very fraternity boy in his neat khaki shorts and oxford with the sleeves rolled up. He looked a little nervous but also pleased as punch to be with Emerson. I had helped Mom set the table with rattan place mats, her Juliska Petit Singe—the boys loved the little monkeys it was named for—and wineglasses. I couldn't find the joy in it, but there was something soothing about the monotony of putting out all those gold forks and knives and spoons, of placing a wineglass at every seat. Mom had made arrangements of fresh hydrangeas from the yard and placed them down the table in vases of varying height. It was simple and beautiful.

Kyle and Kimmy had prepared a summer feast. Tomato sandwiches, string beans and boiled potatoes, corn on the cob, strawberries with fresh whipped cream, blackberries, squash and onions, field peas. It was a simple, healthy Southern spread. Grammy leaned over to me and said, "This reminds me of the dinners I used to make when you girls were little." I wanted to smile at her. I swear I did. But I just couldn't.

"Those were the best summers, weren't they?" How I longed to go back in time to one of those carefree, sandy days before life had gotten hard, before love had begun to hurt.

As we passed the dishes around, family style, Caroline said, "This time next week, you'll be doing this at Seafarer, Viv."

"Yay!" Vivi exclaimed.

All of us had attended Camp Seafarer in North Carolina. We learned to sail and run powerboats, became expert swimmers, sang silly songs, played tennis, practiced archery . . . The list goes on. We had all loved camp, but Caroline particularly adored it, which was kind of funny since rustic cabins and no air-conditioning didn't exactly fit Caroline's overall vibe. But it wasn't the accommodations she loved. It was the water. She was one of the best boaters to ever come out of Seafarer, earning all her ranks and winning the Captain's award. She even did a semester at sea during college and got her captain's license. That was Caroline. When she loved something, she went all out.

"You're going to have the best time," Emerson said. "We loved camp so much."

Part of me couldn't imagine this Park Avenue girl in the crowded dining hall. But if she had even an ounce of her mother's love of the water, Vivi would be OK.

Out of the corner of my eye, I noticed Emerson whispering something to a laughing Mark as Caroline said, "Girls, I had the best, best idea."

I felt nervous butterflies in the pit of my stomach. Whenever Caroline had the best, best idea for "the girls," it somehow included me and it somehow put me way out of my comfort zone.

"No," I said.

Everyone at the table laughed.

"Good girl, Sloane," James said. "When this one has an idea, it's best to just get out of the way." He kissed Caroline's bare shoulder.

"Ha. Ha," she said. "No, my great idea is that Emerson, Sloane, and I take Vivi to camp."

That didn't sound so bad. I could probably handle that.

"By boat," she added.

Ah, there it was. "No way, Caroline," I said. "I can't leave the boys for that long."

She and Emerson shared a glance, and I knew it meant, *You didn't so much as look at them for over a month. Why so concerned now?*

They weren't wrong.

"It's only three days there and three days back," Mom said.

I scowled at her, and she looked back down at her plate. "Sorry," she said. "Just trying to help."

"That would be marvelous," Grammy said. "We used to take you girls by boat sometimes."

"Oh, I remember," I said. I mostly remembered being seasick while Caroline handled the mast and the jib like she had been born on a boat. It was just one more tiny way that Caroline was better than I was, as if being smarter and more beautiful and more popular wasn't enough.

"I'll be here with Preston," James said, "and I'm happy to help Ansley with AJ and Taylor."

"That's so sweet, James," Mom said. "And Linda begged me to let her have them, so I told her I'd bring them to Athens for the last few days of the trip."

I looked around the table, realizing I had been ambushed. "Wait," I said. "Wait just a minute. You all plotted against me, planned how I will leave my children and possibly miss an update about my husband? That's really nice." I paused. "And it's really not happening."

I looked at Caroline's face, and I could tell it *was* happening.

"We're not going to Cuba, Sloane," Caroline said. "For heaven's sake. We'll be completely reachable at all times."

I could feel my mind resigning itself to this plan, forgetting I was an adult, slipping back into the old pattern of Caroline being the big sister, me being the little sister, and my role in life doing what she said.

"We're going to have a really good time," Emerson said. She was sitting across from me, holding Mark's hand, yet, somehow, it felt as though her voice was coming from another life, a time when Adam was here and I was happy. A time when my children laughed and I laughed with them. A time when I could remember who I was.

"Mommy," AJ said excitedly. "I love tomatoes!"

I ran my hand through his hair.

"See?" Kyle asked. "I told you you would."

"That's how you learn," I said. "When you try new things, you discover all sorts of things you love."

"Exactly," Caroline said. "Which is why this trip is going to be so much fun!"

From down the table, Vivi said, "Please, Aunt Sloane. Pretty please with a cherry on top?"

I looked at her. She was so adorable. And she wrote that beautiful essay. "Fine," I said. "I won't like it, but I'll go."

"Wait," Mom said. "What boat are you taking?"

"Well, Jack's, of course," Caroline said, as if it was the most obvious thing in the world that we would be taking the boat Mom's old boyfriend named after her.

Poor Mom. She could never hide her feelings. She turned redder than the fresh tomatoes. I shot her a very satisfied look. She thought she was tricking me, but Caroline was tricking her, too. I wondered if James was ever scared of her, especially now that he had crossed her. She was just a little smarter than absolutely everyone, so even when you thought you had her figured out, she could still ambush you.

"Oh, I . . ." Mom stammered and trailed off. "I didn't know Jack was even in Peachtree Bluff."

Caroline looked at her like she was dense. "Of course he's in Peachtree. Where else would he go?"

I was about to chime in when I heard, "Happy birthday to you," trailing from the kitchen. It made me think of all of those birthday parties I had been watching on the home movies, all those happy times when Adam was here and life was good. But I had to push the thought out of my mind. I was lost without him, but if I kept dwelling on him every single second I was going to destroy everything we had spent years building.

So I joined in. "Happy birthday, dear Ha-al, happy birthday to you."

Hal smiled and blew out the candles as we all looked on. His beard almost got into the cake but missed it by a centimeter. "Thank you all so much," he said. And then, much to my surprise, he got choked up. Caroline put her hand on his arm. "Hal? What's the matter?"

He wiped his eyes and said, "I'm sorry. It's just that no one has remembered or celebrated my birthday in more than twenty years."

I looked across the table at Mom, whose eyes were now filling with tears too. She put her arm around Hal and hugged him.

I wondered how that was possible, how this wonderful man could have gone more than twenty years with no one celebrating his birthday.

I looked around the table at my two boys beside me, Grammy on my other side, Mom across from me, Emerson, Mark, James, Caroline, Vivi, even Hippie Hal, Kimmy, and Kyle. I had all these people who loved me, all these people who supported me no matter what, all these people who would remember my birthday. I took them for granted sometimes and just assumed everyone had what I did. But it was at times like these that I remembered how rare it was to have a family like mine, to have love like this.

I knew Adam would come back to me. I knew he would. But having these people surrounding me, bolstering my spirits, not letting me disappear into myself again while I waited, was an absolute blessing in the meantime.

~~~❧~~~

civilized

ansley

Our Peachtree Bluff neighbors had brought sixty-two casseroles since we got the news that Sloane's husband Adam was MIA. That meant it had been sixty-two casseroles since I had told Jack it wasn't the right time for us, that, with all I had on my plate, I couldn't commit to a relationship too. As I stared at all those uneaten casseroles in my deep freeze in the garage, I could poignantly feel every second that had passed since my first love, the one I had met in this very town, told me that he had waited long enough for me, that he had put his life on hold for thirty years and that was more than generous.

And now, he was gone. Well, gone from my life, anyway. The fact that Caroline, Sloane, Emerson, and Vivi were getting ready to embark on their drop-Vivi-off-at-camp-and-rehabilitate-Sloane mission on Jack's boat meant that he wasn't gone from Peachtree Bluff. I had to admit that soothed me. The thought that he was still here but not in my life did not soothe me.

On the bright side, my mother's episodes of confusion, though more frequent, tended to last a shorter time. We were hoping we could attribute her mental inconsistencies to her pain medication usage after the car wreck and broken ankle that had brought her here to me.

On the other bright side, it seemed like, despite my incredible skepticism, Caroline and James were getting along splendidly and Emerson was well on her way to being totally in love with Mark. Two out of three happy daughters wasn't bad.

"Caroline!" I called, walking up the stairs into the guesthouse.

"In the kitchen, Mom," she called back.

I loved this guesthouse. I had made it a sanctuary from the real world. Before all the girls had come home, I would come out here for a couple of days and feel like I was on a mini-vacation. It was less formal than the main house. Both floors had wall-to-wall seagrass carpet, marble mosaic tile in the bathrooms, and pale sky-blue walls.

As I walked into the kitchen/great room area I admired the beaded chandelier hanging from the vaulted ceiling. I loved the exposed beams in here, the casual, rustic air they lent.

"Do you need help packing, sweetie?" I asked.

It was a thinly veiled offer. The truth was, since our dinner a few days earlier, all I had been able to think about was Jack and that he had stayed away from me for six weeks—which probably meant he could do it forever. It was not my favorite thought.

Jack. I hadn't imagined he would let me go like this. After all these years, all these secrets, all the life we nearly shared, I thought he would understand. So I was caught in a tangled web between sorrow and anger and acceptance. Some moments I could convince myself that his giving me two of my three daughters, keeping my secret for all those years, and never forcing his way into our lives was enough. Then, in the next moment, I would think he was being selfish and insensitive in not being more compassionate or understanding about my predicament with Sloane.

"We're all ready to go tomorrow," Caroline said. She was spraying the kitchen counter. She looked around to make sure no one was in earshot and then whispered, "I'm so nervous about Vivi being gone for an entire month."

I nodded. I remembered the feeling. "I know, sweetheart, but she's going to have the best time. She will learn so much and make friends she will have forever."

She shrugged. "I know. It's just the selfish part of me that wants her here."

"It might be good. You and James could use this time to yourselves." I paused. "Well, I mean, yourselves and Preston."

She laughed. "I know what you mean. Who would have thought a baby would be easier to manage than an eleven-year-old?"

Her face fell slightly.

"You OK?" I asked.

She bit her lip. "I'm all over the place. I'm happy and then I'm sad and then I'm mad. It's a never-ending rotation."

"It probably will be for a while." I took the bottle from her and continued spraying while she fluffed the pillows on the couch.

"So, Jack's boat?" I asked what I hoped was casually.

"Yes," she said. "You know. Fifty-eight Huckins, fully restored thanks to you."

"How did you swing that?"

She shrugged. "I simply explained I had my captain's license and needed to save my sister." She paused. "It was actually way easier than I thought."

Probably because he didn't want to tell his daughter no. Carter had been terrible at that too. I felt that stabbing pain around my heart. It's not a new revelation, necessarily, but it seems that whenever there is one loss, the others are felt more poignantly. Watching what Sloane was going through, seeing how she was suffering, brought back the memories of losing Carter so fiercely that, at times, it was hard to breathe.

"Was he surprised you had your captain's license?" I asked.

Caroline hadn't gotten her driver's license until right before her son Preston, who was now three months old, was born. She insisted that no one needed a driver's license in New York City. But in Peachtree Bluff, her sisters had finally refused to drive her, so she had no choice.

"I don't think he believed me. But I said, 'Jack, you and I both know that driving a yacht is so much more civilized than driving a car.'" She smiled.

I shook my head. "Caroline, for goodness' sake. Only you would ask a man to borrow his pride and joy."

"His pride and joy named after *my* mother." She winked at me.

Then it hit me. "If you're taking the boat, where's Jack going to stay?"

Her look revealed nothing, but I felt it. She knew something she wasn't telling me. "Mother, I have absolutely no idea. I'm not Jack's travel agent."

"Gransley!" I heard from down the hall. Caroline's dark-haired little clone came in, breathless and red-faced.

"What, darling?"

Vivi was wearing her tennis skirt and tank top. For a moment, I panicked. I had dropped her off at the courts. Had I forgotten to pick her up? But then I remembered James had. It's amazing how it all comes back to you, the minutiae of raising children, of coordinating their schedules, of remembering who needs to be where when. "I saw a moving truck pull in next door! Who do you think our new neighbor is? Do you think they have kids?"

Caroline turned too quickly and walked into her room. Despite the positive advances, it was still only her room. James's room was in the house on the corner.

"Caroline!" I called after her. "What are you not telling me?"

"Nothing, Mom. I just need to finish packing."

I walked outside, deciding it was no use hounding her. I went upstairs in the main house and turned into my room. I swiped some blush on my cheeks, reapplied my lipstick, and ran a brush through my short, chestnut hair, realizing I needed to get my roots touched up soon. I was fortunate not to be completely gray, even at fifty-eight, but I still had a few intruders to keep at bay. I hoped I had many more years before I had to start fully coloring my hair. I couldn't fathom what it would be like to look in the mirror and see a blonde. *Maybe I'll look like Emerson.* I laughed out loud. With her dewy skin and legs up to her neck? Nope. She was the daughter who had finally looked like me, but never again would I look like Emerson.

I turned around in the mirror a couple of times, examining my white shirtdress and belt around my waist. No visible stains despite making homemade Play-Doh with AJ and Taylor that morning. Not too wrinkled. I smoothed my hands down my front, turned, and screamed.

Caroline was standing in the doorway, watching me with an amused smirk. "You have a date or something?"

I scowled at her, inadvertently remembering how Jack was gone and how I'd been the one to let him walk away. I'd been avoiding the dock like the plague, just in case he was still in Peachtree, afraid of running into him like we were teenagers again after a stupid fight. But we weren't teenagers. And this fight wasn't stupid.

"No," I said. "You know I've been wanting to decorate the house next door forever. I'm going to run over and introduce myself."

I was so grateful I had picked up a loaf of banana bread at the farmers' market. I had planned on bribing Sloane to eat with it, but I'd take it to the new neighbor, schmooze a bit. Sloane wasn't *that* thin . . . Yes, she was. I was an awful mother.

Caroline rolled her eyes. "Tactful, Mom. Don't even let

them get the first piece of furniture off the truck before you assault them with your portfolio and baked goods."

Had I said that out loud?

"I'm not even going to mention it," I lied. I might casually slip in what I did for a living and the vision I had for the house. But that was a far cry from pulling out my portfolio. Although, if I happened to leave a copy of my latest spread in *Coastal Living* . . . No, no. *Rein it in, Ansley.*

"You know, Mom," Caroline said. "I think you should wait a few minutes. I need to run to the store to pick up our last few provisions."

I shrugged. "So? James has Preston, and Sloane has the boys on the beach. Vivi is certainly fine if I go next door."

"But you could wait a few more—"

I stepped out the door and turned, my look stopping her mid-sentence.

"What have you done?" I hissed.

She gave me her most innocent look, the one that was so innocent it wasn't innocent at all. She put her hand over her heart and said sweetly, "Mom, I haven't done a single thing."

I felt eyes on me, and I knew, even before I turned, exactly whose they were. What I didn't know is what those eyes living right next door meant.

NINE

all in

sloane

Three weeks isn't a long time to know someone. But that's how long I had known Adam when he returned to post, two nights before he would leave on his next deployment. After that moment in the post office, it was like my entire life, and certainly our entire love, was on fast forward. I had Christmas Eve dinner with his family. He spent Christmas Day with mine. We spent every waking moment of my break from UGA together at my apartment, which was completely devoid of roommates, who had gone home.

This kind of behavior was completely out of character for me. But there was something about Adam and the way he looked at me that very first day. Even though I was in my crummy exam clothes, he made me feel like I was the most beautiful person he had ever seen. No boy I had ever been with had made me feel that way or could have tempered the sting of growing up in the shadows of two extraordinary sisters. Caroline was pretty and smart and so confident and self-assured that the world seemed to revolve around her, and Emerson, let's face it, was essentially a gift from God, so unusually beautiful and talented. I always felt lost somewhere in the middle.

I should have been grateful, I suppose. I was smart enough, pretty enough, a good artist. I had good friends, and my parents did all they could to make sure I felt special and unique, like I was just as important as Caroline and Emerson. But, come on. How could I ever be? And now, here, with Adam, I was.

Maybe that's why, very, very unlike me, I said "I love you" first. It was the night before Christmas. We were at his parents' house, sitting by the crackling, real wood fireplace in the basement of their house on Lake Hartwell, outside Athens. It had a rustic, cabin-like feel to it. It was the kind of place where you just *had* to drink hot chocolate with extra marshmallows.

His parents were incredible. They were funny and warm and welcoming, and I felt so at home in his world, as though I had been there forever. In stark contrast to my mother, who would have risked life and limb to make sure we didn't share a bedroom, they hadn't even considered that we wouldn't. I felt weird about it, especially since it portrayed the notion that we were having a type of relationship that we weren't, a type I had never had with anyone, in fact.

That night, after the Christmas presents and carol singing, Adam and I were all alone in the basement by the fire. We had talked so much that I felt like I knew him better than I'd ever known anyone. But there was still one thing I needed to know. Looking up into his soulful hazel eyes, I said, "Adam, what made you decide to enlist? I mean, how could you just leave school and everything behind?"

He was leaning against the couch, his legs out in a V that I fit into perfectly. I leaned up against him, my back against his chest. His strong arms were wrapped around me and for the first time since 9/11, for the first time since my father was taken from me, I felt safe.

He kissed my ear and said, "You know, Sloane, I watched those planes crash into the towers, and it made me sad. But it also made me furious. All I could think about was the people in those towers, my people. They left for work that morning expecting to come home that night, kiss their husbands and wives, and tuck their children into bed. Even the survivors' lives had changed forever." He paused, and I let his words sink in because he was right. I was one of the survivors. And every minute of my life since that second tower fell had been just a little bit worse.

He pulled me closer to him, and I could tell he was thinking. So I looked up at him again. "What?"

He smiled at me. "I want to say something, but I'm afraid it will scare you away."

"There is nothing," I said, "that could possibly scare me away at this point, Adam. I'm pretty much all in."

He nodded, and I knew he felt the same. "I've spent some time wondering why I felt so compelled to right this wrong. I mean, I didn't have a loved one in the tower. I had no real stake in any of it." He paused for a moment, his fingers trailing lazily up my arm. "And this is the crazy part. When I saw you in that post office, when we had lunch that day, when I knew your dad had been killed, it was like all the pieces of my life finally fit together, all the things that didn't make sense suddenly did. I think, even though I didn't know you yet, Sloane, I had been fighting for you all that time, like my heart knew that one day I would meet you and I had to be able to tell you I hadn't watched this atrocity happen to you without trying to fix it."

By this point I had scooted away from Adam. I was sitting on my knees looking at him, rapt with attention. My heart was beating wildly, the butterflies in my stomach having baby butterflies. When I didn't say anything he said, "I'm sorry. I knew it was too much. I wish I hadn't said anything."

But I shook my head and moved closer to him until our faces were only inches apart. "Adam," I said.

"Sloane," he replied.

"I love you."

He smiled and pulled me to him, kissing me. "I love you too," he whispered. "I know it seems crazy, but I absolutely do with everything I am."

I wrapped my legs around his waist and kissed him again. I began unbuttoning his shirt, pausing to pull my own over my head. My rational mind would have reasoned that his parents were right upstairs, but I was way past being rational.

"Sloane," he whispered. "Are you sure about this?"

He knew I was a virgin, knew I had never had feelings like this for anyone.

"I have never been so sure of anything in my entire life."

I knew I had only known Adam for two weeks and I might never see him again, but I didn't care. If he left and, God forbid, something happened to him, I would always regret that I hadn't shared this moment in time with him and him alone.

His poor mother probably didn't have this in mind when she picked that soft sheepskin rug for in front of the fireplace. In that moment, our worlds collided, and I knew he was it for me. I was made to be with Adam.

The night before he left, through our tears and heartache, he got down on one knee in UGA's Founders Memorial Garden and said, "Sloane Murphy, you are the love of my life. Will you marry me?"

It was a proposal exactly like Adam. Simple and direct, but passionate. And I knew I was the luckiest girl in the entire world when I said, "Yes."

He slid a gorgeous ring on my finger. "My grandmother's," he said.

I smiled. "So, your parents?"

"My parents couldn't love you more," he said. "They said they knew from the moment they met you, just like I did, that we were perfect for each other."

Six months later, my sisters, on the other hand, still thought I was crazy. And my mom was a wreck. They didn't think we had known each other long enough to get married, didn't think we understood what we were getting into. What they didn't understand is that when you're getting to know someone normally, there are so many distractions. You go to movies, parties, cookouts, baseball games. You share the inane details of your days at work, binge-watch trashy reality TV shows. But is any of that connection? Does it help you know what's inside the other person's heart? Not if you ask me. At least, that's what I told my mother nine weeks before Adam came home, and, contrary to what my family believed would happen, our wedding was still on.

Every day for eight months, I had written my future husband a letter and received one in return. I had spent eight months asking those important questions, sharing things about myself that I had never shared with anyone, and sending them off to the US Postal Service's care, hoping my words and, much more importantly, my love would reach him.

So, while my family begged me to change my mind and pleaded with me not to be so hasty, I believed with all my heart that I knew this man better than anyone. I knew his soul, the recesses of his mind.

I knew he wanted a small wedding, just like I did. Nothing like Caroline's five-star Manhattan blowout, paid for by James, despite our mother's protests that his picking up the tab was tacky. So we booked the church, picked out a dress, put deposits down on a band and a caterer, and ordered tents for the front yard. All the while, my mom put on a happy face. But when it came time to order the invitations, the veneer cracked. That's when I realized that her happiness for me and her proclamation that nothing would make her happier than having Adam for a son-in-law was a farce.

"Sloane, honey," she had said hesitantly, "you don't have to do this, you know. You don't have to go through with it."

I was shocked and so hurt. "Mom, why would I not go through with it? He's the love of my life. I've never been surer of anything."

She had crossed her arms and leaned on the counter, looking around as if one of my sisters might jump out from the cabinets and save her. "But you don't know him, Sloane. You knew him for three weeks. I know the whole soldier-off-at-war thing is romantic, and I can see how you could get swept up in a proposal, but let's take a step back."

Caroline had called me later that afternoon. "No one's saying you shouldn't get married," she said. "Just let him come home. Date for a few months. Make sure he's who you think he is."

It ruffled me that my family would even say such things to me. But it didn't change my mind. It didn't change the fact that I knew Adam was the one for me. I knew what a commitment I was making.

The way I felt the day he came home that first time was a feeling unlike any other. Relief washed over me with a vengeance. I felt whole again, complete.

I must have stood in his arms in the airport for an hour, relishing the way he felt, the way he smelled. I knew I would never let him go again.

When I stood at the altar in the St. James's chapel and pledged to love him forever, I knew I would. Maybe I hadn't yet considered what that would look like. Maybe I didn't truly understand what that would come to mean. But I would love him anyway. And it would be OK. I had pledged to be with that man for better or for worse.

And this? This was worse. This was worst—well, almost worst, which felt close enough. But despite how it had turned out, I knew one thing without a doubt: even knowing what I knew now, I would do it all again. Adam was a soldier, but, in a way, so was I. And I, like him, like his best men, would be loyal until the very end.

georgia

ansley

After the years Mr. Solomon and I spent feuding over the fence that separated our yards, I swore that if I ever had a new neighbor, I would do whatever it took to make sure we were friendly. We wouldn't have to have cocktails on the porch together; I just didn't want any tension.

I wished more than anything when I saw Jack walking out the front door of the house, then grabbing a box out of the moving truck, that he hadn't seen me. But he had. And I couldn't hide or pretend I didn't know he was there.

Even before I crossed the short distance between my yard and the one next door, I felt the chill. Jack had always had this air about him, a manner that made him seem perpetually amused and never surprised. It was like he always knew what was coming next, even when it was unfathomably shocking to the rest of us. But now, he barely ventured a smile.

It was as though Mr. Solomon had never left. History was repeating itself. I wondered, briefly, if things weren't what they seemed. But, while people say things are never as they seem, I would beg to differ. In my fifty-eight years, I've found that things are almost always as they seem.

It *seemed* like Jack was moving in beside me. My heart raced and my stomach sank all at once. I had no idea how to feel because I had broken up with him—if that's even what you call it when you're a grown-up. But it had felt more like taking something I had always carried inside of me—something that defined me, that was the very essence of me, that I would be irreparably different without—and removing it from my life. That's what I had done to Jack. I had removed him.

Although, not all that well, I decided, as I smiled shyly.

I had known Jack for forty-three years, and I knew his smile. I saw it when I closed my eyes. Even during all those years we were apart, the thought of it and the warmth of it carried me through many a cold night. So I knew what he shot my way wasn't a Jack smile. At least, it wasn't a Jack-and-Ansley smile. It might have been a smile he gave to someone else, someone he didn't love or feel unbreakably connected to. Did that mean he didn't feel those things toward me anymore?

I knew I was going to cry. I wanted to turn and run, but he was walking toward me in his perfectly pressed khaki shorts and blue-and-white-checked Peter Millar button-down with the sleeves rolled up. Despite his age, his hair was still the same lush dark brown it had been when we were kids, the same color as his eyes that, just like Sloane's and Caroline's, had tiny flecks of yellow that made them impossible to look away from. As he walked across the yard, I noticed he was wearing a new pair of driving shoes—and he still had the same strong, muscular legs I had watched run across the sand to catch a football for countless hours as a teenager. Forty-three years later, the man could still take my breath away. I tried to quickly wipe my tears and scolded myself. This was a situation of my own making.

"What's wrong?" Jack asked.

His voice lacked its usual warmth, which made me cry even harder. This had now crossed the line from bad to humiliating.

"I'm sorry," I said, trying to maintain a smidgen of my dignity. "It's harder than I thought that Mr. Solomon is gone."

I really was sad about him being gone. But that wasn't what had made my emotions overflow. That was reserved for seeing Jack for the first time since we had parted ways.

He smirked and shook his head. "Just the reaction I was looking for."

I didn't know what to say. I felt frozen to the ground. I had never experienced this from Jack, never imagined that someone I loved so much, whom I had so much history with, could turn so cold toward me.

The last time he had acted like this, in fact, had been the summer I turned seventeen, right here, in Peachtree Bluff, on the boardwalk across the street. Jack and I had had a summer romance. No. More than a summer romance. A summer love, the kind that, once you left it, woke you in the middle of the night, yearning for something, searching for it, reaching for it,

85

until you realized that what you really wanted, what you were really asking for, was someone who lived several states away. Too far to visit, too long distance to call. A love too impractical to try to keep, though your heart had really been his since the first time his hand brushed yours.

I hadn't seen or talked to him in nine months that summer, and as you do when you're young and insecure and unaware that crushes fade but true love lasts a lifetime, I had convinced myself he wasn't interested in me. And so, when I found out the boy I had been dating for the past two months was going to be in Peachtree Bluff for the first week of summer, sure, Jack crossed my mind. But I scolded myself for thinking he would still want to be with me. So, there I was, walking down the boardwalk to a local seafood restaurant, holding the hand of Stan whose last name I can't even remember, when I caught a glimpse of Jack. My blood ran cold, and I dropped Stan's hand. But it was too late. Jack had seen me. I couldn't walk away. So I smiled and said, demurely, "Hi, Jack."

Time stopped as I looked into his eyes. Something had happened to him in the nine months since I had last seen him. He had grown into himself, transformed from an awkward teenager with limbs too long for his frame to a tall, broad, handsome man. He looked from Stan to me and back to Stan, and it wasn't so much that I saw his jaw set; I felt it. "Hello, Ansley," he said, without venturing a smile. He turned his cold expression to Stan, who took a step back. He wasn't wrong to be afraid. Stan was, after all, a good five inches shorter than Jack.

Something broke inside of me as I realized the boy I had kissed good-bye through tears and promises of next summer only months earlier hated me. When he said, "Looks like your summer plans were different from mine," and walked away, I could scarcely breathe. I realized then, knew in my head what my heart had felt all along: his summer plans had been me.

It took me a moment to catch my breath before Stan and I continued walking down the boardwalk in silence. As we reached the door of the restaurant, I looked at him and said, "I'm so sorry. You're very nice, but I don't think I can do this anymore."

I slipped off my sandals and took off running down the boardwalk. I could hear Stan calling behind me, "Don't you at least want to get some shrimp?" But I was already gone. In fact, I realized, I'd never really been with Stan to begin with.

I still remember how rough the wood felt underneath my feet that night, the warmth of the boards that had spent all spring sunning themselves. I didn't know where Jack had gone, but I felt like if I ran fast enough, I would catch up to him. At the end of the boardwalk, my gut told me to turn right, and when I did, I could barely make out his tall frame in the setting sun. I sprinted down the sidewalk, the crowd parting like seagulls so I could get through.

Someone called, "Hey, where's the fire?" and, if I hadn't been so out of breath, I would have replied, though it was intolerably cheesy, "In my heart!"

When I got close enough, I managed to eke out, "Jack!"

He turned, and I stopped running, gasping for breath. I

was sweating and sure my hair was a mess. The spaghetti straps of my sundress had slipped down my shoulders, but I didn't care. I jumped into Jack's arms, and I kissed him like I would never stop.

He laughed and, putting me down on the ground and pushing my disheveled hair out of my face, said, "So you missed me after all?"

I smiled, so relieved to hear his laugh.

"Hey, Ansley?"

"Yeah?"

"I know I haven't seen you in nine months. But I think it puts me in a pretty good position to be able to say I love you."

I felt my jaw drop. All those nights I had lain awake, pained over the loss of this boy, wanting to say those very words to him, I hadn't been alone in my feelings. I kissed him again and said, "Really?"

He nodded.

"Well, I hope you know I love you too."

The mere memory of that night made me want to cry all over again, standing on Jack's new lawn. But I didn't. Instead, I said, "It was so nice of you to let the girls take your boat. I don't know how I can ever repay you."

"Well," he said dully, "two of them are mine even if they don't know it. Seemed like the least I could do."

I looked around and hissed, "Jack!"

He shrugged and whispered, "OK, OK. It's not like anyone can hear me."

A silver BMW convertible with the top down pulled into

the driveway, a foot from where I was standing. The car stopped, and squinting in the sunlight, I watched the driver get out. A woman. Not a sister or an aunt or a harmless friend. A beautiful woman with a tight skirt, well-highlighted hair, and far fewer wrinkles than I would have liked.

Jack waved. And smiled. He smiled at her. Couldn't muster more than a grimace for me, his first love, the mother of his two secret children, the woman who, not five weeks ago, he had wanted to marry. Now here he was giving *my* smile to a woman in Valentino pumps. Who wore Valentino pumps in Peachtree Bluff? Well, except for me. I did, of course, but that was only because Caroline made me.

The thought of Jack being with this other woman turned my stomach. But this was what I got. I had let the best man I had ever known go.

"Hi, sweetie," she said, walking toward him.

I wondered if it would repel her if I threw up in the yard or if it would bring them closer together, make me the common enemy. All I knew was that I couldn't stand around and watch this. But it was the proverbial car wreck from which I couldn't look away. They exchanged an air kiss.

It had only been five weeks. Five weeks, and he had already found someone else? Of course he had found someone else. He was gorgeous and well off and didn't have children—well, that anyone knew of. Very little baggage. What a fool I had been to let him go!

"Ansley," Jack said, the warmth he had given to *her* gone when he turned to me, "this is Georgia."

I laughed, and she joined me.

"I know," she said. "What are the chances I would have moved to Georgia?"

"Georgia is my decorator," Jack said.

I couldn't hide my shock. It was a blow when I thought he was with another woman. But he had found another *decorator*? This was entirely too much.

"Wait," I said. "I'm sorry. Did you say she was your *decorator*?"

He shrugged. "Yeah. So?"

"So, I don't know." I had suddenly lost all sense of propriety. "It's not like I've been talking about how much I want to decorate this house since 1974 or anything."

Georgia with her annoyingly perky breasts looked from Jack to me, confused. "Oh, right," I said. "You probably weren't even born in 1974."

"Yes, I was," she fired back. "In 1974."

I felt genuinely hurt, not only that he might be moving on romantically, but also that he couldn't put our differences aside. Jack knew, unequivocally, that this would hurt me almost as much as being away from him. He could stand there all frigid and angry in the yard, but the man knew I loved him. He knew turning away from him to take care of my family and protect the secret that could destroy all our lives was the single hardest decision I had ever made. In the top five, anyway. To do this to me was petty and cruel.

And I said so.

"Petty?" he said. "Really? OK, Ansley. Think whatever you

want. But why on earth would you think I would let you decorate my house after all you put me through?"

"Wait," little miss tan legs said. "You aren't Ansley Murphy,
are you?"

I crossed my arms, sizing her up. She readjusted her skirt,
which I found satisfying. I had made her uncomfortable.

"Yeah," I said. "I know. Startling that there is only one decorator named Ansley in a town with a population of three
thousand people."

She put her portfolio over her heart. "Oh my gosh!" she
gasped, all breathy and girlish. I wanted to say, *You're over forty.
Give it a rest.* "You are my inspiration. That shoot you just did
for *House Beautiful.* The yacht. It was unbelievable. The before
and after."

"*My* yacht," Jack chimed in.

I had softened to Georgia a bit now.

"Oh," she gushed. "Wow. I was excited about this job, but
now to know that I'm following in Ansley Murphy's footsteps . . ." She ran her free hand through her hair. "It's just too
much!"

I smiled tightly. "Well, thanks, I guess. If you need any
pointers, I've been dreaming of decorating this house," I turned
to Jack, "since I was fifteen years old.

"Nice to meet you," I mumbled, though it was anything but
nice to meet her.

I turned to walk away and was almost back to my gate
when I heard Jack call, "Ansley."

I ignored him. I was done for the day. I had a shred of

Damn it. I could tell he was walking toward me now. And I had nowhere to hide, so I turned around. He was smiling. Not a Jack-and-Ansley smile, but not a hideous grimace, either. I wasn't sure if it was menopause or the emotional stress I had been under lately, but I teared up again. As long as he would still smile at me, it would all be OK.

"I'm teasing you," he said.

I wrinkled my brow.

"Georgia isn't a decorator."

She shook her head. "I'm a Realtor from Atlanta. I'm the one who sold Jack the house."

Now I was confused. "What?"

"But I really am a big fan of yours," Georgia said.

"Oh, yeah," Jack chimed in. "That was a great addition to the script, G."

"What do you mean, 'script'?"

"It's a joke, Ansley. I haven't hired a decorator, but if you would like the job, I would certainly love to see what you have in mind before I make my decision."

It was ridiculous, considering I had just turned his half-sunk and fire-ridden boat into a palace at sea. But fine. I could play by the rules. He was punishing me a little bit, and that was OK. I could take it. I was so relieved. I could tell that if left to her druthers, Georgia would have used the fabric equivalent of a floral-print Hawaiian shirt in there.

So, no, with the girls leaving me in charge of AJ and Tay-

Kristy Woodson Harvey

lor, this wasn't the ideal time for me to pitch designs for this house I had dreamed of decorating for most of my life. But how hard could it be? I mean, the kids had to sleep sometime, right?

"I'll have something ready for you next week," I said.

Jack nodded. "Do you want to go inside and get a feel for the floor plan?"

I waved my hand. "I know the floor plan. I know the whole house by heart. And I know exactly how to make it fabulous."

"We'll see," Jack said.

Fine. That was fine. He could be like that. "See you around, Georgia," I said.

"Oh, I sure hope so," she replied. "Call me, Jack."

It nearly broke my heart in two when he said, "Thanks, Georgia. I will." It wasn't great. But it was better than her decorating the house, which I think said something unflattering about me and my priorities.

As I crossed back into my yard, I thought again that this wouldn't be so hard. Little did I know what these next few days held for me.

I WAS ANXIOUS TO get to the store the next morning. I had arranged for my two best friends, Sandra and Emily, to keep AJ and Taylor for two hours so I could get in there and grab all the fabric swatches, rug samples, and look books I might need for Jack's house. When I had asked Sandra, she had said, "Honey, Em and I will be thrilled to watch those sweet boys. We would

---

do absolutely anything to make sure you get to decorate Jack's house." Sandra and I had been close since we were children, so I knew what she wasn't saying was that they would do anything to make sure Jack and I spent some good, long, quality months together.

Whatever it took to get her here was fine by me. But I didn't want Sloane to know I was leaving her kids with sitters—even sitters who were practically family—so I needed her out the door. And fast. I went out to the guesthouse and called, "Caroline!" But I ran into James first.

He put his fist out. I bumped it with mine and laughed.

"It's you and me, Ans."

"It sure is," I said, feeling a little conflicted about that. "In fact, could you do me a favor?"

"Anything," he said, obviously, because he seriously needed to get back into my good graces.

"Could you please take AJ and Taylor out to breakfast?"

He went a little white. "All three of them?"

I slapped him on the back. "Oh, James. I know you can handle it. I'll have Emily and Sandra pick them up from you. It'll only be like half an hour."

I had lain awake all night thinking about fabric and furniture, and I had to get moving on this right now.

"Caroline," I called again. "I'm leaving."

I heard her footsteps on the stairs. "But don't you want to see us off?"

"Yes, darling." I grinned at her. "I want to see you off very, very much."

She opened her mouth in shock and swatted at me. "Mom! That is so rude! I can't believe you want us gone!"

"Kiss your sisters for me. See you in a week." As I opened the back door I yelled, "And call me!"

Just like that, I was out the door, the wind in my hair and the sun on my face. For two entire hours, I was going to be free.

ELEVEN

real living

sloane

November 16, 2009
Dear Sloane,

There is no substitute for the sea. I feel its absence when I'm away, tugging at me, even when I'm land-locked for months on end. I can feel the tide within my soul.

It's the same with you, Sloane. I see it already. Like the sea, you are a part of me, a loss I would feel indefi-nitely, the rolling tide for which I would eternally search . . . We're not supposed to admit it, but there's this fear that runs through us all the time, this low level of dread. What if I don't make it home? What if my mother has to fold the flag at my funeral? And then, even worse, what if my wife has to? It certainly comes to mind from time to time. I wouldn't be human if it didn't. Even still,

I know in my heart that I will always return home to you.

    All my love,

    Adam

THEY SAY HEARTBREAK IS soothed by the sea. Well, not they. Jimmy Buffett. It would have sounded more intellectual for me to quote Thoreau, maybe Shakespeare. Anyone, really. But it was Jimmy Buffett's lyrics I thought of on that trip.

And Adam's words in that letter that I remembered. I knew them as well as the sound of my own breath as it entered and left my body. How many times had I read those words? How many times had I handled his letters?

I have always thought I could feel Adam, that his pulse and my pulse were connected, that his soul and mine were one. It eased my fears when I woke up startled in the night, searching for him on his side of the bed, because I could feel him. Whether he was in Iraq or Afghanistan, off the coast of Carolina or the mouth of the Danube, my heart beat in time with his. Maybe it was his letters that made me feel that way; maybe it was his words, the rhythm of them, that made me feel his presence.

That's what scared me the most. Once those uniformed men visited me to deliver the unthinkable news, I quit feeling Adam. So I read and reread his letters trying to feel him, to bring him back to me, wherever he was.

When Caroline pulled me out the door that morning, I felt conflicted at best. As we walked through the front yard to the gate, I started to feel a tightness in my chest. My head felt light and woozy, and my breath came in short gasps. Emerson, who was on my left side, supporting me while Caroline pulled, stopped suddenly, alarmed. "Caroline," she scolded. "Stop!"

I leaned over, trying to catch my breath.

"No," Caroline said. "No. We are fifty yards from the boat. We're not stopping now."

"Are you OK, Aunt Sloane?" Vivi asked.

I stood, about to cross the street to our dock. I could turn back. I could get into bed, close the draperies, and go on like I had been. I could continue to neglect my children and obsess over the myriad ways in which my love might be suffering. Or I could take Caroline's hand. I could cross over, not only to the other side of the street, but also to the other side of my life, real living.

I thought of Adam, of what he would want me to do, and even though I'd had such a hard time feeling him these past few weeks, I knew he would want me to put one foot in front of the other and keep going. Because, without him, I was all my children had. I was our only hope.

I had to do this for me, for my boys, for my niece watching me. She needed to see me swim, not sink. I stood up and leaned on Emerson. I looked up into her clear blue eyes, the color of the Caribbean. "I'm ready," I said.

It wasn't much, but I knew my sister understood. I was ready to start living again.

Two hours later, scopolamine patch behind my ear, I was happy with the choice I had made. Caroline was expertly captaining Jack's yacht. I, for one, was grateful we weren't sailing. It had been bad enough to untie the lines and let out the dinghy. Jibs and masts were more than I could take.

I sat on the bench beside Caroline's captain's chair, Vivi and Emerson behind us on the blue-and-white-striped bench that was sofa-comfy.

"You should have seen her in her little Seafarer uniform," I was saying. "Your mom was amazing. She moved through the ranks so quickly that they thought they were going to have to invent new challenges for her."

"The water's in her blood," Emerson added. "Against all odds."

Caroline laughed.

"I'm so excited," Vivi said. "I'm excited about camp, but I'm also excited to have all of you to myself for three whole days."

Having my entire family's attention on me didn't happen often, but when it did, I savored it too.

"Aunt Emmy, here's what I want to know."

I was expecting her to ask something about camp. Instead, she said, "What's the deal with you and Mark?"

Caroline glanced back at Emerson as if to say, *You can tell her, but keep it clean.*

Emerson smiled, and I swear she looked fifteen again. "I kept telling Mark I didn't want to date him, that it was distracting and not in my plan."

Caroline shot a look at Emerson that I knew meant, *And then he started sneaking in your window, which isn't distracting and is in your plan?*

"So we were seeing each other here and there, but nothing serious at all." She paused, taking a sip of her Perrier. "But remember that Internet series I starred in, *Make It Happen*?"

Caroline and I both groaned, and Caroline said, "How could we possibly forget?"

I pulled the cellophane wrapper off a bag of popcorn and put it in the microwave.

"What's that?" Vivi asked.

She got to keep her clothes on, but in terms of writing, lighting, and production value, that show was just a notch above porn. "It was this awful show Aunt Emmy starred in."

"Mark told me he had watched that entire series nine times just to see me."

"Nine times?" Caroline asked, horrified. "How? Why? And, again how?"

I groaned. "If he watched that trash nine times, he is head-over-heels, can't-breathe-without-you in love," I said.

"I can't wait to grow up and be in love," Vivi said, sighing wistfully. "You and Mark are so cute."

Caroline shot me a pleading glance. She couldn't say anything because she was the annoying mother and would be immediately disregarded. But I was the cool aunt, so I could say, "Oh, Viv, don't rush it. Being young is wonderful and so fleeting."

"Yeah," Emerson interjected. "Love is complicated."

"You can say that again," Caroline added.

"You and Mark don't seem complicated," Vivi said.

As I removed the popcorn from the microwave, I decided

to change the subject. I turned to Emerson. "What's next for you after this movie?"

"I'm trying out for a new part . . ."

I nodded, and Caroline said, "But?"

"But I'm not sure. I mean, it's not that I'm not sure about the part." She sighed and rubbed her fingernail with the pad of her thumb. "It's kind of hard to explain. It's just, like, how much longer do I have as an actress, you know? Ten years if I'm super lucky and have an amazing dermatologist."

"Well, of course you'll have an amazing dermatologist," Caroline interjected. She turned back and winked at her sister.

"I won't be relevant that much longer and I'm not even that relevant now. And then what do I have?"

I reached over and took her hand, swallowing the feeling that, compared to what I was going through, this was trite, insignificant bullshit. But to her, this felt real. "You'll never be irrelevant, Em."

She looked up toward to the sky. "I'm sorry," she said. "Vivi, let's talk about camp some more."

"No," Caroline said, "it's OK. She should hear this. I think we shelter our girls from our real feelings, and it makes them grow up thinking there's something wrong with them when they feel self-conscious."

"Yeah, Aunt Emmy. I want to know everything," she said, rapt with attention.

Emerson sighed. "I've been doing this for eight years, and I haven't had my big break. Maybe I need to look at life after Hollywood. I want what the two of you have, you know? I want someone who loves me unconditionally. I want to have something when this is over."

I opened the paper bag, and steam and the smell of butter rose. I couldn't imagine being Emerson. The cameras, the lights, the people following her around, wanting to take pictures with her, wanting her autograph. Everyone wanted a piece of my little sister. It must have been exhausting. There were plenty of days that I envied the money and the perks that came along with her life. But there were some major drawbacks, too.

She shook her head and grinned the tiniest bit. "That, Vivi, if you must know, is what's complicated about Mark. He'll never leave Peachtree Bluff, and if I'm not ready to quit acting, then we could never be together."

"It could be kind of romantic," Caroline said. "A bicoastal life."

"What would that even look like? I'd fly in on the weekends, see my husband like a third of the time? What kind of life would that be?"

Both my sisters turned to me at the same time, as if it only now occurred to them how much time Adam and I spent apart.

I looked down into my popcorn bag, and Emerson sighed. "I'm tired and frustrated with being so average. Maybe it's time to give it up."

I thought back to the dreams I had had. I could see my work hanging in galleries and picture myself in New York, surrounded by fans and selling out at openings.

And then . . . what? I fell in love. I had children. And I couldn't find my way back to me. I had obsessed over them so completely, feeling the pressure of being a picture-perfect wife and mother getting heavier and heavier. Now I was in the opposite predicament of Emerson. Where she was beginning to realize that once her career was over, her life would be suddenly, fiercely empty, I was realizing that once my children were in school, I would be forced to admit that I had sacrificed my entire life for them. That was why I was so intent on homeschooling. If they were still at home with me, I didn't have to face the fact that I had watched all my dreams evaporate into thin air.

"Don't give up," I said. "I wish I hadn't."

Caroline turned to look at me. We were both wives and mothers. She was the pampered, Park Avenue housewife whose week revolved around Pure Barre and blowouts, and I spent my days in sweats cutting coupons on post. But we were the same. We both knew what it was like to completely sacrifice ourselves for the good of someone else.

"Really?" Emerson said, looking as shocked as I felt that I had just admitted that, even to myself. "Wow." Emerson and Caroline had always been closer than Emerson and I had been. But I couldn't help but feel like, with a few simple words, our bond had just been forged more deeply. I was the one who understood the crossroads Emerson was facing.

"Hey, Sloaney," Caroline said. "We're almost to Charleston. Could you help get us docked for the night?"

I smiled delightedly even though this wasn't really my thing. "Come on, Viv," I said. "You need to learn the ropes." I winked and added, "We'll have you boating like a pro before you even get to camp," as Caroline called, "We're docking stern to bow!"

"Your mother," I said, "is the best boat docker I've ever seen in my entire life. Even in the roughest currents or trickiest channels, one engine or two, it's nothing for her to slide right into any dock or slip."

Vivi grinned proudly.

I thought again about how I had given up everything else I loved in pursuit of one passion. My stomach churned when I considered that, perhaps, my husband had done exactly the same thing.

TWELVE

the natives

ansley

The girls had been gone one day, but as I looked around my kitchen, it was hard to believe it hadn't been longer. Mail was stacked on the island. Peanut-butter-and-jelly crusts, along with sippy cups and a jug of chocolate milk, were still at the boys' spots from lunch. The paper towels AJ had dropped had unrolled and made a trail from the sink to the fridge. In short, there was stuff everywhere. And that was just in the kitchen.

The back door opened and James walked in, Preston strapped to his chest. "Whoa," he said, looking around the kitchen. "Ans, the natives are winning."

I smiled at him tiredly.

"What can I do to help?"

I sighed. "Taking them to breakfast was a huge help, James. Thank you so much."

I glanced longingly at my design bag in the corner of the

room, wondering how I would have any sketches or mood boards for Jack by the end of the week.

"Well, I'm at your service," he said. Then he paused. "When do they go to Linda's again?"

We both laughed. I was still angry with James, of course, but today had cemented us as partners in crime. We only had each other. He might look a little too pristine in his collared shirt and pressed shorts, but no matter what I could say about James, there was no denying he was a great dad—and uncle.

He walked into the den. "How's *Doc McStuffins*, AJ?" I heard him ask.

"It's the one where the fire truck gets dedydrated."

"Oh yeah?" James asked, laughing at his mispronunciation. "Hey, where's your brother?"

My ears perked.

When AJ didn't respond, I ran into the den. "Where's Taylor?

"Taylor!" I called.

"Taylor!" James also called, running upstairs.

I checked the front door. It was still locked.

"Taylor!" I heard James call again.

Mom walked out of her bedroom.

"Good land of the living! What is all this commotion?"

Before I could answer, I heard a gasp and I went running.

When I reached Emerson's room, I gasped too. There were thick, black smears all over the wallpaper, bamboo coverlet, windowsills, and doors. "Taylor, no!" I said, lunging at him. I grabbed the tool of destruction out of his hand as he screamed.

"What is that?" I asked, as if he were going to respond.

I looked up at James. "Ah," I said. "Eyeliner."

Mom appeared in the doorway. "That's going to be tough to get out."

Emerson would be thrilled to hear her nephew destroyed her favorite eyeliner, but that was nothing compared to the havoc he'd wreaked on my favorite guest room.

"No, Gwansley. No!" Taylor was still screaming.

James scooped him up in one arm, Preston still strapped to his chest, and said, "All right, you little monkey. Let's get you downstairs into the holding area." He tickled his belly with his other hand, and Taylor giggled. "Do we need to take you to the zoo?" James asked, making a funny face at Taylor. "Because we only draw on paper, not the house."

He trotted down the stairs, and I stripped the coverlet and shams off the bed to take to the cleaners.

"Noooooo!" AJ shrieked. Biscuit started barking, adding to the chorus of obnoxious noises.

OK. Wall eyeliner would have to wait.

I ran downstairs. "Buddy," James was saying, "we can only play with Play-Doh in the kitchen."

"But I want Play-Doh while I watch *Doc!*"

I closed my eyes and slowly looked down to see Play-Doh ground into the gorgeous loose weave of my Stark Natura rug. I leaned over and grabbed the mound off the carpet, cringing at the orange residue jammed well into the fibers.

There was no doubt about it: the kids were winning.

James grimaced.

"It's OK, it's OK," I said. "You know what? I say we pack it up and drive over to the beach."

James nodded. "Excellent plan, Gransley."

"I want to go," Mom chimed in.

"Beach, beach!" Taylor said.

"Yay, beach!" AJ agreed.

"Gransley, I need to tinkle!" AJ exclaimed.

"Let's go, let's go," I said.

I smelled it before he said, "Uh-oh."

James attempted to cover his laughter with his hand as a puddle of golden liquid formed at AJ's feet. Well, at least it was on the hardwoods.

"Come on, Taylor," he said. "We're going to go out to the guesthouse while Gransley handles this situation."

Before he could even take his nephew's hand, I heard a loud burp, and as I turned, a stream of spit-up shot out of Preston's mouth.

"Oh my God!" James yelled, unstrapping the Baby Björn and holding Preston away from him, the baby's little legs dangling in the air. James looked down at the spit-up covering his clean, pressed shirt. And the poor guy couldn't even see the rivulets running down his back.

"Nope. That's not coming out," Mom said. Now it was my turn to laugh.

James cocked his head to the side and looked at Preston, "Really, buddy? I keep you clean and fed all weekend and this is how you repay me?"

Mom and I shared a glance. This was a make-or-break moment. Would James get mad, hand us the kid, and run off?

But he just laughed and said, "Let's go get you cleaned up, big guy."

"Wow," Mom said. "I'm impressed."

James shrugged. "He's my kid, Grammy. I even love his spit-up."

———

THAT EVENING, WHEN EVERYONE was clean, changed, and blowing bubbles on the front porch, James looked over at me and said, "I have a surprise for you."

I should have bit my tongue, but I couldn't. "I've had about enough of your surprises for one year."

"Ouch," he said, wincing. "OK, I deserved that. But I promise you'll like this one. I met a preschool teacher last week—"

I raised my eyebrow.

He laughed. "Come on, Ans. A sixty-five-year-old preschool teacher. She's coming to watch the kids and put them to bed while we go out for dinner."

I gasped. "You're kidding."

He looked at me seriously. "I would never kid about something as serious as bath time."

———

TWO HOURS LATER, SHOWERED and mercifully childless, we were sitting on the patio at Azure, one of my favorite restaurants, sharing a bottle of Opus One. James ordered it and he was paying, so I figured, why not?

"You impressed me today," I admitted.

"I did?" he said, taking a sip of the decadent wine.

"Yeah. I honestly thought you'd leave Preston with me, claiming some work emergency or something."

He laughed. "I know I have flaws, Ansley, but I take my kids seriously."

I wanted to roll my eyes and ask if that's why he abandoned them earlier this year for a supermodel.

"Plus," he said, "I promised Caroline I would do this for her." He looked at me intently. "I know I screwed our life up royally. But Caroline is my world. I would do anything for her. I will do anything to get back in her good graces."

The waitress filled my wineglass again and placed our tuna tartare between us. The wine had made me a little loose lipped, so I asked, "Are you shocked she's giving you another chance?"

"Honestly?"

I nodded.

"Beyond."

James motioned for me to help myself first. Despite his unfortunate Yankee upbringing, he did have good manners.

I served myself two slices of tuna, a few of the soba noodles, and a bit of the seaweed alongside it, and said, "I know she's a lot, James. I know she is. I still blame you, but I think even Caroline knows marriages fall apart because of two people."

He smiled. "She's a handful, that woman. But her complexity is what makes her so beautiful." I noticed tears in his eyes as he said, "She is everything, Ansley. She is my life. I will fight to win back her trust until the day I die if that's what it takes."

I could feel my heart shift just the tiniest bit. I thought maybe he was sincere, maybe I should be on his team. "That's good to hear," I said. "It really is." Then, trying to lighten the mood, I said, "And the day you die may be really soon if you ever cross her again."

We both laughed. I took another sip of wine and felt myself relax—until I saw Jack walk through the front door of the restaurant. With Georgia.

James followed my concerned gaze and shook his head.

Maybe it was the wine, maybe because he had been such good company, but for some reason I found it all spilling out to James. The breakup, how I missed Jack, how awful it was to see him with someone else.

He paused for a few seconds, long enough for me to feel like a totally irrational, middle-aged fool of a woman. I was about to formulate some excuse, blame the wine. But then James said, "She's just some woman, Ansley. For Jack, you're . . ." He paused. "You're the moon."

I smiled and took a sip of wine. As I swallowed, I hoped against hope that James was right. I hoped that someday, some-how, Jack would find his way back to me. That he could find it in his heart to choose me again. That despite what I had put him through, he would take the moon over Georgia.

THIRTEEN

top of the food chain

sloane

It was the first time I had slept through the night since I got the news about Adam. Maybe it was the rocking of the boat, the way the waves tossed you ever so gently, like a baby in his mother's arms. I woke up that morning to the sun coming through the porthole in my room, and praise the Lord, I missed my children. I wanted to squeeze them close to me, run my fingers through their hair, and kiss the tips of their little noses. The hardest part about Adam being gone was the numbness, the coldness, the horrible fear. My emotions had shut off. With the water surrounding me and the light streaming in, I felt like a mother again. I felt my heart ache for my boys. I felt stronger, cleansed, as only the sky as seen from the sea can do.

I walked up the stairs and out through the main cabin. I could see my bikini-clad sisters, sipping mimosas at the table.

"There's our girl!" Emerson exclaimed when she saw me. Even in my self-absorbed sorrow, I couldn't help but notice how prominent her collarbones seemed.

She handed me a croissant. "They're so divine that even Caroline ate one."

I knew she wanted me to respond with fake shock that Caroline had eaten anything resembling a calorie and play into the repartee. But I couldn't smile and laugh and pretend nothing was wrong. I didn't have the energy. Caroline didn't say anything, but she pointed to the corner, where they had set up an easel and a canvas, along with brushes and paints.

I shook my head. "No."

"You know it will make you feel better," Caroline said.

She wasn't wrong. I looked out at the sun glazing the blue water, the wind cooling the air. It *would* make me feel better. Eventually. But first it would absolutely wring me out, gut me to the point I wasn't sure I would survive, and bring me, like a chemo patient, to the brink of death before reviving me at the last second. I wasn't there yet.

Emerson reached for my hand. "Where's Viv?" I asked.

"Sleeping," Caroline replied. "Reveille is going to be a rude awakening for her."

Reveille. Each morning, at six thirty sharp, those notes rang out through post with a shock of cannon fire that startled me every time. The memory made me homesick.

I looked at Caroline, and for the first time in a while, I really saw her, the girl she had been, my best friend, my partner in crime, my support system in everything I did. She had saved me so many times. It seemed fitting that she would be trying to save me again.

I looked out over the water, and it hit me. "Does anyone else find it a little strange that we're on a boat called the *Miss Ansley* when our mother mercilessly dumped the poor man?" They knew I was the only one not totally thrilled about Mom dating after Dad passed away. When we were young, it horrified me to my very core, and I still had my misgivings. But we all loved Jack. He was perfect for our mother.

"Well, Mom wants to be available for all of us . . ." Caroline said.

She trailed off, and I felt a pang of guilt because taking care of all of us meant taking care of me. But my husband was MIA. For once, I felt like I deserved the extra attention.

"Do you think she's scared or something?" Emerson picked up. "Of falling in love again? Of losing another man she loves?"

Caroline bit her lip. "I try not to think about it because when I do, I come up with so many far-fetched reasons why she won't be with Jack."

I cocked my head to the side. Maybe it was my near comatose state, but I hadn't thought about anything like that. "Caroline, your imagination is too vivid."

Even though she was trying to be upbeat and witty, she seemed distant. "Car, you OK?" I asked.

She shrugged. "It's just sad, you know?"

"What's sad?"

"Everything. Mom loves Jack, yet she thinks she can't be with him. You love Adam, and he's MIA. I love James, and he betrayed me . . ." She bit her lip, like she always did when she was trying to hold back tears, and looked out over the side of the boat.

"I hate seeing you like this, Caroline," Emerson said. "It's your life and your decision, but I just feel like you should move on. It's not worth being miserable over."

Caroline and I shared a look. Emerson wasn't a mother. She hadn't been married. She didn't understand.

"Em," Caroline said, "have a brand-new baby and let some judge tell you he and your other kid are going to be away from you every other weekend and Wednesday nights, and then call me."

Emerson rolled her eyes. "I know, I know. You two are wives and mothers, and I don't understand anything. I just wonder if maybe it shouldn't be easier."

I wanted to point out that her relationship with Mark didn't seem terribly easy, but I bit my tongue. Caroline rolled her eyes.

"The hard part," Caroline said, "is that I still love James so much. But it will always be different now. For all these years I've had this sort of warm glow of knowing he loves me more than anything. And now it's gone. I'm mourning the life I lost."

She looked at me and winced. "I'm sorry. Poor choice of words."

I crossed my legs on the bench and shook my head. "No. You're mourning. I get that. Just because I'm going through something doesn't mean you aren't going through your own thing."

"So what if you make something new?" Emerson asked, and I finally felt like she was getting it.

"You didn't exactly help with that, Emerson."

She looked shocked. "How does this have anything to do with me?"

Caroline laughed incredulously. "Are you serious? Gee, I don't know. Maybe because you played Edie Fitzgerald in a movie and made the media storm a million times worse?"

Emerson had been apologetic then, but she wasn't now. "Like you wouldn't have done the same thing? I've seen you do way worse to get ahead. So don't act all holier than thou."

"Girls," I said. "Let's just calm down and talk this out."

"Talk it out?" Caroline said, and I immediately regretted turning her fury toward me. "She played my husband's mistress on TV. What's there to talk about?"

Emerson crossed her arms. "It was a *part*."

They both looked at me. "Look," I said, "I can't answer this one, but I wouldn't have done it, Emerson."

"Of course *you* wouldn't have," she replied.

I was taken aback. "What's that supposed to mean?"

"What it means," she shot back, "is that you're just like our mother. Vanilla. Predictable. Never done a shocking thing in your life."

I smirked because, believe you me, I could blow that theory right up.

"Fine," Emerson said, stomping into the salon. "Just gang up on me like you always do."

"Do we always gang up on her?" Caroline asked.

I scrunched my nose. "I'm pretty sure we don't." I paused. "But she isn't wrong about finding happiness in a new way."

Caroline softened and nodded. "I know. I'm going to try. I really am."

"Do you think you're going to let him move back in?" I asked.

"I don't know," Caroline said. She paused. "Maybe when the summer is over."

"There she is!" I said, interrupting Caroline, as Vivi emerged from the cabin, bleary-eyed. Her hair was messy from sleep, and she was wearing a huge T-shirt and gym shorts. But she was still beautiful, with that fresh face you really couldn't appreciate until you were older. She was a little Caroline, no doubt about it. But she was sweet—an upgrade if you asked me. This was a conversation she definitely didn't need to hear.

TWO HOURS LATER, EMERSON had reappeared, and I heard her quietly apologize to Caroline. I felt like I deserved an apology too, but I wasn't going to rock the boat.

I announced on the radio: "Camp Seafarer tower, this is the vessel *Miss Ansley* requesting permission to dock."

I laughed when I heard the signature response, "Ahoy, there, *Miss Ansley*!"

"Ahoy, there," I said.

Vivi rolled her eyes, and I said, "Oh, sugar. Get used to it."

"Take a southwest approach," the voice on the radio said. There was a pause, followed by, "Welcome back to camp, Captain Caroline and mates Sloane and Emerson."

We all laughed.

This was one monster of a boat to dock, and the current was ripping through the channel. Emerson was in charge of the bowline, and I had the stern. "Bow to stern," Caroline said, the steering wheel spinning through her hands. "Actually," she said, reversing the port engine at the last minute, "stern to bow. The current's got me."

"Switch the lines!" I yelled to Emerson, as I pulled the rope out of the port cleat and moved it starboard. I always wondered why you couldn't just keep lines on both sides of the boat, but Caroline always chastised me, saying that wasn't proper yachting.

I recognized the camp director as she hustled down the dock. "Caroline! Sloane! Emerson!" she cried. Seeing the campers captaining their Sunfish and tiny Boston Whalers brought back fond memories of making friends, sharing Reese's Cups from the canteen, writing letters to the boys at Camp Seagull, and sneaking out of the cabin at night to meet said boys on the golf course. It was all so innocent, so simple. I wanted to hug Vivi and beg her to never grow up.

LATER THAT NIGHT, SO late it might have been morning, it was as if it were calling to me, as though I could feel it. The crisp linens and bedding my mom had chosen for the room on the boat draped around me. They made me feel protected and secure in the way only the most comfortable beds can. It was cool and perfectly dark in the boat that night. Yet, I couldn't sleep. Because I could feel it. I ignored it for what must have been hours. But, finally, like a clandestine lover you know is wrong but can't resist, I went up to that canvas.

I rolled up the sleeves of Adam's oxford, soft and thin from being washed so many times, like another layer of my own skin. It felt like his arms around me, and I imagined him whispering in my ear that he loved me. The water was perfectly still, the moon's reflection bright on the surface. As the stars danced and twinkled, I prayed that my husband was fighting, that he was feeling me supporting and loving him. Because I was. With every breath.

My easel set up overlooking the boats in the Beaufort, North Carolina, harbor where we had moored for the night, I tentatively swiped my brush into the paint, and with that one motion, I was gone, consumed by another world that lived inside my head, a world that was trying desperately to get out, to escape the darkness and burst into the light.

I have always been cautious with my paintings. I am a perfectionist by nature and refine and edit until they are perfect. But not that night. That night I tore through the canvases, strokes flying. I didn't care if the paintings were complete, didn't want them to be perfect. They weren't supposed to be perfect. They were supposed to heal me, to give me courage, to set me free.

I let myself feel the thing I thought I shouldn't. It welled up inside me and took over my mind, my body, my brush. Anger. Not only that Adam had left me, that he was sacrificing himself, us, our family, but also about everything in our marriage that had ever been tough, every time I'd wanted to stand up for myself but hadn't, every time I had wanted to speak my piece but held it in. For the first time, I didn't feel guilt, just pure, unadulterated, hot rage. This stroke was for all the times Adam came home and didn't ask if he could help with the kids. This one was for the times he looked disapprovingly at a pile of laundry on the floor when I had cleaned up after babies all day. These were for using my toothbrush, leaving the toilet seat up, refusing to leave his dirty shoes by the back door.

I felt it all, all those emotions I had buried so deep. And when I was done, I cried. Not a cry of fragility, but of cleansing. I knew my husband wasn't perfect. Admitting that to myself made me feel a little better. He was a good man, a good husband. But he wasn't a saint, and neither was I. My only prayer was that the perfectly imperfect world we had created together would continue to spin.

AS THE SUN ROSE, bright and bold and beautiful, I heard Caroline's panic-laced voice calling, "Sloane!"

"I'm up here," I called, yawning.

She appeared in the doorway, clad in a short silk and lace nightgown.

"You're wearing *that* to sleep alone on a boat?" I asked.

She grinned at me. "You scared me to death."

"What did you think? That I'd jumped or something?"

She shook her head. "Not jumped. You wouldn't kill yourself and leave your children. But maybe swept out to sea in your grief like in a Victorian novel?"

She finally looked down around my feet. "Oh my gosh. Wow."

She sat down on the deck of the boat, crossing her legs in a very unladylike manner for someone wearing a tiny nightgown. "Caroline, honestly," I said.

She gasped, ignoring me. "These are amazing. The best paintings you've ever done. For real."

They were all shades of gray, silver, and a little white. Not as much black as I had expected. That was how my life felt now. Less dark, a little brighter, but still completely devoid of color.

"Pain will do that to you, I guess."

"Girls," I heard Emerson groan. "It's like six a.m." She stopped in her tracks and picked up the first painting I had done. "Whoa." She held it to her chest. "This one's mine. Sign it now. I'm taking it to my room."

I laughed. "You can have it. You don't have to hoard it away."

"Get your bikinis on," Caroline said, clapping. "We have big plans today."

"I'll get breakfast ready," Emerson said. She pointed to me. "You keep painting."

"Then I guess I'll drive," Caroline said, as if that weren't a foregone conclusion.

"Should we check in with Mom and the kids?" I called to Caroline.

"Later!"

I stretched my shoulders and wrists. I had one more painting in me. The brushstrokes became less precise as Caroline cut through the waves. But that was the beauty of it. This was the painting that would always remind me of this trip, my sisters, and how they saved me, pulling me out of the sea when I was certain I was drowning.

Thirty minutes later Caroline was expertly docking in front of some tennis courts and a gazebo while a very taut, tan twenty-something boy grabbed our lines and tied us up.

A large sign read, *Private Club. Docking for Members Only.* "Caroline," I whispered, "what are we doing here? You aren't a member of this club."

She looked toward heaven like I was dense. She and Emerson were already out of the boat and held their hands out to me.

"She's a beauty," the boy on the dock said.

Caroline put her arm around me and said, "She is, isn't she? She's my sister."

I rolled my eyes. "I think he meant the boat."

"Ah, yes. Well, she's a beauty too."

"Do you have your membership card?" dock boy asked.

My heart raced.

"Tanner has it," Caroline said.

He grinned. He was very, very cute. I turned toward Emerson, but she didn't seem to notice. "By all means, go right ahead."

Caroline linked her arms through mine and Emerson's.

"It's good to have friends in high places," she said.

"Who's Tanner?" Emerson asked.

"Top of the food chain," Caroline said. "The person who runs it all."

I assumed she meant the owner or manager, but when Emerson cocked her head to the side, Caroline said, "The bartender, of course."

Before we had even reached the clubhouse across the street, yellow-and-white-striped beach loungers with matching umbrellas had been swept out for us.

"Ms. Murphy," our beach attendant said to Emerson, "someone is bringing down morning refreshments for you right away."

"Oh, OK," she stammered. "Thank you."

I laughed and shook my head. "You used Emerson's name to get us in the club for the day, didn't you?"

"Of course I did," Caroline said, as if offended I would ask something so obvious. "I do it all the time." She grinned at Em.

I settled into my cushioned chair.

"Maybe you aren't so insignificant, after all," Caroline said to Emerson. Suddenly I was more certain than ever that Caroline was always up to something. She was making sure her sister knew that while, no, she might not have made it as big as she had dreamed, she had made it pretty far.

Emerson was already sunning her long, tanned limbs, and I admired—and envied—the line of muscle that ran from her ankle all the way up to her hip bone. She was spectacular. The beach club probably granted us entrance so people could stare at her all day. "We'll talk about this later," Emerson said, "when I'm not so relaxed."

"Excuse me." I looked up to see a woman about our mother's age in a huge hat and sunglasses, standing over Emerson with a napkin and a pen. "Emerson Murphy? May I have your auto-graph, please?"

Emerson smiled. "Of course."

"I just loved you in *Secret Lovers*. You *made* that movie. I can't wait to see what you do next."

Caroline and I smiled at each other.

"Miss Murphy," another beach attendant said quietly, "your publicist told us when she called that Bellinis were your favor-ite. These were made from organic, local Georgia peaches and Moët and Chandon, as requested."

Emerson lowered her sunglasses at Caroline, who was try-ing to avoid her glance. "Really, Caroline? Moët and Chandon in a *Bellini*?"

"Take a sip and see what a difference it makes."

It was terrific.

"I will ignore, just this once," Emerson said, "that Bellinis are *your* favorite, not mine. If you're going to use my name, at least get my drinks right."

"They don't carry Smirnoff Ice here, Emerson," Caroline joked.

Only, that's where Caroline was wrong. An hour later, a very handsome young beach waiter was asking, "A fresh towel, Mrs. Beaumont?"

Caroline unrolled it and, hiding inside, was a Smirnoff Ice. A hot one.

The game of "icing" someone had been out of practice for years as far as I knew, but it was something my sisters and I used to love to do to each other. Like a champ, Caroline, perfectly coiffed and manicured, got down on one knee in the sand, popped the top, and chugged that hot Smirnoff Ice. She dramatically wiped her mouth—while Emerson howled with laughter.

And then it happened. The thing I was afraid I was no longer capable of, the thing I thought I might never do again. As a laugh escaped from my throat, I realized that no one— and no Bellini—in the world could make me feel as carefree as my sisters.

———————

A FEW HOURS LATER, back on the boat, my sister was saying, in typical Caroline fashion, "Girls, the beach walk was great, but we need a little Yogilates before we get going."

Emerson and I groaned. "No one wants to exercise after drinking on the beach all afternoon, Caroline. That sounds awful."

She was already setting up the mats on the bow. I gave Emerson a withering look. "Why?" I asked. "Why do we keep her in our lives?"

"I don't know," Emerson said. "I can't figure it out."

"It's because you love me and you know I'm right," Caroline said.

"Damn it," Emerson said.

We were only into our second sun salutation when I noticed Emerson's form looked a little off. Caroline must have noticed it too because she jolted up and screamed "Em!" right as Emerson collapsed to the bow, landing solidly on her right side.

"Oh my God!" I cried, running over to her.

"Did she pass out?" Caroline asked as we crouched around our sister, who had opened her eyes and was looking at us, confused.

She tried to sit up. "No, no. Wait!" I said.

"What is it again?" Caroline asked.

"If it's red, raise the head," I said.

"If it's pale, raise the tail," Emerson finished. No permanent brain damage.

"She's definitely red," Caroline said, sitting Emerson up. "I'm so sorry, Emerson. I'm so sorry."

"It's not your fault," she said. "I think I'm just dehydrated."

I looked at Caroline skeptically. "I think we need to get you to a doctor just in case," I said. Caroline nodded in agreement.

"You *guys*, absolutely not," Emerson said. "It's hot, I haven't eaten much today, and I've been drinking. I'm totally fine."

"I say better safe than sorry," Caroline said. "We can get an Uber, run to urgent care . . ."

"I said no," Emerson said, taking charge.

I ran into the salon and grabbed a water for her. As she sipped, she said, "OK. Yoga is over. Caroline, you go drive. I want to wake up in Savannah."

Caroline looked at me warily. "Emerson," she said, trying again. "We are going to be out at sea. If you need help, the Coast Guard is going to come, and it's going to be very dramatic."

"Is that what you want?" I teased. "A dramatic rescue at sea by a hot sailor?"

She smiled. "No. I'm fine. I'm ready to get home. I miss Mark."

I shrugged at Caroline.

"If you're sure," she said.

"Totally sure."

Emerson turned over her water bottle, gasped, and threw it to the ground like it had suddenly grown fangs and bitten her.

"What?" Caroline asked.

"Are you kidding me? You're feeding me water out of a number-six plastic? Have I taught you nothing?"

I rolled my eyes at Caroline and said, "Yeah. I think she's fine," as Emerson chanted, "Five, four, one and two, all the rest are bad for you."

"I will get you nonpoisonous water immediately," I said sarcastically as we helped Emerson up and into the air-conditioning. I handled the lines while the boat idled, and we were off again.

It wasn't until I went to go check on Emerson that I saw them. My heart almost stopped beating. Her cheekbone had a deep, dark bruise, and her arm was covered in what looked like a rash, but upon closer inspection was a cluster of tiny bruises.

"Oh my God, Emerson," I said.

She shrugged. "You know I bruise really easily."

Caroline took a couple of steps toward us and gasped. "Emerson, that is not normal."

I agreed.

She bit her lip. "I haven't felt great lately. Kind of dizzy, and

I'm always exhausted. Just walking up the stairs makes my heart race."

She pulled down the side of her bathing suit bottoms to reveal a huge red and purple bruise.

Back at the helm, Caroline said, "Look, the moment we get back to Peachtree Bluff, you're going to the doctor." She paused. "In fact, James and I have to go to the Hamptons for a benefit. Why don't the two of you come with us, and we can get you to one of our doctor friends?"

Now my heart was racing for two reasons: There was no way—especially now—I could get on an airplane or face New York, neither of which I'd done since 9/11. And there was definitely something wrong with my little sister.

Emerson shook her head. "No, no. I don't want Mom to know anything is going on. I'm sure it's nothing. I'll just run to a doctor in Peachtree."

"And if it's something more, I want you to be seen in New York," Caroline said.

"Fine," Emerson agreed, exhaling. She looked at us. "Promise me," she said. "Not a word to Mom. She has enough on her plate."

Caroline and I simultaneously put our three fingers up in scout's honor.

I hated keeping secrets from my mother. But we had done it before. One more time probably wouldn't hurt.

scary small person

ansley

"We made it," I said to James over my car's Bluetooth speaker, as I was pulling out of Linda's driveway in Athens's charming Five Points neighborhood.

"We sure did," he said. These last few days had really brought out a different side of James. I was beginning to see him not as the slick, suit-wearing lawyer, but a family man capable of standing by my side when the chips were down—like when I was drowning in poop and finger paint.

Against all odds, I had even managed to put a presentation together for Jack. "You should know that Jack's coming by the house at three."

"So what you're delicately telling me is to keep it clean?"

I laughed. "Exactly."

It would have been more professional to have our meeting in my shop, but I wanted Jack to be in a home I had put my stamp on from top to bottom. And I knew it was childish, but after seeing him with Georgia a few nights earlier, I wanted him to remember what it was like for us to be more than client and decorator.

At three on the dot, Jack walked through the front door, Biscuit licking his bare ankles with gusto. I snapped my fingers at her. "Biscuit! Stop that!"

Jack laughed as he walked into the living room. I was sitting cross-legged on the floor surrounded by paint chips, wallpaper books, fabric swatches, and furniture catalogs.

"Wow," he said. "This is not what the other decorators brought by to show me."

"They aren't as brilliant as I am," I deadpanned.

He nodded. "Clearly." He paused. "Are the girls having fun?"

"Oh, yes," I said. "It was very, very kind of you to let them use your boat."

He sat down on the floor across from me. "How are they, Ansley? Are they OK? I want to do something to help. I really do."

I smiled at him, that familiar warmth running through me. He was such a kindhearted soul, a generous man. That was what had always drawn me to him.

"Caroline is just going to have to feel it, I think. And Sloane . . ." I shook my head, hoping he didn't hear the crack in my voice. But he must have, because he scooted beside me and pulled me into him.

"I want so badly to be mad at you," he said. "I want to hate you for not giving me what I want. But then I think of all you're going through and I understand you a little more. And I can't hate you as much as I want to." He kissed the top of my head, and a little laugh broke through my tears.

"This is the least professional interview I've ever done," I said.

"Ansley, we both know I don't know a thing about being a parent. But I know about you. I know they are your life, but don't lose yourself in this." I looked up into his earnest face. "Please."

"I'm trying," I said. "That's why I want to do this house so badly. It will help me focus my attention somewhere other than on Sloane and Adam and even Caroline and James. Their unhappiness is so consuming."

"How's your mom?"

I shrugged, and as if she heard him, she called from her room, "Ansley!"

"I've got her, Ans," James called from the kitchen. He walked into my mother's room, saying, "Ansley is with a client. Remember?"

As I was saying, "She seems better," James walked in. "I'm sorry, Ansley," he said, "but I think you'd better come in here."

I got up, and Jack followed me. Mom was looking around the room and glanced up at me when I came in. "What's wrong, Mom?"

I could tell she was confused. "Whose suitcase is that?" she asked, pointing to the corner of the room.

"What?" I asked.

"Whose suitcase?" she repeated.

"Well," I said slowly, "it's yours, Mom. You've had it for like twenty years."

"It's not mine," she said indignantly.

I looked at Jack helplessly. He rolled the suitcase to her. "See?" he said, pointing to the plate at the top of the suitcase.

"Those are my initials," she said.

"Right."

"My initials, but not my suitcase." Then she peered at Jack. "And who in the world are you?"

"Oh my God," I said. "Is she having a stroke?"

"Ansley, for heaven's sake, I'm not having a stroke." Then she looked up. "Jack, why in God's holy name do you have my suitcase over here? It belongs in the corner."

Jack looked concerned. I was sure I looked horrified. This was what I had been talking about for months now, what the doctors assured me was just old-age confusion.

"Mom? Do you know where you are?"

Now she really looked confused. "Darling, of course. I'm in the same bedroom I've had since I was a little girl at my parents' house in Peachtree Bluff, which is now your house in Peachtree Bluff, much to the chagrin of your brother John." She grinned at me. "And this is Jack, the man you have loved since you were a teenager but are too foolhardy to let back into your heart now."

Jack laughed. "She seems fine to me."

I sighed in relief. "Thanks, Mom. That's great." Whatever it was seemed to have passed.

I wanted to take her to the doctor or at least call, but every time I did, they acted like I was this delusional woman who couldn't accept that her mother was aging.

"I'm so sorry, Jack," I said when we were back in the living room.

"It's OK," he said. "It's hard. When that started to happen to my dad, it nearly broke my heart. The first time he didn't remember who I was . . ." He looked away from me, and I wanted to wrap him in a hug and kiss him. It was one of those moments—not the first and probably not the last—that made me realize what Jack and I had had as kids was nice, but what we could have as adults could be so much more. He was different. I was different. But we still shared so many important things.

"Before crisis strikes again . . ." I said, holding up a handful of swatches.

Jack softened and put his hand up to stop me, the hostility of move-in day behind us. "Of course I want you to decorate my house, Ansley. That was half the reason I bought it."

I smiled coyly. "You won't be sorry."

"I know I won't be sorry," he said. "I . . ." He trailed off, smiling. "Do you remember that night we fell asleep on Starlite Island?"

I laughed. "Remember? Oh, I'll never forget. And we woke up, and it was four thirty in the morning?"

He nodded. "We paddled as fast as we could from Starlite back to the dock, and as we were running across the street, you stopped in front of my new house and said, 'Man. That one could really shine in the right hands.'"

That had been a perfect night, as so many of those young

nights with Jack had been—besides the fear that my parents would wake up and kill me for spending the night out with a boy, of course.

"That night, I remember thinking I would give anything to buy you that house, to live there with you and make it our own."

"Jack . . ." I said.

He shook his head. "No, I get it, Ans. This isn't me coming on to you. It's just I could tell in the yard that I had hurt you, that you thought I didn't remember. But I did. I remember."

"Well, thank you."

He smiled. "And, also, Caroline told me to buy it, and she's a really, really scary small person."

Between my laughter I said, "Caroline told you to buy it?"

He winked at me. "She had some notion that maybe you would fall in love with the boy next door."

All those years ago, I had. I had fallen in love with the boy next door—or the boy down the street, anyway. Sitting with Jack now, I had the feeling that maybe, just maybe, I could fall in love with the man next door too.

FIFTEEN

the brightness of the stars

sloane

November 28, 2010

Dear Sloane,

Even out here, in a dry desert that it feels like God surely has forgotten, the stars shine bright and the moon hangs low, and for a moment, between the gunshots and the shrapnel, the wounded soldiers and the innocent civilians lost in the mix, there is a moment, just a moment, that still feels like a miracle, that still feels like life can be beautiful and good. I'm convinced that these moments are what make up our lives, that the moments that are nothing short of miraculous are the ones that define who we are, that we will remember always. At least, that's what I tell myself. Because I'd hate to think that I will remember the fighting but I will forget the brightness of the stars.

All my love,

Adam

I PRAYED ALL DAY, every day that God would bring Adam home to me, unharmed. My faith was my sanity, and I wondered, not for the first time, how my mom survived everything she had without belief in a higher power. My faith was one of the greatest gifts I had. Because of it, I knew that even when I couldn't quite see the end, everything would work out the way it was supposed to.

That didn't keep me from feeling utterly terrified and devastated, but it helped me put one foot in front of the other when I didn't want to. That day, I wanted to. I could practically smell my children, feel their sticky little hands on my face, and hear their sweet, small voices, so filled with excitement and joy.

When I walked through the door, my two boys flew into my arms so quickly that they almost knocked me over, giggling and covering my face with kisses. It occurred to me that, in a world where children's laughter exists, all can never really be lost. I hadn't even finished kissing them before I looked up and saw that Caroline had hung one of my paintings from the boat over the mantel.

"It's perfect," Mom said. "It changes the entire room."

"Aren't the grays so good?" Caroline asked.

Emerson walked through the front door, canvases in her arms.

"Sloane!" Mom gasped, admiring each one. "You should sell these."

I was going to say no. These canvases were too important to me. They were my heart and soul, all of my emotions draining out from my fingertips and onto the canvas. But then I remembered: I needed the money. This could be the answer to my prayers. It could get me out of the mess I'd made and help me start over. I picked up one of the canvases. Sure, these paintings may have helped bring me out of the darkness. But if I could let them go, I would be free. Not forever. But for now. "Not yet, Mom. I'm not ready. But soon."

Grammy walked in wearing a beautiful yellow pantsuit. Her hair was freshly combed and her makeup expertly applied with a steady hand, but I would never get used to seeing her with a cane. I didn't like it. It made her seem old. I didn't want her to be old. I wanted her to be young and so very alive. I wanted her to walk on the beach with us, take the boat over to Starlite Island. I wanted her to be immortal. As foolish as it seems, I almost believed she was.

She hugged me and kissed my cheek. "We had so much fun with the boys, darling. They are precious."

Then she hugged Caroline. "And that James." She paused. "I hate him much less now."

We all laughed as Mark burst through the door. Emerson jumped into his arms like she hadn't seen him in months, kissing him passionately.

"Darling, for heaven's sake," Grammy said.

Mark backed away from Emerson, assessing her. "Why do you have on long sleeves?"

Caroline and I shared a glance.

Mark was studying Emerson's face. As he said, "Oh my

God, Emerson," she pulled him out the door, and I knew he had noticed her bruise. I looked at Caroline again and she mouthed, "Doctor. Today."

I motioned toward the front door with my head, and Caroline followed them. She could handle that one.

I had other things on my plate, namely paying my bills.

———

TEN MINUTES LATER I was sitting on the end of the bed, thinking about miracles. My dad always believed in them. Adam certainly did. And me? I did to an extent, I suppose. But, while a lot of great things had happened to me in my life, I wasn't sure that any of them would qualify as a miracle. I mean, *miracle* is a pretty big word, something that defies logic, that defies explanation, something that you seemingly willed into being. But that was the only, single explanation for what was happening now.

I just kept staring at *$0.00 due*. How was that possible? After years of feeling sick every month, of making minimum payments and watching the overall balance climb higher and higher, of being terrified Adam—or anyone, for that matter— might find out this terrible secret that, while, on the outside, I appeared to be this wonderful steward of our family's money, in reality, I was nothing more than a fraud, I had been given a clean slate.

I heard Caroline's voice. "You're going to burn a hole through it."

She sat down beside me, and I clutched the paper to my

chest so she couldn't see. "Is that your credit card bill?" she asked.

I wanted to lie. I was so embarrassed about my spending habits and how it had been nearly impossible for me to support our family on our salary. But she was my sister. Maybe there shouldn't be big secrets between sisters. Besides, this was Caroline. I could tell her now, or she would pull it out of me later.

I looked at her in amazement. "It's gone," I said, still totally mystified, looking at the zeroes again and praying it wasn't a glitch in the computer system.

"Your credit card is gone?"

"No. My balance."

She looked at me like I was dense. "Well, yeah, it's gone," she said. "I paid it."

I could feel my eyes widen. "You paid my credit card bill?"

She nodded. "Somebody had to pay your bills while you were in a coma in here." She paused. "And, no offense, but how in the hell did you ever, *ever* think you were going to pay it?"

I threw my arms around her neck with so much force that I nearly knocked us both off the bed. I could feel the tears in my throat. "I will pay you back. I promise," I said. "This is the nicest thing anyone has ever done for me."

"Sloane, what were you thinking?"

I shrugged, ashamed. "I don't know. It's what I do to keep the boys from feeling sad their dad is gone. I buy them stuff they don't need and I can't afford." I sighed. "I always assumed we were going to get the money Dad had left us, and it would be fine. Then I couldn't stop, and the bill kept getting higher. And I would save up a little to pay it down, and then something would happen and we'd need the money . . ." I trailed off, envying my sister's life. She didn't have these worries. She had an endless amount of money at her disposal. I couldn't imagine what that felt like, how freeing it must be to know that, no matter what, you were going to be OK. You could pay your way out of whatever mess you spent yourself into.

We didn't have that luxury. I didn't want to wound Adam's pride, but I needed that security. I needed to know that if something happened, I wouldn't have to go running to my mom or sister. I could in an emergency, of course, but a run-up credit card bill didn't feel like an "emergency" per se. I needed a job.

Caroline took my hand. "I totally get that, Sloane, but they don't care about all that stuff."

I nodded, tears gathering in my eyes. "The worst part is that it felt like every month I was lying to Adam. I was living in fear that he would get to the mailbox before I did, open my credit card bill, and see what I had done."

She ran her fingers through her hair, patted my leg, and said, "It's all cleaned up now. Don't worry. But don't do it again."

I shook my head. "Car, I'm paying you back."

I couldn't begin to imagine where I would get that kind of money, but I would. Little by little, I would pay my sister back the debt I owed.

She shook her head. "No, Sloane. I don't want you to. I had put something aside for a rainy day, and this was a rainy day." She cleared her throat. "So now you will owe me and, trust me, I will cash in the favor in a big way."

I threw my arms around her neck again. "Whatever you want, Caroline. Honestly. Anything."

She raised her eyebrow, and I realized I shouldn't have offered that. But I felt free, like I was running through an open field of daisies. And now the credit card would be used solely for emergencies, just like Adam and I had always intended.

Part of me felt bad for not paying my sister back, but I also knew it was completely fruitless to argue with her. It always had been. Even when we were kids.

Even about the big things.

In the fifth grade, when we were studying genetics, I became obsessed with the idea that my father didn't give me any of my DNA—and I desperately wanted to know who *had*. Where were my brown eyes from? The dimple in my chin? Was my biological father good at math like I was? I had gone to my parents, but they told me that Caroline and I had to agree about whether to find out who our biological father was since we had the same donor. I thought that would be simple. Why wouldn't Caroline want to know who her father was?

Only, she didn't. She was adamant. "Why would you do that to Dad?" she had asked me. "What if he came to you and said he had another daughter he wanted to meet? How would you feel about that?"

She always knew how to get to me, to appeal to my emotions, of which I had many. "He seemed OK with it," I had said, a little hurt.

"Well of course he *seemed* OK with it. He didn't want to hurt your feelings." Then she had crossed her arms and sighed. "Fine. If you want to crush our daddy by trying to have someone take his place, then fine by me. But that's on you, Sloane."

I remember how the tears stung my eyes, and I vowed right then and there that I would never hurt my dad by finding out who my real father was. After he died, I considered it, but then I didn't want my mom to feel like I was trying to replace him. So I went on about my life—and watched a lot of Lifetime movies where the daughter gets a disease and has to search out her biological parents. I didn't *want* a disease. But I had to be prepared.

"I've never been able to argue with you," I said now. "Not even about finding out who our sperm donor was."

Caroline scrunched her nose. "I'm sorry."

I put my hand over my chest and made a face like I was having a heart attack.

"Ha. Ha," she said. "My apologies are not that rare. But it wasn't right of me to talk you out of finding out who our sperm donor was. If it was something you felt like you needed to know, I should have gotten on board."

I smiled. "Of all the bitchy things you ever said to me, the one about replacing Daddy might take the cake."

"That's really saying something." She paused and looked down at her hands, the massive apology diamond James had bought her catching my eye. "But Dad wasn't the reason why I didn't want to meet our sperm donor."

"Were you scared?"

"Maybe a little. But I was most worried about Emerson. It would be like you and I had this whole family that she wasn't a part of. I didn't want her to feel left out."

I squeezed her hand. "Caroline, that may be the most self-less thing you've ever done."

She swallowed and nodded regally. "I know," she said very seriously, and we both burst out laughing.

"If you want to know now," she said, "I'm OK with that. I could handle it."

I smiled and raised my eyebrows. "Do you want to know?"

"No, but I will if you want to."

I shook my head. "Nah. I'm fine. I don't need to open that door. My life is complicated enough." I paused. "Plus, I mean, I know she's twenty-six, but I kind of feel like it would be worse for Emerson now than it would have been when we were kids. I mean, it's like we get this replacement father, and hers is still dead."

Caroline shrugged. "Yeah, I guess."

"Moooooommmmmmmmeeeeeeee," I heard AJ call from down the hall.

"Good timing," Caroline said.

We stood up, and I hugged her again. "Thank you," I said. "Thank you, thank you, thank you."

She smiled. "I love you."

"I know," I said, before turning and rushing out the door to hear what the second "Moooooommmmmmmeeeeee, I need you!" was all about.

I realized then that I felt almost strangely relieved I would never have to talk about my sperm donor again. I could spend the rest of my life content in the knowledge that my father was my father, and that was all that mattered. In some ways, it was as big a relief as knowing that my final balance was zero.

———

IT WAS NO BIG secret Caroline hated doctors' offices. She hated the germs, the people, the general smell. I swear I didn't think we would get her through her hospital tour when she had Preston.

Needless to say, she wasn't the first one volunteering to go to the doctor with Emerson. I, on the other hand, wanted to go, but we weren't sure what excuse we could use to leave together without Mom wanting to come along. Plus, once Mark saw those bruises on his beloved Emerson, there was no way he was going to miss her appointment.

Mom had taken Grammy to lunch, Taylor was napping, and AJ and I were playing what felt like our hundredth game of Candy Land when Mark's car appeared in the front driveway.

I grabbed AJ's hand and Taylor's monitor and flew down the stairs at top toddler speed to the guesthouse, where we'd all decided to meet after Emerson's doctor's appointment. A somber-looking Emerson was leaning against a protective-looking Mark.

"So?" Caroline asked breathlessly.

"So, it's not great," Emerson said.

Mark interrupted her. "But we don't know that for sure yet."

She shrugged. "OK. True. But he said from my initial blood work and the pattern of my bruising that it looked like it was aplastic anemia."

The part of me that was sure she was going to say "leukemia" or "cancer" was relieved, but the part of me that wasn't sure what these scary medical words meant was terrified.

But Caroline knew what they meant. "Do they know why you aren't producing new red blood cells? I mean, could it be a virus? Autoimmune disease?"

"Back up a minute here," I said, looking at Caroline in disbelief. "One, how do you know so much about aplastic anemia? Two, what even is that?"

Caroline bit her lip. "Well, when I saw her arm, I did a lot of Googling. It's like anemia, but on steroids. Basically, your body quits making new red blood cells, which is a problem because, you know, oxygen."

"So is it treatable?"

Mark interjected. "They aren't even positive that's what it is yet."

"Yeah, right. We got it, Mark," Caroline said.

He was annoying me too. This was our little sister. He was the brand-new boyfriend. Well, I mean, brand-new if you didn't count the three years in high school. We would be asking the questions here.

"There are treatments," Emerson said.

"I don't even have to ask Sloane," Caroline said. "Either one of us will give you our bone marrow without a second thought."

"Of course." Now I was starting to worry. Bone marrow transplants were not a simple matter, and this was really major if she potentially needed to have a bone marrow transplant.

I could tell Emerson was trying not to cry. "But even still," she said, "I probably can't have children."

Mark pulled her closer into him.

My heart sank for her. I couldn't imagine that. I had seen what Caroline had gone through trying to have another baby—and she already had Vivi. "I will have a baby for you, Emerson. I have a beautiful uterus." I cleared my throat. "My doctor's words, not mine." We all laughed.

"I know," she said, nodding. "I know you would do anything you could. I love you both so much."

She stood up, and Caroline and I both hugged her. "I will have a baby for you if you're OK with having a hippie LA home birth, but I'm not going back in that hospital."

I patted Caroline. "It's OK. I've got that one." I winked at her. "Let's just hope you're the better bone marrow match so it's fair."

Caroline nodded. "Deal."

Emerson was wiping her eyes and laughing now. "Listen," I said. "Mark's right. Let's not get worked up about something we don't even know yet. OK?" She nodded.

"Right," Caroline said. "And in the meantime, just know that the two of us will do and give you anything you need, and we will make sure you get the best doctor in the world."

Emerson nodded again. "I know."

"Good," I said, hugging her again. "Chin up, little one."

"And, guys," she said. "Just please don't let anything slip out to Mom. I don't want to worry her."

I nodded in agreement, but I didn't feel all that confident. When Mom found out we had kept this from her, I had a feeling our biggest concern would no longer be who was going to carry Emerson's baby.

SIXTEEN

life

ansley

I don't think I've ever been as shocked as I was when my husband, Carter, came to me and said he thought we should start trying for another baby. Because I saw the way he watched Caroline, the way he studied her. I saw the way he hoped she would develop some feature or mannerism that would indicate she was really his. It had all been a bad dream, what he had asked me to do. I knew he wanted to believe that we had defied what the doctors told us, that we had created this beautiful miracle all on our own.

I had also known, from that very first rainy night I ventured back to Peachtree Bluff, back to Jack, back to try to get the one thing Carter and I wanted that we couldn't have on our own, that it was a bad idea. Jack and I had loved each other. We had shared so many of our teenaged summers, stealing kisses on the boardwalk, spending lazy days holding hands in the sand, throwing footballs with our friends, sneaking beer at the pier at night. The only thing that had eventually torn us apart was his proclamation that he didn't want children and my insistence that I would have them. Our life together had been so carefree, so much fun—except when the summers were over and we had to leave each other, of course. But, no matter how happy you are in your marriage—and, believe me, I was— marriage is real life and it's real work. There are bills to pay, taxes to figure, laundry to be done, decisions to make. The love is real, but the stress is real, too. While I was deeply happy in my life with Carter, there was no doubt that my mind wandered every now and then to that simpler time.

I understand with every ounce of my being that this is why people have affairs; this is how they convince themselves that they are in love with someone else. It's easy to resurrect that forgotten feeling when you have no responsibilities.

I knew this. Logically.

But it had taken me five months to get pregnant with Caroline. That was five sections of time carved out for Jack and me. Five stints of seventy-two hours that weren't only about making this baby. They were about spending time together, reliving the past, and, in some ways, getting a glimpse into what might have been if I had never met Carter that summer before my senior year of college. If, instead, I had spent that summer with Jack.

I knew in my heart of hearts that what I had with Carter was a once-in-a-lifetime love. But it had been tainted by the day-to-day of marriage. What I had with Jack hadn't. Even though my head knew this, my heart still felt that dangerous pitter-pat whenever I was in his presence, which is why I realized, after I became pregnant with Caroline, that I couldn't see Jack anymore.

So, no, technically, I didn't need to fly to Peachtree Bluff to tell Jack that I was pregnant. But, for heaven's sake, I owed the man that much, didn't I? He had been the one to create this child with me. Didn't he have a right to know?

I was sitting in Jack's living room when he walked in from work. His face lit up. I had promised myself that I wouldn't have any physical contact with him. I was already pregnant. It had to go back to friendship. But I stood when he walked into the room, and he rushed to me, kissing me with that intensity I had come to know so well.

"Hi," he said, a smile playing on his lips. "We have to stop meeting like this."

I kissed him again. He was so close, so warm. I couldn't help it. "Well," I said, hearing a hint of sadness in my voice, "I think we're going to."

He pulled away from me, and his face fell. "Oh. Right." His posture shifted from confident and happy to distraught. "So that's it, then? I've done my duty, and now we're over."

"Jack," I whispered.

He shook his head and ventured a smile. "I'm not angry," he said. "I knew this was the deal. I knew you would get pregnant and you would be gone."

I had planned to go back home to New York, tell Carter I was pregnant, and have the celebration to end all celebrations. We were going to have the life we had always dreamed of:

strolling through Central Park with our baby, holding hands walking to preschool, Carter parading his son or daughter around his office.

"Maybe we have this one last weekend?" I whispered. "Maybe we can pretend we don't know."

"Know what?" he asked, winking at me.

My head was screaming that this was wrong. But, hell, the whole thing had been wrong, hadn't it? Of course it had. I knew that. It's amazing how convoluted your thoughts can become, how a seemingly reasonable mind can convince itself that the worst things are right, that, in between the very clearly black and white, there might be shades of gray.

But even I couldn't convince myself there were shades of gray in what I was doing now. The baby was made. This was cheating on my husband. Yet, I couldn't break away from Jack's arms. Not yet.

As day turned to night, the light drifting away, slipping from the sky like this love from our fingers, the sadness started to creep in between us. Our banter shifted to serious conversation about what the future could hold. But I never expected Jack to say, "Stay."

"What do you mean?"

I rolled over on my side, suddenly chilled, covering myself with a sheet, our faces inches from each other. "You know what I mean, Ansley. Leave Carter. Leave New York. Come home. We'll get married and raise our baby together."

I shook my head. "You never wanted children, Jack."

He shook his head. "I know what I said, but if it's you and

me and the baby, I think it could be kind of great." He paused and looked at me again. "Stay, Ansley."

Another chill ran through me, a dread that this was not what we had agreed to, a horror that I had made a colossal mistake. But, in that, I realized: I was thinking about it. And that was what scared me most of all.

It took only a few minutes of considering leaving Carter, bringing this baby back to Peachtree Bluff, and living with Jack for me to realize that if I was meant to be with Jack, I would have been. But I wasn't. I was meant to be with Carter.

And now I felt like I was where I was meant to be once again. The girls were home. I was going to decorate Jack's house. I wasn't even nervous about leaving everyone for Mom's doctor's appointment. She had fought me tooth and nail on this for weeks. But after the episode a couple of days ago, that feeling in my gut that this was more than just normal, old-age forgetfulness kept nagging me. We were going to a neurologist in Athens late that afternoon, and I wouldn't hear another word about it.

"Hey, Mom," I said nonchalantly, walking into her room. She was making her bed. I had hated it when she arrived in Peachtree Bluff in that cast and was so reliant on us. Her independent streak was one of my favorite things about her, and even at eighty-three, she was going strong. That same independent streak was, of course, the thing that had driven this deep, seemingly impenetrable wedge between us. But so many of the things in our lives are a bit of a double-edged sword. The mere thought of her losing her mind was too much for me to take.

"Let's go out to lunch," I said.

She looked at me suspiciously. "Your three daughters just got home from six days at sea and you want to take me out to lunch?"

I shrugged. "Yeah." Then I winked at her. "If I'm gone I don't have to help with the laundry." I paused. "Plus, we've had practically no quality time together since you got here."

She perched herself at the end of her freshly made bed and said, "Speaking of, I wanted to talk to you about that. I'm as good as new, and I think it's time for me to go home."

I could feel the shock on my face, though I wasn't sure why. Of course my mom was going to want to go back to Florida, to her friends and her life. But as my brother Scott and I had discussed many times, her age was starting to show, and she needed to be here where I could keep an eye on her. Scott's travel reporting kept him on the road or in the sky all the time, and it wasn't like my brother John even spoke to any of us. This was the only option. Only, none of us had had the nerve to break it to Mom yet. And, quite frankly, if I was going to play caregiver for the rest of her days, I didn't feel like it was my responsibility to break that news to her.

I gave Mom my most pitiful look. "Couldn't you stay a couple more weeks? Until I get Sloane back on her feet? There's so much going on here, and I could really use your help."

Mom took the two steps to her walker, patted my shoulder, and said, "Sure, sweetheart. Whatever you need."

I couldn't believe that worked.

I helped Mom into the car, and she said, "Why don't we go to one of those divine waterfront restaurants? My treat."

Eighty-three-year-olds and three-year-olds are essentially the same. Slow. Stubborn. Extremely opinionated. But eighty-three-year-olds generally have better table manners, so, overall, they're better lunch companions.

Verbena was our favorite waterfront restaurant, but I hadn't been there in a while. White tablecloths and two-hour lunches weren't exactly my speed these days. Mom and I both ordered tea service instead of lunch. There was nothing better than those little sandwiches with the crusts removed and tiny brownies, lemon squares, and macarons.

"So how long do you think it will be?" Mom asked.

I knew without clarification that she meant until we heard about Adam. "I hope soon," I said. "The waiting is the worst part."

She nodded. "You know all about that."

The waiting when Carter died had nearly killed me. And I was never one of the lucky ones who knew. I never had remains or a DNA sample; I had no wallet, no shoes. Nothing. I never had any real closure. Of course, I had known the entire time that he was gone. But there's always that voice in the back of your head that tells you to keep hoping, keep searching, keep believing.

Mom smiled at the waitress as she served us. "Thank you."

I placed my green tea bag in the white porcelain pot. Mom selected Earl Grey, as usual. She was kind of a tea purist, except when it came to Kyle. If Kyle fixed her anything at all, she would bat her eyelashes at him and tell him it was divine.

She took a bite of brownie first. I laughed.

"What? At my age, I'm not taking any chances."

I took a bite of mine too. Why not? The desserts at Verbena were decadent, rich, delicious, award winning. But I would rather have had a Hershey's bar, if I'm honest about the whole thing.

My mother and I always had a deep bond, which is why it had shocked me that she wouldn't let the girls and me come home when I discovered Carter had left me not penniless, but in a cataclysmic hole of debt. I had tried so hard to move past it, but I think this period in my life now only served to intensify the wound because I knew for certain I would never leave my girls out in the cold when they needed me most.

In the quiet, in the dark, in my most private thoughts, the ones I would never say out loud to anyone, I resented the fact that, though she hadn't lifted a finger to help me when my life exploded, I would be the one taking my mother to doctors' appointments, feeding her dinner, bathing her, taking care of her every need until the day she died. But, mostly, I felt lucky I could do it.

We'd never been best friends like some of my girlfriends had been with their mothers, and I was OK with that. I only hoped that, maybe, during this time in our lives, we could repair what was broken between us.

"Darling," she said, taking a tiny sip of her tea, "I meant what I said the other day. Why do you push that divine man away? He's totally in love with you. I'm totally in love with you, but even still, I recognize you are not perfect. He, on the other hand, does not."

I laughed. Mom had always loved him. When I first started dating Carter, she kept asking what had ever happened to that darling Jack.

"Mom," I said. "Carter was the one. If Jack had been the one, I would have married him. But he wasn't."

"I did love Carter. But you didn't marry Jack because he didn't want children. I assume you don't want any more?" She raised her eyebrows.

We both laughed. I wiped my mouth and took a sip of cool water. "It's not that simple, Mom. I loved him all those years ago, but we're different people now."

She looked at me like I was dense. "That's why you give the man a chance. That's why you try to get to know each other now."

She made it sound so simple, but perhaps that's because she didn't understand the entire picture. When Jack came back to Peachtree Bluff, I was panicked that the girls would find out our secret, would find out that Jack was Caroline and Sloane's father. Now I knew Jack would never let that happen. But, even still, how could I lie to my children like that? How could I be with Jack without telling them the truth? I wasn't sure I could.

But that was all beside the point. Today, my mission was to get this woman to the doctor. I decided to level with her.

"Mom," I said, taking a bite of egg salad for courage. "I'm taking you to the doctor today."

She waved her hand. "Darling, my ankle is fine."

"Not for your ankle," I said. This was when it was going to get dicey. "For your brain."

I expected her to freak out, but she barely reacted, still as a cat stalking its prey. That's when I began to worry.

She took a sip of tea and cleared her throat. "There's no need."

I cut her off. "I know you're going to say you're fine, but you're not fine, Mom. There's something going on, and if we can catch it early, maybe get some treatment, it won't progress."

She took a deep breath and reached for my hand across the table.

I knew that she was going to argue with me, so I said, "Mom, you were out of your mind when Jack was there the other night. You didn't recognize anything, didn't know who he was . . ."

"Darling," she said calmly. And that's when I knew something was wrong. Something big. I knew that whatever she said next was going to change my life in ways I wasn't ready for. "I don't know how to tell you this, really," she said. She paused and looked into my eyes as if she were memorizing them. "But, you're right. I'm not fine." She put her hands back in her lap, smoothing her napkin slowly. She took another sip of tea, cleared her throat, and looked up at me. "I have cancer, darling. I've had it for quite some time. It's in my brain."

I felt numb, frozen in my chair. She was so calm, so steady. I wanted to cry, but instead, I sprang into action. "We have to get you to a specialist. Are they going to operate, do chemo, radiation?"

She put her hand up to stop me, and I knew we were about to have the biggest fight of our lives. "We are not going to do any of that. I'm going to live out my days as I please. I will eat my dessert first and watch *Mickey Mouse* with my great-grandchildren. And when my time is through, it will be through."

She was so stoic when she said it. I usually thought of this decision, of this state of mind in the face of death, as resigned. But Mom wasn't resigned. She was almost joyous. And it hit me. My mother was dying. My mother was going to die. Soon. I felt tears well up and dabbed them away with my napkin.

"Sweetheart, let's not make a scene, OK? I'm fine. I'm better than fine. I'm not losing my hair and vomiting. I'm not spending a year in the hospital to potentially buy me two more when I'll never really be right. I've thought about this. I assure you this is the right decision."

"For whom, Mother? Because it doesn't feel like the right decision for me."

She smiled at me sadly. "I will not have you spending your life caring for me and shuffling me back and forth to doctors' appointments. I'm ready to be with your father, anyhow." It wasn't until she said, "You are all terribly boring," that I finally saw emotion breaking through her placid expression.

"You will not go back to Florida. That's it, and that's final."

She opened her mouth to argue, but I think she knew I needed this, in the way that mothers always do. She took a sip of tea and said, "I do so love that beautiful Emerson with that darling Mark. Wouldn't it be wonderful if she married him, moved back to Peachtree, and gave up all that acting nonsense?"

Just like that, we were finished talking about dying. We were, instead, talking about life. While I wasn't sure I agreed with her decision to forgo treatment, I did know one thing for sure: in the entire time I had known her, all my life, except for once, I had never known her to make the wrong decision. And that thought would carry me through until the very end.

SEVENTEEN

war zone

sloane

January 20, 2016
Dear Sloane,

I lost one of my men today. His world is over. I'm still here. How can that be? All there's left to do is keep fighting. All I can do is make sure he didn't die in vain.

I love you,
Adam

SIX MONTHS INTO OUR marriage, Adam and I had slowed the fast, crazy pace of our relationship and begun getting into a routine. He was home, so I wasn't worried. I was painting and working at a gift shop near our post. We would cook dinner together at night. It was a simple life, the kind of life I'd never known I wanted but, now that I had it, felt absolutely perfect.

Perfect, that is, until the night we were lying in bed and I was drifting off, when Adam said, "When do you want to start trying to have a baby?"

I had jolted up. "A baby?" I asked, panic surging through me. "No one ever said anything about a baby."

It was true. No one had. In all those months of talking and writing letters, Adam and I had never talked about having children. Obviously, this was not a good idea. Having kids is one of the most life-altering things that can happen in a family, and I knew we should have talked about it a million times. It was always on the tip of my tongue, especially because I knew I seemed like someone who wanted that traditional life, that role as mother and caregiver.

Only, I didn't. Being with Adam had, ironically, soothed that fear that had embedded itself into me like a tick in flesh after my father died. Whereas before, I felt terrified of getting too close to anyone, scared of loving or letting anyone in, paralyzed by the mere thought that I might receive another phone call that someone I had loved more than life was gone in an instant, now, with Adam, I felt safer.

It was strange since he had a job where he could be taken from me at any moment. But I knew that. In his line of work, people died. People were killed. It's not that I expected he would be killed in the line of duty by any stretch of the imagination, but it was always a possibility. It was always something that was in the back of my mind.

While I realize this doesn't sound totally rational—tragedy will do that to a mind, I think—I liked that the element of surprise was gone. If Adam were to be killed, it would rip my heart out of my body. It would break me in ways I couldn't even imagine. But it wouldn't be a total shock. And so, in that way, I felt prepared. But I wasn't prepared for this.

"We've only been married six months," I said. The reality was not that I didn't want to have kids because Adam and I hadn't been married long enough. I knew without hesitation that Adam and I would be together, happily, in love, until our dying breaths. The reality was that I didn't want to have kids at all. And if I was honest with myself, I had never brought it up before because I was selfish. I had never brought it up because I knew it might be a deal breaker for Adam—and I wanted him more than I wanted anything else on the planet. If I was with Adam, everything else would work out. Or so I thought.

He laughed and kissed me on the cheek. "I know, babe," he said. "But I'll be deployed again soon, and wouldn't it be great to be pregnant before I go?"

I looked into his earnest face. He was so happy, so enthusiastic, so charming. Who wouldn't want to pass along those genes?

Well, I mean, I wouldn't. I could never handle the level of fear and anxiety that would hide out inside me every minute if I had children out there walking around.

Were they safe? Were they sick? Would they get cancer? Break their leg? Get an infection that went into their bloodstream? Would they get hit by a car crossing the street? I could play "what if" all day, every day, all night, every night. And I didn't even have them yet. There was no way. But Adam was so happy and he looked so expectant. I wanted to please him. I wanted to make him smile.

But I didn't want children. I should have told him. I considered telling him. But I couldn't bear to send him away, into a war zone, with this huge burden weighing on him. I couldn't send him away distracted. I needed him focused on his security, his safety. I needed to give him a reason to come back home. I could have suggested we wait until then, but I looked into his eyes and I remembered what he had given me, what he had sacrificed for me. I couldn't bear to break his heart.

So I said, "That sounds great, honey."

Adam didn't know I had an IUD. And what he didn't know wouldn't hurt him.

EIGHTEEN

well-behaved women

ansley

Mom called the boys to tell them about her cancer. Scott was reporting on a crisis in Venezuela, and despite the major flooding there, he promised he would be on the first flight back to the US. John was at work just an hour and a half away. He didn't promise to come, didn't even mention it, in fact.

Carter was a terrific judge of character, and it used to bother me that he didn't like John. He never said as much, of course, but I could tell. He was usually so warm and open, but around John, he closed up. I'm not saying John is a bad person, necessarily, but I see now that Carter's assessment of my brother was correct.

John and I have been distant for a long time. I always believed we would evolve past that, but when Grandmother left me the Peachtree Bluff house, I realized John and I would never have what Scott and I had. Because, at our core, we are fundamentally different people. Who would abandon his own sister and practically never speak to her again over a house?

All of that came rushing back to me when I got a text from him that morning: Let me know when Mom gets really bad off so I can come.

I texted back: She's dying of cancer, John. I'd say time is of the essence.

I could feel the chill through the phone. His lack of response didn't surprise me, but it would have been nice to be able to tell my mother that her son was coming.

Just like that, she appeared in her robe, fresh from a shower. I was sitting at the dining room table, sipping my first cup of coffee of the morning and sketching a room—something I hadn't done in quite some time. Over the past several years, I had created mood boards for my clients so they could see exactly what furniture, fixtures, and fabric I was contemplating for their rooms. But I knew already that Jack would let me have free rein, and sketching the rooms I was designing was how I best dreamed them. I liked to think I was drawing them into life. Plus, the sketches were beautiful and would make a terrific thanks-for-letting-me-decorate-your-house gift.

Mom's cane was tapping rhythmically on the floor as she walked into the kitchen. "Don't you need to get to your store, darling?"

I needed to go to my store very, very much, but I had seemed unable to pry myself away from my mother's side since she told me the news. The store would still be there when she was gone.

"I can work on these sketches right here," I said, standing up. "Let me get your breakfast. I made bacon and eggs for the kids, so I kept some warm for you."

She touched my hand gently. "Please let me do it while I'm still able."

I didn't want to let her. I wanted to take care of her, to make this go away, to have her for years and years more. But that wasn't the hand we had been dealt.

"I'd like to go with you to the store after breakfast," she said.

"Are you feeling up to that?"

She glared at me.

Note to self: don't ask Mom if she's feeling up to it.

"Great," I said. "I'd love that. I know Leah would love it too. You can be our design assistant today."

She shook her head. "You design. I'll wait on customers. I've always wanted to run a cash register."

I doubted she realized the "cash register" was now an iPad with a Square reader attached. But there was still that drawer that popped open and made the satisfying "ding."

"What else, Mom?"

"What else what?" she called from the other side of the wall.

"What else have you always wanted to do?"

She peeked her head around the doorway. "Oh, let's not do that. I don't want to be one of *those* dying women."

I laughed. "You won't. But if there are things you want to do, let's do them. Why not? We have time."

She smiled at me and disappeared again. "I have traveled

the world," she called. "I have no desire to jump out of any airplanes, but I would like to ring a cash register."

I couldn't imagine a dying woman's request being any simpler than that. I heard the clang of the plates through the wall and could picture my mother serving eggs and bacon—for what could be one of the last times. How many times had she made bacon and eggs for me? How many times had I watched her, always perfectly dressed, scrambling eggs, and avoiding grease pops from the bacon? And now she was going to be gone.

I wiped my eyes just as she reappeared. "I'm going up to get dressed and then I'll drive you down to the store."

She crunched her bacon and said, "Ansley, my abilities have not completely deteriorated since I told you about the cancer yesterday. I am perfectly able to walk one block to your store."

———

TWENTY MINUTES LATER, MOM was perched on a bar stool behind the counter of my store, Leah was teaching her how to use our point-of-sale system, and, despite my excitement over designing a pair of custom chaise lounges for Jack's house, I could feel my eyelids starting to get heavy. As if he sensed my exhaustion from several blocks away, Coffee Kyle appeared.

"Oh," I said, practically running to meet him. "Bless you!"

He laughed. "And to think, my parents wanted me to be a doctor, lawyer, or missionary. There's no way those things could have been as satisfying as this."

He handed me a cup and I said, "Trust me, you'll save far more innocent lives doing what you do now."

Kyle smiled. "Now, before you take a sip, you should know you three ladies are my guinea pigs. I'm trying to switch some of my regulars on to drinks with less sugar." He looked at me pointedly and said, "Prevent cancer, all of that."

How did he know? I hadn't told anyone except Sandra and Emily. But this was Peachtree Bluff. No one could keep a secret around here. Well, no one except for Jack and me.

"I want the sugar," Mom said. "If I'm going down, I'd like to go down with a mocha Frappuccino in one hand and a Hershey's bar in the other."

We all laughed.

"Just hear me out," Kyle said. "This is my new latte made with unsweetened cashew milk, raw cocoa powder, cinnamon, a dash of chocolate stevia, and a touch of matcha tea and maca powder for added health benefits."

I was going to hate it. I knew it. Leah, Mom, and I took simultaneous sips. I was expecting a flat, thin latte with practically no flavor and that disgusting stevia aftertaste, but what I got was a cup of heaven.

"This is my new usual," I said. "Kyle, you are a genius."

Mom nodded. "Yeah. I'll go down with this in one hand instead."

"It's so creamy," Leah said.

I loved the authoritative air Kyle took on when talking about coffee, as if he were discussing a new species he had discovered in the Amazon. "I've been experimenting with homemade nut milks for a while now, and I've discovered that cashew takes on the perfect density for lattes. Macadamia does as well, but the flavor combination isn't as good."

"Oh!" Leah exclaimed. "White chocolate macadamia!"

Kyle laughed. "It's in the works."

Mom took another sip and said, "You know who would love this?"

"Oh, Emerson," I chimed in.

Kyle cleared his throat, the way he tended to do when he was nervous, and I could have sworn his ears reddened the tiniest bit. Oh my gosh. He had made this for Emerson.

"I'll have to get her to taste it when she gets back. When will the girls be back?" he asked with forced nonchalance.

"Oh, they're back."

He grinned. "Then I'll take her one right away."

I felt bad for him, but maybe it was all in my head and I just assumed every man was interested in my daughters. But maybe that wasn't the case with Kyle. In fact, when I said, "She's probably at Mark's," he didn't even flinch.

"OK!" Mom said exuberantly. "Kyle, you need to buy something. I'll ring you up!"

"Mom," I scolded. I turned to Kyle. "You don't need to buy anything."

"Grammy, is this your first sale?"

Kyle's hair seemed even blacker today, his arms more toned, his jawline more defined. I wasn't sure it was possible for him to get more handsome, but it seemed he had.

"It certainly will be, darling. I've always wanted to work the cash register." She scrunched her nose. "Well, not this newfan-gled contraption. But I suppose it will have to do."

Kyle shook his head. "The cash register in my coffee shop is from 1962. I'd be honored if you would help me out over there for a bit."

She gasped and put her hand to her mouth. "Well, if you don't know how to make a lady's dying wish come true, then I don't know who does."

"Mom," I scolded again. "The girls don't even know yet."

"My lips are sealed," Kyle said.

I looked at my mother. "We have to tell them today."

Mom waved her hand. "Fine, fine. You're such a bore some-times, Ansley."

Such a bore. I guess I was. But there wasn't much that was exciting about dying.

Kyle carefully hoisted Mom off the stool and winked at me. "I promise I'll take good care of her," he said. "I'll bring her back before lunch."

"Mom," I said, feeling as if I were sending one of my girls off to school again. "Behave."

She turned and put her hand on her heart, as though she were offended. "Why, don't I always, darling?"

I shook my head. "No. No, you never do. Which is why I have to say it."

"Well-behaved women rarely make history," Kyle whis-pered.

And then they were on their way, Mom's arm wrapped around Kyle's, her other hand on her cane.

For the briefest of moments, I just knew the doctors were wrong. There wasn't one thing wrong with my mother. There couldn't be.

And, while Kyle had always been the adorable boy who brought me my coffee, this was one of those times when I couldn't help but see him as something more.

NINETEEN

mother's morning out

sloane

The boat trip with my sisters had done me a world of good. Coming home made me realize what a world of good Vivi did me. I had taken for granted over the past few months how much my sweet niece played with Taylor and AJ.

Now, this afternoon, sitting in my bedroom that seemed to be getting smaller by the minute, I realized I needed to get out of there. Me. The girl who didn't even want her children to go to school because she was so terrified something would happen to them and it would be all her fault felt like she needed a break.

AJ was sitting on the floor arranging coins from biggest to smallest, and Taylor, whom I was trying to read to, was knocking over each of AJ's stacks as soon as he finished them. AJ had made a particularly tall tower with probably fifteen coins. I was very proud of his motor skills. I thought Taylor was completely

177

engrossed in a Shel Silverstein poem—until he wriggled in my lap, kicked out his leg, and the stack was gone. "Mommy!" AJ wailed.

"Taylor, that's enough," I said, a little too forcefully. "I've had it. I've told you five times not to do that, and now you're going to your room."

"Noooooo!" Taylor screamed, flailing on the floor. I grabbed him by one arm and one leg—I'd learned from experience that during a full-on tantrum, I couldn't hold him the regular way. One arm and one leg made him madder, but it gave me a safe grip with which to remove him from the situation.

I walked into his room, set him on the bed as gently as I could, and said, as if a mid-tantrum kid could even hear you, "You stay here until I tell you to come out."

I closed the door behind me, and the screaming continued. He'd calm down. Eventually.

AJ was still stacking when I got back to my room. "Look, Mommy," he said proudly.

He had completed his task once again. "Good job, bud," I said. "Now I want you to make a pile of change for me that equals one dollar."

He nodded.

"One hundred cents is one dollar."

"Exactly," I said. I wanted at least one member of the family to be good with money. I smiled thinking again of that zero balance and smiled even bigger when I realized that since my debt had been cleared, despite my stress levels with Adam, Emerson's illness, and the kids, I hadn't bought one single thing.

Not so much as a juice box, which Mom was handling right now. It would be a good chance for me to build up our savings.

Caroline walked into my bedroom, Grammy on her heels. "Well, hello there," I said. "Did the screaming bring you up?"

"Something like that," Grammy said, looking around at the floor. The room was fairly neat, but AJ's school things were spread everywhere. I thought again how much easier it would get when Taylor was three or four and could do work at the same time as AJ.

I sensed an ambush coming, but I wasn't sure what sort of ambush it would be. "So," Caroline started, "I have the best idea."

"No," I said.

Caroline crossed her arms, looking hurt. "Not no," she said. "You don't even know what I'm going to say."

"Right," I said, "but I can already tell I don't like it."

Grammy laughed.

I ran my hand through AJ's hair while Grammy said, "Wow, AJ, I'm going to bring my change up here and let you sort it."

He lit up. "OK. That would be so cool. Wouldn't it, Mommy?"

I nodded and grinned at him. "Hurry up," I said to Caroline. "I need to go get Taylor out of time-out."

"I was just thinking that our poor mother has hardly been able to work for months and the last month wasn't able to work at all."

I wasn't sure what she was getting at.

"I thought it would be nice," Caroline continued, "if we

helped her at the store so she could get caught up on all her design projects."

I still didn't say anything but eyed her warily.

She continued, "I could run the store, you could paint a little." She paused. "I thought we could market these cool live paint sessions with you, and it would really help sell your art."

"What a waste of your breath," I said, getting up off the floor.

"What do you mean?" Caroline asked.

I walked toward the boys' room and said, "I mean, I said 'no' to begin with. That's still my answer, and everything in between was just a waste of breath."

Caroline leaned against the door jamb, arms crossed, as I knelt down in front of a now-calm Taylor. "Taylor, you were in time-out for not listening to Mommy. When Mommy speaks, we listen, and we always do what Mommy says right away."

The new discipline book I was reading said this was more effective for kids under the age of three than trying to explain why the exact behavior was wrong, i.e., pushing over AJ's coin stack.

"Do you have anything to say to Mommy?"

Taylor nodded, his little lip stuck out. "Sorry, Mommy."

He hugged me, and I said, "Thank you, Taylor. You may go play now."

I was so relieved. Some days this routine took an hour because the child absolutely refused to apologize, and we'd have to keep repeating the cycle. It was exhausting. But it was working.

When I got up, Grammy was standing behind me. "Darling," she said gently, "I know you've been having some money troubles, and it's time for you to stand on your own two feet. You need to be able to support yourself in case . . ."

She trailed off, and I could feel the anger welling up inside me. "In case what, Grammy?" I paused. "There's no 'in case.' Adam is coming home. Adam supports our family. That's it and that's final. I don't want to hear about it again."

"No," Grammy said, putting her hands on her hips. "I'm going to say this. I love you, Sloane. You're a beautiful, talented, artistic bright light. It has bothered me for years that once you married Adam, you became this . . ." She paused, searching for the words, then finished, "this Stepford wife."

I gasped, and Caroline scolded, "Grammy!"

The anger was rising in my chest. "How could you say anything negative about Adam at a time like this?"

"Darling," Grammy said. "I'm not saying anything negative about Adam. Adam is perfect. It's *you* who's the problem."

I wanted to protest again, as tears of humiliation sprung to my eyes. I wanted to fight her on this. But I knew she wasn't wrong. I had lost myself, and I needed to do something for me—before it was too late.

All the same, I was indignant as I walked back to my bedroom. Who was she to even consider that Adam wouldn't come home? Of course he would. It was preposterous to consider any other scenario. Still, it would be nice to get out of the house a little bit more. And going back to work would get me to my savings goal much faster.

I turned so quickly Caroline almost bumped right into me.

"I will help Mom at the store, but I will not paint in public." I was really enjoying painting. Loving it, actually. But it wasn't time.

Caroline put her hands up. "Fine," she said.

"That's my girl," Grammy said.

Caroline squealed. "I've already signed the boys up for Mother's Morning Out."

I looked down at my precious little babies on the floor, the babies who had never been cared for by anyone outside of their family—except for a couple of moms on post who, let's face it, were my family too. How could I possibly leave them?

Then AJ picked up one of my hair ties and flicked it at Taylor. Taylor started crying. I looked at Caroline. "When do I start?"

$$\sim\!\!\infty\!\!\sim$$

georgia girl

ansley

It was hard to believe that, only a couple of months earlier, Jack and I had been planning to take his recently renovated boat out on its maiden voyage. Together. I had been hesitant when he came back to Peachtree Bluff. Maybe "hesitant" was putting it mildly. More like terrified. I didn't know what he wanted, but I did know he was the one person who had the power to ruin everything I had built with my children and devastate my relationships with them forever.

Sure, Caroline and Sloane knew they came from a "sperm donor." They knew Emerson was a miracle child, the only one who was biologically Carter's. But they didn't know their mother nearly died from a rare infection from her first Intrauterine Insemination, and that, from then on out, Carter wouldn't hear of fertility treatments of any kind. Knowing they came from an anonymous sperm donor is quite different from knowing their father is actually the man who lives beside them, their mother's first love—or that he got her pregnant the regular way, not via a syringe. That was a lot of things not to know. A few of those things, namely that Jack was their biological father, I really wanted them to know. But in my time, in my way.

That was why, I reminded myself for the millionth time, I could not be with Jack. I had been standing at his front door, holding my sketchbook for ten minutes, trying to gear myself up to go in. Biscuit was getting impatient at my feet, her little tail thumping on the wood of the front porch. She whined up at me. "I know," I said. "But it's complicated. You're a dog. You wouldn't understand."

Just then, the door flew open. I screamed, Biscuit barked, and I expected to hear Jack's gasp, but that wasn't what I heard at all. Instead, there was a second scream, one of the busty blond variety named after the state in which we currently resided. She was wearing a cocktail dress.

People do not wear cocktail dresses at nine in the morning unless they are, as my girls would say, doing the walk of shame. "Oh, hi, Ansley," she said, grinning at me like she'd been caught with her hand in the cookie jar.

My cookie jar.

I was having trouble regulating my breath. I was trying to smile and make my face look normal. Did my face look normal? I looked down at Biscuit, who was looking up at me. She started barking in Georgia's direction, which is how I knew once and for all that my face did not, in fact, look normal.

Georgia had her clutch in one hand and a wrap in the other. I knew I should say something, but I didn't know what.

"I had a flat tire," she said quickly.

"How convenient," I said under my breath.

"What?"

Her hair was mussed in the back—definitely sex hair.

I could hear Jack's footsteps coming down the hall, and I turned to leave. I couldn't possibly face him. Not now. I should have been sad or heartbroken, but really, I was just mad. So, no, we couldn't be together. I couldn't have him. But I didn't want *her* to have him either. It was a mature reaction.

Unfortunately, as I turned to walk down the porch steps, so did Georgia. "Jack and I went to the most splendid benefit last night. And then we got home, and I had a flat tire. And he was in no position to drive, so . . ."

"We have got to get Uber here," I said, an edge to my voice.

She laughed delightedly and winked at me. "Oh, I hope we don't."

"Ansley?" I heard Jack call from the porch as if there were any question about who I was.

I wanted to pretend that I didn't hear him. But I couldn't. I was twenty feet in front of him. I turned and held up my sketchbook. "I'll come back later," I said, relieved to see he was at least dressed. "When you're not so busy."

"Now is good," he said. "Come on in."

"I can't wait to see what you do to the place, Ansley," Georgia called.

Maybe it was only in my mind, but the way she said it

made me feel like she wanted me to get it all spruced up so she could move right in. I would die. I would die if he were living beside me with another woman, and then my children would have yet another tragedy to deal with. A vision of them sobbing in black at my funeral crossed my mind.

No. I couldn't die. I didn't have time.

The last thing I wanted was to walk through that front door, but I had to.

"You're upset," Jack said.

How perceptive. "No," I said. "Not upset."

Of course I was upset. How could I not be upset? I loved him, for heaven's sake. He named his boat after me, and now he was having sleepovers with Realtors from Atlanta named Georgia. But I had no right to be upset. I had told him it wasn't time for us to be together, that I had to focus on my girls. And all of that was true. When you loved someone, weren't you supposed to want good things for them? I took a deep breath, swallowed my pride, and said, "You deserve to be happy."

A flicker of emotion passed across his face. Certainly not his usual amusement. Something more like defeat, but maybe I was reading too much into it. "OK," he said.

I handed him my sketchbook. "Please be careful with it," I said. "You can look these over. I'll come get it later."

He tossed the book onto the ratty sofa, sitting on the green carpet, in the dimly lit room. This place was awful. But it wasn't going to be. It was going to be pure luxury. For Jack. And Georgia.

"That's exactly what I meant when I said to be careful."

Jack rolled his eyes.

I felt like we were working up to some sort of fight, but there was nothing to fight about, nothing to fight for. We were over, and I just needed to go. "I'll come get these in a few days," I said.

"Ansley, come on," he said.

I stopped, my hand on the doorknob, and turned.

"I know you're not OK," he said. "You don't have to pretend. I get it. We can't be together, but that doesn't mean you have to be OK that I'm with someone else. I would hate that, roles reversed."

I got that same feeling I get when I haven't eaten in too long, and the room went wobbly. So he was with her. I knew what it looked like and I knew that, flat tire or no, if you wanted to get home, you could figure out a way to get home. But a part of me was hoping it wasn't what it seemed. Maybe she had slept in the guest room. Maybe he didn't have feelings for her. Maybe he didn't find her attractive or interesting. Although, what red-blooded, straight American male wouldn't find her attractive or interesting I wasn't sure.

"Biscuit," I called. No paws thumped across the floor. "Biscuit, I'm leaving right now. Come on!"

No paws. Really? I save the dog from a life of off-brand kibble at the shelter and this is the thanks I get? I guess I should have known she wouldn't want to leave the house where she had spent her entire life up until a month ago.

I opened the door. "Send her into my yard when you find her."

"Ansley," he said. "Wait."

But I couldn't wait. All I could think about standing there was *her*. That woman in this house that, truth be told, I had envisioned myself living in from the moment I saw his car pull into the driveway.

I controlled my tears right up until the moment I walked through my front door. Mom was sitting quietly in the living room, the morning sun streaming through the windows. This was, without a doubt, the best time of day in this room.

She didn't say anything, just patted the spot beside her. I noticed that even her hand looked frailer. "Honey, I know this is all a lot on you."

She didn't say anything more, but the unspoken truth that lingered between us was that she was glad about the decision she'd made.

I shook my head. "It's not. It's fine. It's just that Jack is right there, and now there's this other woman. And I realize I sound like a teenager."

She smiled at me and patted my hand. "Darling," she said, "we are teenagers forever when it comes to matters of the heart."

She shifted on the couch and stood up slowly, a pained expression on her face.

I didn't help, and I didn't follow her out of the room. I was trying to give her space, allow her the independence she had asked me for.

Jack burst through my front door, tiny Biscuit tucked under his arm. "Did it occur to you to tell me that your mother is dying? Was that something you thought I might need to know?"

My stomach clenched, and I put my finger to my mouth. But before I could answer, my mother called, "We're all dying, Jack. Some of us just sooner than others."

Mom walked back into the living room, and Jack looked embarrassed. "I'm sorry," he said. "I shouldn't have blurted that out like that."

Mom raised her eyebrow. "You shouldn't have strange women spend the night, either. Look like a damned fool. It's totally inappropriate." Mom paused. "Your mother would want me to tell you that."

Then she turned so only I could see, winked at me, and headed back toward her room. I stifled my laugh.

Jack shook his head. "Again, she seems fine to me."

"Jack," I whispered. "Mom hasn't told the girls yet."

He looked shocked. "Well, she'd better hurry the hell up. I just found out because two ladies I don't even know were standing in front of your house saying what a shame it was and speculating whether the house would be for sale. The whole town is talking."

When was the whole town not talking?

"But I get it now," Jack said. "I forgive you."

I could feel anger rising in my chest. "Forgive *me*? For what?"

He stepped closer, making my heart race in a way I wished it wouldn't. "I forgive you for not being able to be with me the way I want to be with you. I've thought about it, and I understand it a little more now. You have a lot to lose."

"I have a lot to gain, too," I said quietly.

He raised his eyebrow. "What does that mean?"

I shrugged, right as Sloane walked through the doorway. I studied her face to make sure she hadn't overheard anything about her grandmother. She definitely hadn't.

"Hey, Jack," she said. She kissed Biscuit on the head, taking her from Jack. "Hey there, little Biscuit girl. Let's go play in the backyard with the kids."

Biscuit started panting like she knew she was in for some fun.

"I'd better go play with the kids too," I said. "Doesn't matter. You have Georgia now."

Jack shook his head. "I do," he said. "But let's not forget that I came back to Georgia for a different girl."

As I listened to the laughter outside the back door, I realized I'd come back to Georgia for a different girl too. Three of them, in fact.

TWENTY-ONE

more sisters

sloane

I knew from our first lunch together that I'd never met anyone like Adam and that I never would again. Even in those first few days, maybe even in those first few seconds, I knew this was a man unlike any other. He'd quit college to fight for his country; he always had and always would put the needs of others before his own.

That thought woke me in the middle of the night, roused me from a deep sleep as surely as a hand shaking my shoulder. Adam had always put others before himself. What if he was putting others before himself now, too? What if he sacrificed himself for his friends? What if they were the ones who came home instead of him?

I remember being pregnant with AJ, how I knew something would change between Adam and me, how I felt almost sad that I was no longer his only true love and sole focus. I feared he would love this baby more than he loved me and that things between us would be different.

I know Adam loves our boys, but his love for me has never changed, never darkened, never dimmed. If anything, giving him those children made Adam love me more. I feel that. Even now.

As the sun rose, I fell asleep thinking that, no matter how much he felt the urge to sacrifice, Adam would come home to me because I was the one he was always fighting for.

THE NEXT MORNING IN the well-groomed backyard with the boys laughing with Preston, who was having some very serious tummy time, Grammy in a chair on the screened porch, Emerson and Caroline standing beside me, the night before and all those worries seemed so far away. The tears had dried for now. Adam would come home. Emerson would be OK. The sun would keep shining. All would be right with the world.

Emerson walked up the steps to the porch to sit with Grammy, and I turned to Caroline and whispered, "What do you think Jack meant when he told Mom he understood how much she had to lose if they were together?"

"What?" I could see Caroline squinting through her cat-eye sunglasses. I was in a pair of old sweatpants and a T-shirt, while she was in a beautifully pressed linen dress and wedges, her idea of casual wear.

"I just walked in the living room, and I heard Jack tell Mom he forgave her for not wanting to be with him now. That he understood how much she had to lose."

Caroline shrugged. "I don't know, Sloane. I'm not in the business of old-people relationships. I can't even keep my own husband off reality TV."

She smiled, which made me happy. After Caroline, Emerson, and I had sat down and watched James with Edie Fitzgerald on *Ladies Who Lunch*, after the tears and seeing how my always strong, always together sister was so very broken, I truly hadn't believed there was any chance they could get back together. But she had persevered. Her New York friends were livid. They thought she was weak. But Caroline trying to fix her marriage wasn't weakness. It was strength, the kind of strength not many people possess. But that was Caroline.

"Maybe he meant since it was so hard for her to lose Dad?" Caroline asked.

"Maybe," I said, but that didn't make sense. Sure, it was possible for Mom to lose Jack if they were together, but he wasn't dying. Not as far as we knew, anyway. She wasn't in imminent danger of losing him. Any fool could see he was madly in love with her.

Caroline pulled her glasses down her nose and peered at me over the top of them. "All I'm saying is I told you there was more to the story."

"Mommy, watch this!" AJ called for maybe the four hundredth time in the past ten minutes. I smiled. I was here. I was watching. I would always want to watch. I felt guilty for feeling like I wanted a break. But this was the vicious mom-guilt cycle.

"Let me see, buddy!"

He twirled around in the yard and then fell down, laughing. Taylor piled on top of him, trying to emulate his twirl and fall. Soon, we were all laughing. I felt that catch in my chest, that near suffocation that I shouldn't be laughing, not when Adam's fate was so up in the air.

I looked back toward the screened-in porch where Emerson had Grammy crying with laughter. Emerson could tell a story like no one I've ever met. It made sense, really. Of all of us, she was the most Southern.

"This may sound weird," I said. "But sometimes it makes me sad we don't have the same dad as Emerson."

Caroline cocked her head. "He loved us all the same. You know that, right?"

I nodded. Never for one day in my entire life did I feel anything but worshipped by our father. I never had any doubt he loved Caroline and me. "It isn't that," I said. "I mean, I know he loved us so much. I can't put it into words."

By the look on Caroline's face, I thought maybe I'd lost her, but then she said, "Do you think it makes her sad? Like maybe you and I are more sisters?"

I didn't get a chance to answer because I heard the screen door slam, and Mom appeared.

She looked at Grammy, who called breezily, "Sloane, Caroline. Could you come here a minute, please?"

I thought this was going to be our announcement to Mom that we were coming to work at the store.

I noticed how pretty Grammy looked in her slim-legged black pants with a pale pink jacket over top. Her hair was styled, and her blush was on. She was still lovely at eighty-three. I hoped

I would be like that one day. But, if I was honest, with how little time I took to fix myself up now, the chances were slim.

Grammy was seated between Mom and Emerson on the bamboo settee. Caroline and I were each sitting in a bamboo armchair flanking it.

Grammy took one of Mom's hands in hers and one of Emerson's in the other, and I felt my stomach lurch. Had she found out about Emerson?

"My sweet girls," she said, sighing. "I have some news, and it isn't good." She paused, composing herself. "I found out a few months ago that I have cancer, which, at my age, isn't all that uncommon, of course."

I heard myself gasp.

"Grammy, no!" Caroline said.

"You know I'm not one to take things lying down, but when they found it, it was already in my liver, lungs, and brain."

I looked at Emerson, my mouth hanging open, and could feel my tears, ones that matched those streaming down Emerson's face. Caroline's hands were over her mouth, and her eyes were wet as well.

My heart felt like it was breaking in two as it hit me: Grammy was dying. My rock, the woman whom we had loved and adored and looked up to for forever, wasn't going to be here anymore.

Who would I call when I couldn't remember if the fork went on top of the napkin or beside the napkin? Who would I call when I wasn't sure whether to wear black tie or cocktail to a noon wedding?

My boys wouldn't remember my grandmother. That made me cry even harder.

"I have taken some lovely medications to help slow the growth a bit, darlings, but as you probably know, at this stage, there isn't much to do." She paused. "Well, there isn't much to do but live."

She was so composed, so stoic in contrast to the rest of us, who were hysterical sobbing messes.

"You girls are the joy of my life. I'm ready to go, but oh how I hate the thought of not being with y'all." She cleared her throat. "But you can't imagine how much I miss your grandfather, how I long to be with him again." She looked at Mom. "Well, maybe you can."

"Grammy," Caroline said, walking to her, kneeling down in front of her, and taking her hand. "Isn't there anything you can do to fight this?" Her voice broke as she said, "We need more time, Grammy. We have to have more time."

I loved Grammy. We were close, but she and Caroline were attached at the hip. They were practically best friends. This would hit Caroline the hardest.

It didn't surprise me that Grammy's eyes finally flooded with tears when she looked down at Caroline.

Grammy smiled sadly at her, stroking her hair. "You know, sweetheart, I'm sure they could try to do surgery, rip me from stem to stern. But at my age, it would probably kill me. And, even if they tried, it wouldn't help." She swallowed, strong again. "It's my time, girls. This life is not perfect by any stretch. It's hard, and some days it feels long. But as long as you are surrounded by people you love, you have absolutely everything you need." She cleared her throat and patted Emerson and Mom on the legs. "OK. That's that. Let's get back to savoring every last inch of this life we have."

We all got up and hugged Grammy, the voices of our little boys floating around us. There was so much sadness on this porch, yet so much happiness only a few feet away in the back-yard. How could that be?

"Let's go out to lunch," Mom said. "Grammy's choice."

"I think that sounds lovely," Grammy said. "I'd like to take my girls out."

She didn't say it, but we all heard the *while I still can* any-way. I was going to savor every last second with my grand-mother. I was going to take every opportunity to show this family I had how much they meant to me.

Thinking about what Caroline said earlier, I linked my arm through Emerson's. "I love you, little sister," I said.

"I love you too, big sister," she said, smiling and touching her forehead to mine.

"Um, excuse me," Caroline said. "Does either of you love me?"

I scrunched my nose. "Well . . ."

We all laughed the relieved laugh that comes in the midst of so much pain, of too much sorrow. "OK," Caroline said. "Fine. Love me, don't love me. We all know I'm the glue that holds this group together." She paused. "Both of you look abso-lutely atrocious, and I will not be seen at lunch with you until you do something to yourselves."

"Glue?" Emerson asked. "Yeah. Keep telling yourself that."

We all laughed again. Dutifully, like the little sisters we were, Emerson and I went upstairs to change—and I changed the boys as a bonus, too. It occurred to me that, no, we would never have the same father, but, as long as Caroline was on this earth, Emerson and I would always have the same boss.

TWENTY-TWO

gifts

ansley

I don't know what it was about saying it aloud, but telling us she had cancer had released something in my mother—and released something in her disease. In no time, she had gone from the sassy lady chatting with me over tea and sandwiches to a ninety-pound, gray waif. She was so weak and tired. It was time. Hospice was coming in a couple of days to get her out of pain. I couldn't stand it. None of the medications seemed to help.

I've always been very good at being numb. I'm the doer, the fixer, the one to take charge. It keeps my mind off what is actually happening so I don't have to face the sadness.

I had lived through tragedy, so I was in a good position to say this was not a tragedy. My mother had lived eighty-four beautiful years tomorrow, and it seemed she would die quickly after a life impeccably well done. I was proud of her for that, for the way she seized every opportunity, lived every moment to the fullest while she was here. I didn't have to mourn the things she didn't get to do because I knew she was leaving content. She wouldn't have to suffer through years as an invalid or a slow, devastating decline. It was what she wanted, what we all wanted, really, but I couldn't help but feel like a part of me was dying too.

We talked so much during those weeks, and the girls, like they were children again, spent most of their time crowded around their grandmother, trying to get her attention.

"You know," she said to me that night, before she went to bed, "I think I'd like to go to Starlite Island tomorrow."

There were moments, many of them, when my mother was confused, and I chalked this one up to that. We were practically carrying her to the bathroom now and setting her on the couch during the day so she could be a part of the action. Her skin had become translucent and thin over her bones. Even sitting caused her pain. I wouldn't have thought about getting her into a car, much less bouncing her around on a boat.

Mom looked at me intently. "Ansley, I'm serious. I want to go to Starlite Island, where I have my best memories, one more time."

I smoothed her hair across her forehead, kissed her sunken cheek, and said, "Well then, Mother, to Starlite we shall go."

She smiled, her eyes closed. "I want to see your father," she said softly. Daddy's ashes were spread all across that beloved island of his, that place where we were raised, that raised us. But I knew she didn't mean his ashes.

"Did you know," Mom said, looking up at me, "that Starlite was the first place you ever saw water?"

I smiled, my eyes filling with tears. "I didn't know that," I whispered.

She nodded. "You were only four weeks old the first time we brought you to Peachtree Bluff. It was unusual for women to travel with babies so early in that day, but your father couldn't stand the idea that his girl hadn't seen the ocean." She paused and smiled, and I knew she was back in that moment. "He couldn't wait for you to see that spot where the river meets the sea, where the world connects, where we all connect."

"The water binds us all," I said, repeating something my father had said to me so many times.

Mom nodded. "You slept the whole loud, bumpy ride to the island. But the moment we stepped out of the boat, you woke up, quiet and wide-eyed, looking around. You smiled for the very first time. And we knew then that another water lover had been born. Your father was so proud."

I wanted to stay longer and soak up all her stories and memories while she was still here to give them to me. Instead, I tucked Mom in gently, and as I left her room, heard her tiny, frail moan. I wished for a quick and safe passage for her, a gentle exit from this world where she was no longer comfortable. I wished she would sleep and that the pain pills would kick in tonight. I also wished I, like my mother and Sloane, believed there was some sort of beautiful next life where I would see her again. But that idea had left me long ago.

I walked out to the front porch where Caroline, Sloane, and Emerson were all perched, a bottle of wine on the coffee table.

It was quite stunning, actually, how those girls had rehabilitated my Sloane. I wasn't sure if it was the sea, the stars, the wind, or the sisters . . . but whatever it was, she seemed to be a willing participant in her life again, and while I could see the distraction, the wondering, and the worrying written all over her face, she was a present figure in her sons' lives again. I was grateful yet again that this had happened when we were all here, when her family could pick up the pieces.

"Girls, Grammy wants to go to Starlite Island."

"Seriously?" Sloane asked.

I nodded.

Caroline sighed. "I'll ask Jack if we can use his boat again." Then she wiggled her eyebrows at me. "Unless you want to ask him yourself, Mom?"

I shot her a look, but part of me did want to ask him. One, I could see Jack. Two, I could see my favorite house. This project couldn't have come at a better time. It was the only thing I could think of that could take my mind off my mother dying.

Caroline stood with purpose and said, "Oh! We'll have a party." Then she disappeared inside the house.

I sighed. "I guess we're having a party."

It made me think about being on that boat with Jack a few months earlier, how he had said Caroline was like me. In this regard, he was right. She, like her mother, was the planner, the doer, the avoider. Sloane, on the other hand, was wiping her eyes as Emerson said, "Please don't. Once I start crying, I'm never going to stop."

"OK," Caroline said, bursting through the door not five

minutes later. "Kimmy is going to cater, and Kyle is going to provide beverages." She paused. "And muscle."

"Muscle?" I asked.

"For the tables and chairs."

She looked at me like I was dense.

"Car," Sloane said. "You're the only woman in the known world who could put together an entire party at nine o'clock at night."

She looked down at her phone and typed, rapid fire. "Mom, I'm going to need a bunch of those blue-and-white-striped paper straws from your store. Hippie Hal is going to set up tents with Kyle."

She typed some more. "Emerson," she said, without looking up from her phone, "I'm going to need you to go over there and string the lights in the tent."

She didn't say anything. She didn't even look at any of us.

"Caroline," Sloane said. "Is this a bit over the top? She just wants a day on the beach."

Caroline glared at Sloane. "Her *last* day on the beach, Sloane. Her last one. Ever. It's going to be the best damn beach day in history. Understand? Plus, it's her birthday."

Sloane put her hands up in defense. Then we were all quiet. Caroline's chin quivered. Caroline never cries, so, of course, that set us all off.

"How long do you think she has, realistically?" she asked.

I shrugged and pulled her close to me. "You know, honey, I'd say maybe a couple weeks. Tops."

Emerson sobbed.

She and Sloane wrapped their arms around each other. Watching Mom die was going to be terrible, but in so many ways, it would be better than watching her endure treatments we all knew, at this stage, would probably have very little effect.

Jack appeared at the gate and walked through the white picket fence. As he approached, I saw he was carrying two bottles of wine. He set them on the glass coffee table, which, I noticed, really needed to be wiped down.

I stood to greet him, and he wrapped me in a hug. Usually, hugs made me cry harder when I was upset, but this one soothed me. There was something in Jack's nature, his steady, easy way and the strength that exuded from him, that made me feel better. Everything inside of me was screaming that I needed him, that he was what was missing in my life. But it wasn't time. Not yet.

He followed me inside and smiled sadly. "I remember this part," he said.

I nodded, swallowing my tears. It made me sad that I hadn't been there for Jack the way he was for me now. Sometimes I worried the draw I felt toward him was nothing more than a glorified memory. But it was times like these when I realized what I was drawn to wasn't the kid I had fallen in love with all those summers ago. It was the man he was now.

"How do you get through it?" I asked. "I want to be strong for her, Jack, but it's tearing me apart to watch her die."

"I don't think this is much consolation," he said, "but this just has to happen. It's the natural order of things. Whether it's today or six months from now or ten years from now, this is pain you have to feel. It will hurt like hell. But then it gets a little better. And a little better. And, one day, you wake up and you smile and you think of them fondly without feeling the need to sob about it."

I nodded. "I should be better at this. I did it with my father. I should know how to handle it."

He took my hand and squeezed it. "But it's your mom," he said. "And once she's gone, you're parentless."

The tears really came now, because Jack had vocalized what I had been feeling all this time but couldn't quite reconcile. I was going to be an orphan. A fifty-eight-year-old orphan. But an orphan all the same.

He hugged me to him. "I'm sorry," he whispered. "If I could take this pain away from you I absolutely would."

What kind of woman wouldn't want to be with a man like that? But I couldn't lie to my daughters. I just couldn't.

Jack and I walked back out the front door. "Mom!" I exclaimed. My tiny mother was curled up on the couch between Caroline and Sloane, a pale pink pashmina wrapped around her long-sleeved nightgown, a pair of fuzzy slippers Caroline had gotten her on her feet.

"I couldn't bear to miss the action, darling," she said.

I smiled at her. "You never could, Mom." I was bolstered by the fact that she felt like being awake and out here with us.

"Oh my God!" Caroline exclaimed. "I need to go get Vivi from camp. She needs to be here for this."

Mom shook her head and said, "Absolutely not. That sweet girl is not coming home from one of the best parts of her life to watch me shrivel up."

"But Grammy—" Caroline started to protest.

"No," Grammy interrupted. "Life is for the living, darling. Don't you ever forget it."

I cleared my throat, trying to swallow my tears and turned to see Hippie Hal walking through the gate, Kimmy on his heels. I laughed. "It's almost ten o'clock at night, you crazies."

"We come bearing gifts," Hal said.

I pointed to Jack's wine. "I guess everyone thought we needed gifts tonight."

"Oh, we can do better than wine," Kimmy said, winking at me.

I raised my eyebrows. Hal reached into his backpack and pulled out a Tupperware container, and I was no longer confused.

Emerson burst out laughing, and Caroline said, "Those better be gluten free."

"Obviously," Kimmy said. "I would never leave you out."

"No," I said, trying to put on my most serious face. "Absolutely not. There are children in this house, and there will be no drugs here."

"They're not for you, Ansley," Hal said. "They're for Grammy."

"What are you talking about?" she asked.

"Grammy," Hal said, "we brought you nature's very best pain reliever."

"Oh, hogwash," she said, wrapping her pashmina tighter around her shoulders. "If oxycodone isn't killing the pain, I doubt some herb is going to."

"It's pot, Grammy," Kimmy said, pulling the chairs from the dining table on the other side of the porch across from the couch and sitting down in one.

Mom cackled, deepening the expression lines in her face that had become more pronounced as she lost weight. "Well, why didn't you just say so?"

"Count me out," Sloane said. "What if we have to go to the emergency room in the middle of the night?"

"James fell asleep on the couch," Caroline said. "He can be our emergency driver."

I could see the smile playing on Sloane's lips. I started to protest, but they weren't children anymore. They could decide whether they wanted pot brownies.

We all took our seats in a circle around the side of the porch. I looked out over the low tide, taking in the sliver of crescent moon perched in the sky. Hal passed the brownies around and when they got to me, I kept passing them.

"Mom, come on," Caroline said. "It's just a little brownie. Loosen up."

I shook my head. "What if it makes me paranoid or something?" I gasped. "What if it's laced with something horrible and we all die?"

Kimmy's turn to gasp. "Ansley Murphy, I am offended. I tended this beautiful bud every day of its life, and if you can't respect its perfection, then you don't deserve any."

Hal and Kyle burst out laughing. "Simmer down, Kim," Kyle said.

Jack squeezed my arm. "If you're ever going to do it, now's

the time. You know where it came from, so you know it's the best of the best."

"Thank you," Kimmy said, grinning at Jack. "Finally. Someone who understands me."

"Yeah, Mom," Emerson said. "Come on. Do something fun for once in your life."

"Shock us, Mom," Sloane said.

I couldn't help but share a quick glance with Jack. No doubt about it, I could shock those girls if I wanted to.

"I am *not* eating pot brownies," I said. "Not happening."

"Oh, Ansley, just have a bite," Mom said, chewing heartily, holding her huge pot brownie daintily in her manicured fingers.

I sighed and reached out my hand to Jack. The crowd cheered.

"All right, all right," I said. "Simmer down, all of you." Then, under my breath, I added, "Peer pressure is not just for kids."

I ate mine very, very slowly, as I had rarely done any drugs, and even those were in the late '70s.

After about twenty minutes, I saw my mother's face relax. Really relax. She seemed more comfortable than she had in weeks. I leaned over toward Hal. "Keep the brownies coming," I said.

"Oh, Ans, Kimmy and I have a whole kitchen full of amazing things for Grammy to try. We're going to be ready when marijuana is legalized in Georgia."

Jack burst out laughing, and then we all did, of course. If anyone had ever told me this would be happening, I wouldn't have believed it. But, sometimes, when all seems lost, the last thing you would have imagined starts to seem normal, natural even. I wished I could freeze this moment, all our happy faces, all the people I loved most in the world sitting around my front porch, the flags blowing in the breeze, the lights from the sailboat masts in the harbor reflecting off the water.

"Grammy," Caroline said, "we're going to have the best party ever on the beach tomorrow. I mean, I can't even tell you."

"Oh, darling," she said, "you can give me one of these brownies and tell me I'm at the beach and save yourself the trouble."

That set us all off again. I felt calm and peaceful and happy. All the hard angles of life were gone and we were floating along on its soft, fluffy curves. There had been so much pain the last couple of months. So much uncertainty. So many tears shed, sleepless nights, new worry lines. I hoped beyond hope that when I looked back, I would forget all that. This was the night I wanted to remember.

love connections

sloane

June 27, 2010

Dear Sloane,

I never understood why, but I never felt at home in college. I was searching for a purpose, a passion, something that lit me up inside. I know it sounds crazy, but the day I signed those papers to join the Army, I felt whole. I felt complete. I knew I would never be fulfilled unless I was fighting for something bigger than me. It's only now that I consider what this job really means in terms of what it is I'm giving up. Because being away from you feels like a punishment. Even still, I know this is where I'm supposed to be. Just like I know when I come home, in your arms is where I'm supposed to be. Meeting you, Sloane, loving you, has given me another purpose.

And where, at one time, I lived for my country, now, my
beautiful bride-to-be, I live for you.
    All my love,
    Adam

MARIJUANA SHOULD BE LEGALIZED for military spouses. It's a fair concession. We have to spend years of our lives worrying about our partners—for the good of our country. We should get this in return.

I hated smoking of any sort. But eating brownies was fab-u-lous.

I peeked into the boys' room. They were both still out cold. I don't know what I did to deserve a twenty-one-month-old who slept until nine in the morning. Maybe it was restitution for the fact that AJ was such a terrible sleeper as a baby. I took a moment to gaze at them, the best parts of Adam and me. Clutching their stuffed animals, they looked like little angels. I prayed quickly that I wouldn't have to break their hearts and blow up their world.

I hadn't gotten that with my father. It seemed like a fair request.

The smell of pancakes wafted up from the kitchen, lazily and unhurried, like the morning itself. There is nothing in the world—and I do mean nothing—like having your mom make you pancakes. You don't have to worry about what you're going to feed yourself or how you're going to handle the million re-quests of, "Mommy, I'm hungry," when your little ones wake up. It's all taken care of. Our mom had always just known what we needed, understood what to do.

I wanted to be that effortless. But that nagging feeling that I needed something more had never really gone away. What did that do to the vision I'd had of myself as the ever-present, constantly available mom?

I walked down the hall and slid into bed beside Emerson. She was sleeping so peacefully, her blond hair draped across her beautiful face. She would be horrified when she woke up and realized she wasn't on her back. She was convinced sleeping on her face would cause wrinkles. As the big sister, I had always felt the need to protect. Only, this sickness wasn't something I could fix.

I couldn't even make her go back to the doctor. She kept putting it off and rescheduling. She was afraid to learn the truth. So was I. But there comes a point when even bad news is better than no news at all. She would get there soon. Or maybe she would get tired of Caroline and me harassing her mercilessly about it. Either way.

I got up and walked quietly down the carpeted steps in my sock feet. Mom was alone in the kitchen, crying into the pancake batter.

"The recipe only calls for a pinch of salt, Mom," I said, hugging her from behind.

She smiled at me and sniffed. "I'm sorry. I think this is how it's going to be around here for a while."

I looked around the kitchen, as clean and pristine as ever, even though we were all here, making a dozen sandwiches a day and three times as many snacks. Somehow, in between helping clients, trying to put time in at the shop, and taking care of Grammy, Mom managed to keep it looking like no one lived here. She was a marvel, really, and I wondered if she had always been this way and I just hadn't noticed.

Mom poured batter onto her griddle, and it sizzled, filling the air with the scent of many a childhood Saturday morning. I grabbed a pancake off the "done" plate. It was delicious even without syrup.

She pointed with her spatula. "Grammy's request."

I nodded. "When do we have to start withholding food? I mean, isn't that one of the hospice things?"

She shook her head. "She can eat if she wants to. It's more about giving her a bit of pleasure than sustenance." Her eyes filled again. "We could feed her all day, every day, though, and she'd never come close to a normal size."

I walked to the easel that was crammed into the corner of the kitchen. It probably should have been in my room, at the front of the house, where I could overlook the water, but it seemed my mother and sisters gave me just as much inspiration as the water did. And, once the floodgates opened, they hadn't closed. The paint was pouring out of me now.

The back door opened. Caroline swept in wearing a floor-length white silk robe. "What have I missed?" she said. "Besides carb circles." She scrunched her nose.

"They're for Grammy," Mom said. "Not you."

"I want in on that action," Emerson said as she walked into the room. I smiled at her. She seemed less vulnerable when she was awake, vivacious and so full of life.

I picked up the brush in my hand, and the strokes flowed

from my heart to the canvas. These past few days I'd done the best painting I ever had, the most raw, the most real. Were these strokes of fear? Pain? Independence? Were they strokes of horror? Exhaustion? Dread? I've only ever been able to express what I felt through a brush. The easel was the only place where I could make sense of who I was and what that meant.

Mom was neatly stacking the pancakes, a generous pat of butter between each one, and squeezing syrup on the side, just like Grammy liked.

"Mom," Caroline said, "Sloane and I are going to come help you out in the shop a little. I'm trying to convince her to sell paintings, too, but I'm not as persuasive as I once was, obviously."

She gasped and dropped the syrup, and Mrs. Butterworth bounced on the counter. She put her hand to her mouth. "No! You don't mean it!"

This was not exactly the reaction I had expected, and I wasn't sure what to make of it. "Yeah. We want to help you in the store. Whatever you need. I just feel like something is missing. Adam, obviously. But something else. Like maybe it's time for me to have a little time away from the kids."

"Oh, girls. This means so much to me! It will be so much fun to have you at the store."

I laughed. I hadn't expected her to be so excited. "We all talked about it, and Caroline, Emerson, and I are going to take turns staying with Grammy so her care doesn't fall completely on you."

"And the boys can go to Mother's Morning Out at St. James's," Caroline said.

"St. James," Emerson snorted.

Caroline rolled her eyes. "I know. Ironic, isn't it?"

"He's kind of being St. James these days," Mom said. She disappeared down the hall with her pancake plate.

"He really is," I added. "I would never have imagined he would stay so long in Peachtree Bluff."

"I know." Caroline walked to the stove, filled a pot with water, and turned on the burner. "He has to head back to New York, but I think I want to stay the rest of the summer."

I knew the work James and Caroline had ahead of them was daunting—and far from over. I wondered if being in Peachtree for a little longer might help give them a stronger foundation before they went back to their real lives.

Mom reappeared. "What's up with Mark, Emerson?" she asked.

Emerson only shrugged. She was being uncharacteristically tight-lipped about him. But there were weeks and weeks left of summer. If I knew anything about the sea, it was that nothing had the power to pull things out of you quite like it did. And, at the same time, nothing had quite the power to fill you back up again.

TWENTY-FOUR

six months

ansley

I was already crying when I woke up. I knew my mother wouldn't die as long as she had this trip to Starlite Island to look forward to. After that, I wasn't sure what would happen.

Sandra and Emily were already sitting in my kitchen when I padded in. When I saw them, the waterworks started again, and they both stood to hug me, one on each side.

"She's going to be gone," I sobbed. "Then I'm not going to have anyone."

"Oh, honey, no," Sandra said. "You have us; you have the girls."

Biscuit let out a little yip as if to say, "You have me, too!"

But surely they knew what I meant. That had been the hardest thing about losing Carter, the thing I hadn't expected. When the initial shock and horror of his death had worn off a bit, there were still months and months of realizing how much

I depended on him. For far longer than I would like to admit, I would think, "Oh, Carter will do that," before I would take out the trash or change a lightbulb.

It still crossed my mind to ask my husband for directions, for advice about what to do with the girls, what brand of wine to buy . . . The list went on and on. Not two years later, I went through the same thing with my dad. Now, my mother would be gone. Friends were wonderful and children were terrific, but they were not replacements for your spouse or your parents. A deep sense of vulnerability washed over me, as though, suddenly, I was open to whatever the world wanted to throw at me. I had no one left to protect me, though, frankly, I couldn't imagine what other horrors we could possibly endure. I tried to take that thought back, as though I was tempting fate.

But Jack was right. My mother was going to die. It was always going to be hard. We would grieve, we would heal, and life would go on. The children were healthy, and while, yes, it would have been great for Adam to come home, for today, we had to be grateful for what we had.

Emily handed me a cup of coffee, and I followed my friends into the living room, to sit down in one of the comfortable, patterned chairs.

"I just can't believe she's going to be gone," I said.

Sandra and Emily still had both of their parents, which was quite a feat at our age. "But she's not gone now," Emily said. "And we're going to give her one hell of a going-away party."

We all laughed. That was a good way to think of it. A going-away party. Only, it was one thing to give someone a going-away party when you could hop on a plane to Paris to see her again. But she wasn't going to be in Paris. And I wasn't going to see her again.

"You'll get to be together again one day," Sandra said.

I rolled my eyes. My two best friends were completely undone by the abdication of my faith. In a town like Peachtree Bluff, or a lot of small Southern towns, really, saying you were ambivalent at best about God was like saying you didn't believe in sweet tea.

I stood up. "We need to get ready."

"Is it black tie?" Emily quipped.

"Black suit," I said. "Bathing suit."

We all managed a small smile, and I heard AJ's tiny voice calling, "Gransley." I saw him at the top of the stairs.

"Hi, my big boy! Come down here and see me!"

This time I really smiled. I was grateful I had my grandchildren with me during this tough time. They were such a beautiful reminder that life did, indeed, go on. There was more. And it was wonderful.

AJ was wearing green-and-white-striped pajamas, sucking his thumb, and clutching his blankie. Before I turned around he would be twenty-one. I wanted to freeze time and keep him at this sweet and innocent age when life is full of possibility.

He climbed up into my lap as Sandra said, "We'll see you in a couple hours."

They made their way out the front door as AJ rested his head on my chest. "You're the best snuggler I know."

He looked up at me and smiled. "I love to snuggle."

"I know you do. Will you still snuggle me when you're eight?"

He thought for a moment. "No, Gransley. But maybe when I'm six."

I laughed. "Sounds fair." It broke my heart that in this short couple of months my grandson had started calling me "Gransley," not "Gwansley." He was growing up too quickly. They all did.

I heard voices on the landing. I couldn't make out what they were saying, but Sloane and Emerson sounded like they were deep in conversation.

The back door flung open, and Caroline called, "Who's ready to party?" Mom's weak voice called back, "I am!"

I rushed into her room. It was dark, the blinds were closed, and she seemed so small in the king bed that she was barely detectable. I leaned down and kissed her. "Good morning, Mom. Do you feel like you can get up today?"

"Yes," she said in her small voice. "I have to get up. I have a party to get ready for, for heaven's sake."

Her spirit hadn't waned. Emerson helped me lead Mom, very slowly, into the bathroom to complete her morning routine.

I knew she would be exhausted by the time we were finished. It would take all the energy she had to simply complete her everyday tasks.

"I'm going to get this hair looking good," Emerson said.

I looked down at my watch. It was nearly eight thirty. I heard a light rap on the door. I was still in my robe with no makeup and hair pulled back into the squatty ponytail that was all my shoulder-length hair could manage. "Sloane," I half-yelled, half-whispered. "Get the door and take Jack into the kitchen."

If he was safely stowed away there, I could sneak upstairs and get presentable.

"Where's your mom?" I heard Jack ask.

"Oh, she's hiding in Grammy's room so you won't see her without her makeup."

She would pay for this. I had brought her into this world, and I could take her out of it. Emerson was still with Mom in the bathroom, and Jack peeked his head in. I pretended that I was making the bed, not hiding.

"Hey," he said, winking.

I threw a pillow at him and put another one up to my face. "I will be ready in ten minutes. I promise."

"I think you look great now."

I couldn't see his face because mine was covered with a pillow. On the one hand, it was silly. The man and I had been through everything together, and he had certainly seen me without my makeup before. But I was young then. Fresh. Wrinkle-free. Now I had to keep up appearances, and as much as I didn't want to admit it to myself, keep him interested. You know, just in case.

———

TWENTY MINUTES LATER, JACK and I were standing on the teak deck of his beautiful boat. It felt so rewarding to see one of my completed projects. "So," he said, "brought back a lot of memories getting high with you last night. Good times."

I swatted him playfully. "It was only once, Jack," I said, remembering as clearly as if it had happened the day before sitting in the cabin of Bobby Franklin's boat with Jack, Sandra, Emily, Bobby, and their friend Craig, passing around an ill-rolled joint, feeling very, very rebellious.

"Twice," he said.

"That must have been another girl." It was silly, but I felt jealous, thinking of *Georgia*. Her car had been at Jack's house for quite some time the day before, much longer than your general Realtor check-in. But this was what I deserved. I had told him we couldn't be together. What did I expect?

"It was not another girl," he said. "It was you and me over by the lighthouse. And then we . . ." He wiggled his eyebrows.

I put my hand over my mouth and could feel the blush coming up my cheeks. "Jack!" I scolded. But then I said, "How could I have forgotten that night?"

He smiled up at me, and our eyes met for a bit too long. I couldn't help but think of how something similar had transpired between us in this very boat a couple months earlier. If I was honest with myself, I wanted it to happen again. We were standing so close together, the energy between us so thick you could almost see it. I wondered, briefly, what would happen if I leaned over and kissed him. Just this once. What could it possibly hurt?

Jack clapped his hands as if to snap us both out of it. "OK," he said, leaning down and picking up the big bag from my store I had dropped on the deck.

"Jack," I said.

He looked up at me again, and said, "I can't, Ansley. I can't even think about the start of this road when I know where it ends."

The impulsive part of me, the part that still loved that boy as much as I had that night on the beach by the lighthouse, wanted to tell him the road didn't have to end, that I had been stupid and made a snap decision. But then I thought of all the people getting ready to get on this boat and how much they needed me. My mother was dying, for heaven's sake. This was not the time to be kissing high school crushes on their beautiful yachts. Before I could say anything, Jack handed me a pillow. I had covered the banquette around the dining table in blue-and-white-striped Sunbrella, and combined with these pillows, it would be a plush and comfy place for Mom to hang out.

I turned around to see them all. My mother, frail and tiny wrapped in a blanket despite the heat, James on one side, Hippie Hal on the other. Coffee Kyle was carrying Preston, which struck me as immensely funny. Sloane was holding Taylor, who was already in his life jacket, and AJ was swinging between Emerson and Mark.

Kimmy ran onto the dock. When she reached us, she stopped, her hands on her knees, panting. "Phew!" she said. "I was afraid I was going to miss the boat."

"Me too," Jack said. To everyone else I'm sure it seemed like nothing. But, to me, his words felt heavy, laced with longing and what's more, anticipation.

"I sure am glad you didn't," Hal said. "How would you have ever gotten all the way over to Starlite?"

We all turned our heads and laughed. It was a laughably short distance. With all the preparation, the food, the tents, the lights, the massive amount of planning crammed into a very short window, all of us gathering on this huge boat as though we were off on a grand voyage, we had forgotten this was a journey we could have taken via kayak, or, had we been strong swimmers, no vessel at all.

"More importantly," Mom said, "who would have brought my pot brownies?"

That set everyone off again. It was a good start. I was afraid this would feel like a funeral, somber and heavy. But it didn't. It was a party for sure.

Emerson had done wonders with Mom's hair. She looked lovely in her knit pantsuit. I smiled, but then it hit me what we were here for: her literal going-away party. I was going to wake up one morning, probably soon enough that I could count the days on my fingers and toes, and she was going to be gone. I would never again see her face. Never hear her laughter. Never call her on the phone to ask her opinion.

No, it hadn't been perfect. I would never fully understand her decision when Carter died, and sometimes she wasn't as touchy-feely a mother as I really wanted her to be. Still, although she may not always have been what I wanted, I had to consider that she had always, always been what I needed.

I felt the lump in my throat growing, and I knew I wouldn't be able to control it much longer. As everyone chattered around me like this was another ordinary day on the island, I turned and walked as quickly as I could without arousing suspicion into the luxurious interior of the boat and into Jack's room. I closed the door behind me and sat on the end of his unmade bed, the same unmade bed I had not only picked the linens for but also made love to him in. Then I started to cry. I knew I had to get it over with. I would never get through this day without at least a few tears.

When I heard footsteps and a hand on the doorknob, I tried to gather myself and wiped my eyes. But when I saw Jack's face coming through the door, I lost it again.

As he came closer, I expected him to wrap me in a hug, rub my back, tell me it would be OK or anything soothing that would calm my nerves and dry my tears.

But he didn't do any of that. Instead, he put his hands on my cheeks and kissed me so passionately that I truly felt like I was living that night by the lighthouse all over again. Only, this time, the only thing making me feel giddy and free was Jack.

We looked at each other for a long moment after that kiss, neither of us daring to speak. "You have six months," he said. "Six months to get your shit together, to get over your excuses and your fears, whatever they are."

He'd never spoken to me so firmly or so intensely. "Let's face it, Ansley. Your life is a disaster zone. No one, and I mean *no one*, in his right mind would want to get mixed up with you. But I do. I want you." He paused. "I won't say it again. Six months from today, a 'For Sale' sign will go up in my yard. I will leave. I will wish you well and be on my way. I am too old to play these games."

He turned and, with his hand on the doorknob, repeated, "Six months."

I knew I'd never make it that long.

I WHOLEHEARTEDLY BELIEVE SEEING your husband become a father can only make you love him more. That had certainly been the case with Carter. Bringing Caroline into our world changed him completely, and I was in love with how in love Carter was with baby Caroline.

If seeing Carter with his daughter made me love him more, if watching him change diapers and get up for middle-of-the-night feedings and take her off on errands so I could get some sleep had compounded my love for Carter, then seeing her eyes change into Jack's, watching the way her lips curled when she smiled and the color of her hair darken into his made it impossible for me to forget about him. That was perhaps the unexpected consequence.

It shouldn't have been unexpected, of course. I should have prepared myself for that, closed the wind shutters, battened the hatches. But I hadn't known yet how spending those weeks with Jack and giving birth to his baby would cause a deep longing for what we could have had to take permanent residence inside my chest and remove the light from my eyes.

I never talked to Jack. Never called him. Never visited or wrote a letter. But it was no consolation. No salve existed for the pain of being apart from him, yet I knew instinctively that the anguish I felt over losing him was nothing compared to what it would be if I left Carter and chose Jack like he had asked.

So the night Carter had come to me and said, "I think we should start trying again," I held myself back, but I wanted to run upstairs, tie my shoes, and hop the first plane to Atlanta. I was like an addict who had spent years without a fix, still craving it with every ounce of her being. I was going to give in to my primal need for it again. In the back of my mind, I knew it would only make things worse and prolong this profound loss I felt in every cell.

Time would never erase the memory of Jack and what we shared, would never allow me to get past what I felt for him. And so, seeing him again, asking him this unaskable favor for a second time, might be, as my father would say, a temporary solution to a permanent problem.

If I wanted another baby, which I did, desperately, this was how I would get one. I knew already without hashing it out with Carter again.

At the time, it didn't seem odd to me that he was so against people delving into our personal and financial lives. He had always been private. He had convinced me that if we let an adoption agency dig around, they might find out that Caroline wasn't really his. I could never let that happen.

I realize now that was just a cover. He wasn't worried about them finding out about Caroline; he was worried about me discovering what a disaster he had made of our finances. As soon as he died and I found out about the debt, it all made perfect sense. I should have been angry at him for leaving me out in the cold, for not telling me the truth. But I knew even then that, in his own way, he was trying to protect me. Plus, there was no sense in holding grudges—especially against a dead man.

Much like that rainy night in Peachtree Bluff when I boarded a plane into a great, wide unknown expanse of which I could never have predicted the consequences, that morning, I kissed my husband, stroked my sleeping baby's forehead, and left for what I'd told Carter was a girls' trip. He didn't delve deeper. He knew better.

My stomach was in knots the entire flight, a mix of anxiety and unadulterated, nearly maddening excitement. What if he was involved with someone else? What if he wouldn't agree to this again?

Soon after I landed, I was swigging Pepto-Bismol in the back of the cab on the way to his house. It felt riskier this time, showing up unannounced. By the time I had arrived at Jack's small but charming Buckhead home, admiring the ivy that grew over the trellis around the front door, I was so worked up I had almost convinced myself to go back home.

But the need for his lips to be on mine felt stronger than my need to make the safe choice.

It was a Tuesday evening, so I figured he would be home. Only, when I knocked, there was no answer. I knew immediately I should have called. What if he was away on a trip? What if, even worse, he came home with a woman? I had to be prepared for that scenario, didn't I? I had no claim to him whatsoever, except for, I had to consider, his heart. A hot flash of jealousy ran through me at the thought that someone else might have his heart now and he hadn't given me a second thought.

I walked around the side of the house and into the backyard, the high heels I had laboriously picked sinking into the grass. I leaned to the left to compensate for the weight of the heavy duffle bag on my right shoulder. I smelled the grill before I saw him. I stood quietly at the edge of the patio, on the small pathway surrounded by mature bushes that were probably eight feet tall. I watched the way his mouth curved as he sipped his beer, the way that vein on his forearm I had always loved running my finger down became more pronounced as he flipped the steak, the way his eyes crinkled when he smiled to himself. I took a step forward, into the safety of the bushes and, as if I had triggered some silent alarm that only he could hear, Jack turned. Our eyes met. I smiled.

I expected him to run to me and scoop me up in his arms, or at least walk casually toward me in his completely charming and irresistible way.

But he did neither. Instead, he sat down in a black wrought-iron chair behind him and put his head in his hands. I had the sinking feeling that I had made a huge mistake, that this was going to be nothing like what I had envisioned and I had ruined Jack's life. I had caused him the same pain and anguish I had caused myself.

I dropped my duffle on the edge of the patio, and even in his distress, even though I wasn't sure it was the right thing, I went to him. I had to at least try to ease the pain I had caused. Jack's head was still in his hands, and as I kneeled to look at him, I realized he was crying. I knew then I shouldn't have come. But he looked up at me, put his hands on my cheeks, and said, "Oh, thank God."

I realized his weren't tears of distress. They were tears of relief. All those months that Jack had been the insistent tick-tock in the back of my mind, the beat so persistent and rhythmic that you incorporate it into your life, learn to coexist with it, that the things he had said, the way he smelled, the feel of his lips on mine had been running through my mind on an endless loop, he had felt the same. And now I was here. In that way I had felt like I couldn't live one more moment without a fix, he couldn't either.

He didn't say any of that, of course. But those three words told me more than any long, convoluted monologue could have, because those three words perfectly expressed what I had felt all that time. He pulled me onto his lap and kissed me not with passion but with ferocity, as though he could make us one, make it so I could never leave again. In that moment, as I felt myself ripping the T-shirt over his head, I thought that was what I wanted too, to be with him, to never leave, to be one with him like I had dreamed of since we were children.

Never before and never since have I completely lost myself like that. I've never felt as though I had disappeared into another person and that time and space and direction no longer existed. It was only Jack and me in that private backyard paradise that, in the coming months, would become a place I would lie in to feel the sun on my skin, a place where I would pretend for hours on end that I was going to bring Caroline and never leave, a place where I would experience emotions so complicated, so convoluted, and so intense that I was certain I would completely lose my mind.

But then, it was just Jack and me and the love we'd had since we were teenagers in his Boston Whaler. Just Jack and me in the knowledge that sometimes love really isn't enough.

Just Jack and me. And a horribly charred steak. And the realization that what we had done wasn't making a baby. It was reigniting a flame, an old one, one too intense, perhaps, for either of us to stand. We wanted that fire. We never wanted it to go out. And, lost in Jack that night, I never could have predicted how irreparably we, like that steak, would burn.

TWENTY-FIVE

true south

sloane

March 28, 2016

Dear Sloane,

You can't imagine how much the thought of you keeps me going, how much knowing I have you to come home to makes me know everything is going to be OK. Now that I'm the Sarge, everything feels different. I have to be the strong one now, Sloane. I have to be the brave and fearless leader, the one they look to when they are feeling low. It's hard for me to stay strong sometimes, but I look up at the stars at night, and I picture you there in Georgia, in the land of peaches and pecans and peanuts, of all the things that are right with the world. And I know one thing for sure: you are my true South. No matter where I am, no matter how far away, my heart's compass will always, always lead me back to you.

All my love,

Adam

WHEN I HEARD THE voices downstairs begin to get louder, I finally roused myself to get ready for the day. For Grammy's day. Her last day at Starlite Island.

We think and talk a lot about our firsts, but we never really take the time to savor our lasts. Not enough time, anyway. Maybe it's because they break our hearts so much. I don't actually remember, for example, the last time I nursed either of my babies. I likely won't remember the last time either of them sits on my lap or kisses me on the lips. Maybe that's just as well, because it would be too hard. In the savoring, we would never be able to let it go. And letting go is the essence of life, the thing that keeps us moving forward.

That's what made this morning particularly difficult, realizing it was, definitively, the very last time we would spend the day with our sharp, beautiful grandmother over at the island where we had spent countless hours with her in childhood. That last made me think about the last time I had Skyped with Adam. I had been upset with him, angry even, something I seldom was. I was an expert at putting on my brave Army wife face, but on the inside, I was a wreck most of the time. The thing I respected about Adam most, his dedication to his country, freedom, and his family, was also the thing that bothered me most. Because, in my heart of hearts, I just wanted him to come home. To me. To the boys. He could get a regular job or go back to school. But I never said that. Well, not until that day.

Through my tears, I had said, "Adam, please. Make this your last tour. Just come home already." The look on his face had pained me.

"I know this is hard on you, babe," he had said, to which I had retorted, "No, Adam. 'Hard' is an hour-long spin class. This is unthinkable."

I knew the exact difference between the two, in fact, because Caroline had made me go to an hour-long spin class the day before.

Even through the not-always-wonderful Skype reception, I had seen Adam was hurt. I didn't want to hurt him, especially not when he was living through something so unimaginably difficult. I wanted to make things easier for him and be that strength he needed, and 99 percent of the time, I was. But not that night.

"I can't stand this, Adam. The kids are getting older. They're going to start to remember when you aren't here for months on end. I know your country means a lot to you and so do your men, but you need to choose us."

I knew he wanted to argue with me then because he thought fighting for freedom and safety was choosing us. That was how he saw it. Sometimes, that was how I saw it too. But not that night. He didn't bother to argue with me.

He simply sighed and said, "OK, Sloane. I'll think about it. We can talk about it when I get home."

That had been our last conversation. Oh, I hated that. I always said that last conversations didn't matter when you truly knew how much you meant to each other. But now I understood. It was awful to think that the last time you spoke to someone, especially someone you loved so much, was in anger.

But there was little I could do about that today. All I could do was make sure I didn't have another regret, that I gave my grandmother a proper good-bye, the kind of good-bye that would make me look back with a smile, not with sadness that I hadn't done the right thing.

It was that idea that finally got me out of bed. Sometimes, no matter how you're feeling, how sad you are, how hurt, the only option is to get up and keep going. I had heard it all my life. Now I was living it.

An hour later, Caroline was leading the charge to the boat, and all I could think about was how Mark and Emerson were so in love, giggling and cuddling. It was like stepping back in time, as if I were looking at the head cheerleader and star center from Peachtree Bluff High, the kids they had been when they fell in love the first time. Nothing had changed at all. They didn't even look older. I hated them a little.

"OK, Grammy," I said to my grandmother, who was sandwiched between Hal and James. "How do you think these crazy characters are planning to get you in here?"

"Oh, seems pretty simple to me," Kyle interjected as he slid his arm under Grammy's knees, and she wrapped her arms around his neck. I saw her wince when he lifted her, but, instead of complaining, in true Grammy style she said, a deep Southern accent dripping off her every word, "I've always depended on the kindness of a stranger."

Caroline, Emerson, and I laughed, and she looked back at us, putting her hand up to stop Kyle from walking. "Take note, girls. That accent is the secret to Southern charm."

"Why whatever do you mean, Grammy?" Caroline asked in what was one of the best Southern accents I had ever heard, real or otherwise.

"Come on, Caroline," Emerson said, in her regular voice, which was a little Southern. "You're a New Yorker."

"And yet," Caroline said, still channeling her inner Scarlett, "I do the accent better than any of you."

We all laughed again, and Caroline, Emerson, and I crowded around Grammy, who was lounging in a pile of pillows at the dining table banquette. "This really is the way to ride, girls," she said.

I noticed Jack coming out of the cabin, and when, a few minutes later, Mom followed, Emerson, Caroline, and I all shot each other looks. "That looks pretty suspicious," I whispered first.

"We all see what's happening here," Emerson said. "We aren't twelve."

"Maybe you girls should talk to her about it," Grammy said.

"Maybe *you* should talk to her about it," Caroline said. "She'll listen to you."

"She never has before." Grammy exhaled, and we all laughed. Then she added, "But now I'm dying, so she has to."

Just like that, our laughter turned to tears, as quickly as a summer rain shower bursting from a stray dark cloud.

"Oh, girls," Grammy said. "I'm sorry. I didn't mean to upset you. You have to remember I'm very, very high right now." We erupted into watery giggles.

As I looked over to Starlite Island, I thought about the fairy stones Caroline had found for us there, how we had kept them in our pockets, how Grandpop said they were a gift to us to keep us safe. We had lost them on that same island where she had found them—and we were devastated, to say the least. And Grandpop had said to us, "The fairies gave your stones to someone else, someone who needed them more than you did."

I had found that comforting, but it still hurt to remember what we had lost. They were more than a toy. They were a gift given to us by the land, by the sea, by this place we got to visit every summer that we loved so much.

I looked up at Caroline, whose eyes were on me. It didn't matter now. It had been so long ago. But I still wondered who that man was that Mom was arguing with that day on the beach when we left the stones.

"What are y'all laughing about?" Mom asked.

"Oh, nothing," I said, looking around. Amidst this strange, sort of sad, sort of funny, sort of happy day, I had to pause to realize how incredibly lucky my mother was. These people were here today because of her. They were here, in the morning, on a gorgeous summer day, when they could be doing anything else, because they were that devoted to her and wanted to give her an amazing memory with her dying mother.

I walked inside the boat, where Taylor and AJ were examining how one of the hatches opened and closed, and pulled them both onto my lap, wiggly creatures that they were. I knew this wouldn't be the last time I held them, but I breathed them in anyway. I squeezed them to me, savored their warmth, memorized how good it felt to hold my children.

It was a fleeting moment. AJ, with his Superman cape tied around his neck over his life jacket, wriggled free and, yelling, "I'll save you, Gransley!" was back on the stern in a flash. I kissed Taylor and set him free too.

The beach looked truly beautiful. Caroline had a trellis set up, about triple the size you would see in someone's wedding, and it had yellow-and-white-striped paper lanterns—yellow was Grammy's favorite color—hanging from it. The table underneath the tent was overflowing with flowers, and Kimmy was fussing over the trays of delicacies I'm certain she had been up all night creating. I hoped Grammy would be able to eat a bite or two.

I put my arm around my sister. "You're really something, you know that?"

She grinned at me, popping a cherry tomato into her mouth. "I am, aren't I?"

I noticed how Kyle fussed over Grammy, how he helped Kimmy, how he talked intently to Jack—anything to keep from watching the Mark-and-Emerson lovefest taking place in the corner.

"It's like they never broke up," Caroline said.

"Wait," Mom said. "Maybe that's what's happening. Maybe it's really 2008 again."

We all laughed.

"They look pretty together, though," Caroline said.

Mark was super cute. Not scorchingly hot like Kyle, but cute. And Emerson looked happy. That was all that mattered. "All I've heard from her," I said, "is how she doesn't have time to worry about relationships because all she can think about is her career."

"Well she doesn't look worried . . ." Caroline said.

Emerson took a bite of a ham biscuit Mark was feeding her. She didn't look worried at all.

I walked over to the table, poured us each a glass of champagne, handed one to Grammy, one to Caroline, one to Mom, and said, "Here's to love."

"Here's to love!" Grammy said.

Tears caught in my throat with the realization that, in no time at all, this beautiful woman, this head of our household who had done nothing but love us, would be gone.

Grammy had said earlier that the accent was the secret to Southern charm. But she was wrong. This putting on a brave face, carrying on, helping others, being kind and humble and giving, believing with all your heart that the world could be a better place and that maybe you could make it that way . . . that was Southern charm. Looking around at these women who all embodied those qualities so well, I had to think that maybe Grammy was wrong. Maybe it wasn't a secret at all.

TWENTY-SIX

safe passage

ansley

I know I'll never forget that day. I'll never forget the way my mother smiled, with all the people who loved her most surrounding her. I will never forget the way Jack kissed me, how it was different from any other time I'd ever been kissed. I felt very clearly, in that moment, that the tables had turned in some way. He had the upper hand, and he was serious this time. This was my last chance, and though I wasn't sure if it was the right decision, I knew it was a chance I needed to take.

The best part of the day was when a man on a paddleboard floated up to Starlite and, as I was about to ask Mom, "Who is that?" she practically yelled, "Scott!"

I let him hug her first, but I couldn't wait to get my hands on my little brother. In true Scott fashion, he had perfectly chiseled abs and was shockingly tan for early June. But when you spend so much time south of the equator, that is bound to happen.

"Mom," Scott said breathlessly, her face in his hands. "You look as beautiful as ever."

I could tell he was lying. The tears in his eyes gave him away. He knew she was dying. It was written all over his face.

He squeezed me, lifted me up in the air, kissed my cheek, and said, "How you doing there, big sis?" Then he pulled away, squinted, and said, "Wait. Is that Jack? Like from high school?"

"It sure is," Mom said. "He's standing in for my sorry eldest son. I rather like him. I think I'll keep him, actually."

We all laughed, but Scott and I exchanged glances. I had spoken with John earlier that morning, and he promised he would get here to see Mom early next week. As I looked over at her, so happy but so small in the tall chair made of hammock material that Caroline had covered in flowers, I couldn't help but wonder if early next week would be too late.

Scott squeezed Sloane next. "How are you?"

She shrugged. "Breathing."

Scott nodded gravely. "Listen," he said, turning toward all of us. "You know I've spent a decent amount of time reporting in Iraq over the past few years. I have a lot of contacts there. I know how to get deals done, and I think I can get the cash to do it." He paused. "I'm going over there to look for him."

Sloane cocked her head to the side. "Wait. I'm sorry. What?"

"Adam. I'm going to go look for him," Scott repeated.

My heart thudded in my chest. We already had one family member missing in Iraq. Yes, I had to come to terms with the fact that Scott was always going to be on some adventure or another, and if I spent my whole life worrying about his safety, it wasn't going to be much of a life. But going to Egypt when there's a travel advisory is one thing. Going into a war zone as a hated American journalist was quite another.

"Scott!" I said, not sure what to say next.

Caroline and Emerson were wide-eyed. Mom said, "I'm proud of you, son. I really am."

"How would you even begin to look for him?" Sloane asked.

Scott waved his hand as if this were a minor detail. "I think going over there and trying is better than sitting here waiting." He paused. "I mean, not for you. You've got kids to take care of. Nobody's counting on me."

Me! I wanted to scream. *I'm counting on you.* But I stayed quiet.

This was a bridge to cross another day.

Mark interrupted, saying to Mom, "I got you a little something for your birthday." Mom put her hand to her mouth in surprise and then ripped the wrapping paper with a frail and shaking hand to reveal a beautiful box of Easter egg–colored macarons from Ladurée. They were Mom's favorite things in the world.

"How did you get these?" she gasped, motioning for him.

She kissed Mark on the cheek as he said, "It doesn't matter how I got them. It only matters that you get to have them on your birthday."

Mom pulled out her favorite green, pistachio macaron. She offered the box halfheartedly to us, but we all knew better than to accept. This was Mom's treat. It was her day.

I could tell she was getting tired, so I leaned down to her. "Are you ready?" I asked.

It nearly broke me in half when the tears came to her eyes. "Good-bye, beautiful beach," she said. "You have given us so much life here." Then she swallowed and said, "Don't take it for granted, Ansley. Come here whenever you get the chance. Feel the sand underneath your feet, run your fingers along the water. Don't let this life pass you by." Then she looked up at me and smiled and patted my hand. "I'm ready, darling."

Holding Scott's hand, Mom dozed in between Scott and me on the ride back to the dock.

As she drifted off and the girls were in the salon finishing the rest of the champagne with Jack, Kimmy, Kyle, Mark, and Hal, I practically hissed at Scott, "You are not going to Iraq!"

He shrugged. "Ansley, her husband is over there, probably trapped in some god-awful cave."

"So what are you going to do about it?" I asked. "Write him to safety? Pen his journey to freedom?"

"Maybe," Scott said. "Maybe I will. But all I've been able to do since I heard the news is think about that pitiful girl sitting over here worried to death and her poor husband. I know people. I might be able to help, and I'm going to try."

I shook my head. "Great. That's just great. So now I'll have a husband killed by terrorists, a son-in-law killed by terrorists, and a brother killed by terrorists."

He grinned at me. "On the bright side, you don't have too many different things to hate. Simply saying you hate terrorists pretty much covers it."

I couldn't help but smile. He reached over our tiny mother and squeezed my shoulder. "I won't die, sis. I didn't die in that avalanche on Mont Blanc. I didn't die from that green tree viper bite on Machu Picchu. I didn't die those nights we played Edward Fortyhands in college. I'm gonna be all right."

I smirked. "So what about our brother?"

"Ans," he said. "You've got to let it go. You can only control you, and John can only control John."

It was an inopportune time for our mother to wake up, but with her eyes still closed, she said, "I love all of you unconditionally. If he doesn't come here to tell me good-bye, I've made my peace with that."

I believed her because I had no other choice.

I whispered, "But you love me the best, right, Mom?"

I winked at Scott. He leaned down too and said, "Mom, just tell her she's your favorite daughter. That will appease her. Don't break her heart by admitting I'm your favorite child."

We smiled at each other, and though her eyes were closed, our mother smiled too. This was a game we had played with her nearly our entire lives. A game we would likely never play again. It was so small, so simple, so insignificant, but even the insignificant becomes terribly important when you know it's going to be over. I squeezed Scott's hand, and I realized it didn't matter now who won or lost, didn't matter who Mom's favorite was. This was a pain Scott and I would share, a pain only we could truly understand. I closed my eyes and took a deep breath. I would worry about that when she was gone. For now, I was going to savor every second we had left.

the lifetime movie version

sloane

August 5, 2011

Dear Sloane,

I know you said you weren't upset earlier on the phone, but I can't express to you how much I wish you had gotten pregnant before I left. I'm sorry I couldn't give you the baby we want so badly. But when I get home, we will try again, and this time it will work. This time, we will get everything we have ever wanted. I already have you, Sloane. This baby will just be the icing on the cake. Wonder if the icing will be pink or blue?

All my love,

Adam

IT WAS ONLY A few months between the time Adam and I had started "trying" for a baby and the time he was deployed again.

It wasn't enough time for us to be worried—or for him to be suspicious. It was very unlike me, this big lie. I was never one who could keep a big secret, but I had managed to keep this one quite splendidly.

It wasn't until Adam was gone that the gravity of what I was doing really set in, that the level to which I was compromising my marriage hit me. My adoring husband who trusted me implicitly believed that when he was making love to me, we were trying to make a baby. Only I knew he was alone in that.

It was that letter that really did it for me. All I could think was, here is my husband halfway around the world, fighting for my freedom, and I have betrayed him in the worst possible way.

I thought about writing him a letter, explaining to him my position and that I was sorry. I would try to make him understand my reasons for what I had done, explain that I wanted to make him happy but I did not want children, under any circumstances.

But I knew this wasn't something I could write. I couldn't hide behind a letter. I had to tell him in person. So, for the six months he was gone, I wrote to him under the pretense that I, too, couldn't wait to have a baby. I reasoned that if, God forbid, something happened to him, he should get to be happy just a little longer. I never told anyone what I had done, how I had lied to my husband, how the secret I kept from him had nearly cost me my marriage and the love of my life.

Now, sitting on my mom's screened-in back porch with my two sisters, that seemed a world away. I could hardly remember a time when I didn't want children, couldn't imagine I had ever envisioned my life without these little people who, while frustrating at times, made my world go around.

Earlier that night, for the first time in weeks, I hadn't rushed through putting my children to bed. I didn't feel the urge to get back in my pajamas as quickly as possible to get the day over with. Maybe that was the gift in this whole thing. I remembered this was the only life I was going to get, and one day I was going to be gone and wouldn't get to spend time with my boys. I read to them, snuggled into my side, until Taylor fell asleep and AJ could barely keep his eyes open. Then I sang their favorite songs until AJ drifted off as well. I stared at them, trying to remember them as babies, trying to memorize them now, as though I could tuck this perfect moment somewhere deep inside myself and save it, like Adam's letters, for a time when I really needed it.

The screen door squealed open, breaking me out of my thoughts, and as it slammed shut again, Scott appeared, a beer in his hand. "Nothing will make you want to drink quite like your mother dying."

I didn't want it to, but my mouth opened and words flew out: "Try having your husband Missing in Action."

Scott grimaced.

"Scott," I said, "it was nice what you said earlier, but you aren't really going to Iraq, are you?"

"Oh, I assure you I am," he said, taking a seat and crossing one leg over the other. "I'll book a flight as soon as . . ."

He trailed off, and I swallowed away the tears for what that "as soon as" meant.

"So what will you do when you get there?" Emerson asked, leaning toward him intently. I had a feeling she was picturing this all unfolding on the big screen and what her part would be. Probably me. Because the terrified wife in the Lifetime movie version would most certainly be a tall, blond, thin twenty-six-year-old.

"Civilians tend to know a lot," Scott said. "And I have a lot of friends in Iraq now. I'll do a little digging into where the boys were when they crashed, and I'll do what I do best: ask questions."

"Does that really work?" Caroline asked.

I sighed.

"Sorry," she said. "I'm sorry. Of course it works." She turned to Scott. "This sounds like a great idea, uncle of ours. I have the utmost faith in you."

"Thank you," he said.

"I think it's the craziest damn idea I've ever heard," I said, "and if you're killed by a land mine or left to die in a prison somewhere, I will blame myself forever."

He shook his head. "No, you won't. I'm doing this for completely selfish reasons."

"How is this possibly selfish?" Emerson asked.

"Because if I go over there, find them, and report on the whole thing, no doubt I'll win a Pulitzer."

He winked at me. "For real, though," he said. "I'm going of my own accord for my own reasons. Do I want to save Adam and get my niece her family back? Absolutely. But if it all goes awry, that's on me, not you. I know what it's like."

It was borderline stupid that knowing Scott was going made me feel better. I mean, my husband was God only knows where in that dusty desert land of caves and rock. It wasn't like my uncle, who was trained in journalism, fly-fishing, and very little else, was going to track down my husband and bring him home safely to me if the world's finest military hadn't managed it yet. But, after months of sleepless nights, my teeth ground down, my eyes bagged, my shoulders slumped, the color drained from my face, I needed something, anything, to hold onto. Scott loved me and he loved Adam. And, sometimes, that's as good a reason as any to believe everything is going to be OK.

Scott squeezed my knee and said, "OK, girls. Uncle Scott is going to bed."

"Yes," Caroline said firmly. "You're going to need your strength." She paused. "Grammy and Mom are on the front porch. Let's go out there with them."

Emerson nodded. "Perfect. My wineglass has been empty for like a half hour."

Grammy was snuggled on the couch in a nest of pillows with blankets all around her. Mom was right beside her, as though if she got close enough, she could breathe for her, keep her here.

There were so many things I could say to Grammy in that moment, but I only squeezed her tightly and said, "I love you so much. I hope you had the best day."

"I love you too, sweet girl," she said. "This was the best day of my life."

"Hey!" Mom exclaimed. "What about the day I was born?"

Grammy laughed. "The best normal day where no one was born or married."

The door opened, and Emerson flopped dramatically on the couch, while Caroline spread out on Mom's new outdoor chaise. It seemed fitting she would get the best seat. Queen Caroline, past, present, and future.

In that moment, with all the women I loved most in the world crowded around me, it didn't feel like anything was out of the ordinary. It didn't feel like anyone was dying. It didn't feel like life was about to change in ways we couldn't even imagine.

And so, when I look back on my life, that moment, just Grammy, Mom, my sisters, and me, sharing stories and laughing until we couldn't breathe, is one I want to remember. When I think of Grammy now, when I imagine her in heaven, she is having a night just like that.

TWENTY-EIGHT

prodigal son

ansley

When the girls finally went to sleep that night, I knew Mom had to have been beyond exhausted. I tried to take her to bed, but she refused.

"Darling," she asked, instead. "Could I trouble you for a cup of tea?"

"It's no trouble at all, Mom," I said, walking back into the house.

A few minutes later, I was about to open the door when I heard Jack's voice on the porch. I stopped, my back pressed against the wall inside. I could just make out Jack saying, "I honestly don't even know when I would ask her, if we will get to that place. But I can't bear the thought of marrying Ansley without your blessing."

Mom laughed. "Oh, darling, I can't think of anything much finer than that." I couldn't see her, but I could imagine the way her eyebrow rose as she said, "It would be lovely to have your family back together again."

I heard Jack choke. My heart was racing. Oh my Lord. She knew. My mother knew. "I'm not sure what you mean," Jack recovered.

"Oh, Jack," Mom said. "Anyone who has ever seen you and Caroline side by side would know you possess a shocking likeness."

There was silence, and then I barely heard Jack say, "I thought that was only in my mind."

I held Mom's hot cup to my chest and gasped quietly. She knew, and he had corroborated. I was about to burst out the door to confront Jack.

But then he said, "You have to understand. Ansley needed something, and I gave it to her." He paused. "I would do anything for that woman, then, now, and forever. I would move heaven and earth for her—"

Mom cut him off. "You would keep a secret that would eat away at your soul for nearly thirty-five years."

It took my breath away to hear her say that, and I felt the tears gathering in my eyes. After everything we had been through, everything we had lost, everything we had shared, Jack had still been there for me. And I couldn't help but think that maybe it was high time I shared some of myself with him.

"To be honest," Jack said, "I wish I could let her go."

"But true love lasts a lifetime," Mom said.

"Exactly."

She said quietly, "And now I'm ready to be reunited with mine," as I opened the door.

I smiled brightly at Jack. "Oh, hi," I said casually, not wanting them to know I had overheard. "What are you doing here?"

"Just saying good night to your mom," he said. He stood, leaned over, and kissed Mom on the cheek. She patted his arm. "You're a darling boy," she said. "You've always been my favorite."

"Mom!" I scolded. She was nonplussed. "I'm sorry," she said. "I love Jack. So what?"

I shook my head, and Jack laughed as he wrapped one arm around my shoulder and kissed my head. "I'm here if you need me," he whispered, before walking off the porch.

Of course I need you! I wanted to yell after him. But I didn't. Not for the first time and not for the last, I watched Jack walk away, his silhouette disappearing down the street. I handed Mom her tea and sat down beside her.

"I've said it before and I'll say it again: you really should marry him."

"For heaven's sake, Mother. We aren't even dating."

Her eyelids grew heavy, and for a moment, I thought she was about to fall asleep. But then I realized she was glaring at me. "I know true love when I see it, Ansley, and it doesn't take too much to make a man forget you are his. Men who will love you like that, sacrifice for you, do anything to make you happy don't come along all that often. I suggest you beg for his forgiveness before he runs off with a forty-year-old who isn't moody and menopausal."

I couldn't help but laugh. "Moody and menopausal. Thanks, Mom. Glad to know what you think of me."

"I think you will both feel much better once you tell the girls he's Caroline and Sloane's father."

I nearly spit out the water in my mouth.

"Jack tried to deny it," Mom continued, "but the man is a terrible liar. That is a wonderful quality in a husband."

"If that day ever comes, I will say yes, Mom."

She smiled and nodded, realizing I had overheard their conversation.

She always knew the right thing to say. Always. Which is why I would never understand. I had needed her advice, her encouragement, and her fortitude for all those months when it felt like I was suffocating, when it felt like Carter wasn't the only one who had died.

Now she was dying. And I didn't have much time. So I took a deep breath. "Mom," I said, "all these years, I've never brought it up, but I can't let you go without asking. Why didn't you help me when Carter died?"

She smiled calmly at me. "Look around you, darling. Look at the life you have, the life you built." She leaned in closer to me. "You. Not me. Not Daddy. You."

I began to understand then that we were different parents. But her methods weren't selfish, just how she showed love.

"You built this life for yourself, honey. Your store. Your town. Your friends. You raised those girls and you fought through your pain and you came out the other side. You survived. Hell, you thrived. And you did it all on your own."

Mom sighed and said, "I know it came between us. But, Ansley, if you had come home and wallowed in your self-pity and your fear, that's all you ever would have done. Look at you, my girl. You are magnificent."

That day she told me I couldn't come home was the scariest day of my life. I had this jewel of a house my grandmother had left for me, but that was it. I had no job. No plan. No idea where the world would take me. But I had to wake up every day. I had to get out of bed and take care of my girls.

I thought of Sloane, and I wondered if maybe I had done the wrong thing. Maybe my mother was the one who had known how to handle tragedy and adversity. Maybe I should have taken a page from her book. But there was no right way to parent. We all just have to do our best.

She smiled at me sleepily, and I knew she was about to drift off. "That's a good girl," she said.

"Can I take you to bed, Mom?" I whispered.

"No, darling. I need to be here with the sea and the stars and the sky." Then she fell asleep, breathing heavily, no doubt dreaming of the near-perfect day she'd had on the beach. I put more pillows around her so she wouldn't fall. I sat by her for quite some time, and I'll admit it, I prayed. I was still ambivalent at best about God's presence, but I prayed for her safe passage into another world, where she could be with Daddy and check on Carter, where she could be happy and out of pain.

I didn't know that was the last conversation I would ever have with my mother. But it was perfect. It wouldn't have felt right for our last conversation to have been dripping in "I love you's" and "You're the best thing that ever happened to me's." No. She told me what she thought, gave it to me straight, and left me with something to chew on. She was making sure I would be OK after she was gone. It meant more than anything else I could have imagined.

She should have had weeks longer to live. Hospice wasn't even coming until the next day. But that night, my mother closed her eyes and didn't open them again. None of us was with her, but she wouldn't have wanted us there. In fact, I'm quite sure that if we had kept vigil over her bedside, she would have held on longer, too long even. I love that the last memory I have of my mother is her smiling, surrounded by her children and grandchildren, on the beach. I love that she closed her eyes for good in Peachtree Bluff, one of the places she treasured most in the world. She would have told us not to cry, would have told us to dance instead. But how could I dance when my mother was gone? Simply knowing she was there made me feel like I had someone.

The last person on the planet who loved me unconditionally was gone. Forever. I would never see her again. At first, it terrified me to my core. But then I realized that was my job now. My job was to love the other people in my life unconditionally. I could give that so fully because I had received it so very well.

If anyone had asked, I would have told them that was the thing my mother taught me best of all.

OUR HOUSE HAD BECOME a command center. So many people were filing in and out that I couldn't remember everyone's names. As it turned out, the Peachtree "Funeral Fairies," which were instated when my grandmother was alive, were still thriving. They were here to help, like it or not.

They stuffed the already full freezer with yet more casseroles, defrosted frozen lemonade for the funeral punch, and generally made a lot of noise to keep me from hearing my thoughts. I was most appreciative, as my thoughts were not ones anyone would want to hear.

Well, except for one. The one I kept hearing over and over again, between the bouts of crippling devastation: *you have six months.*

"Ansley, dear," I heard Mrs. McClasky say. My skin crawled. I wasn't wild about having all these people in my house.

I heard the back door open and saw Hippie Hal with a bucket of wildflowers in one hand. He took one look at Mrs. McClasky, made a horrified face at me, and jetted back down the steps. I had to put my hand over my mouth to keep her from seeing my laugh. Hippie Hal and Mrs. McClasky were on-again, off-again mortal enemies because, in addition to a variety of other very useful skills, Hal refurbished bikes—and generally had no fewer than 150 of them scattered about his front yard, which Mrs. McClasky found reprehensible and deemed it appropriate to say so at every single town meeting.

If she noticed my laughter she didn't let on. "Darling, the altar guild brought these dreadful black napkins. I thought your mother would much prefer white linen."

I smiled supportively. "Thank you so much. I appreciate your attention to detail. I have 150 linen napkins starched and hanging in the coat closet." I paused. I needed to give her a job, preferably a time-consuming one, if I was going to make it through this. "Mrs. McClasky, would you be so kind as to fold them for me?" I whispered behind my hand, "I'm certain none of these people knows how to do it properly."

She smiled authoritatively. "Oh, of course, darling. I'll do them all myself."

I peered into my dining room where there were women polishing silver, women arranging flowers, women standing in the corner admiring or criticizing my light fixtures, women fussing over the punch bowl. In the living room were yet more women, who I assumed were waiting to receive gifts, food, and flowers from whoever stopped by. I wanted to tell my mother about it. She would find it terribly funny, all these women making such a fuss. And then I remembered my mother was gone. I would never talk to her or laugh with her over one of life's little absurdities again. I wanted my mother. It was as though the rest of my life was stretching out in front of me, long and bleak and empty.

I suddenly felt so sorry and so stupid that I had wasted time resenting her for not being there for me. And now she was gone. All I wanted was the time back. The typhoon of all those emotions washed over me.

I knew all these people meant well, and in some ways, I was grateful for them. In others, I just wanted a quiet house where I could mourn my loss. When no one was looking, I opened the pantry door, thankful I had opted against the French style with the glass panes, and sat down on the overturned mop bucket, my head in my hands.

My mother was gone, and I was all alone with these three daughters who were my responsibility and, in some ways, that felt harder and bigger and even crazier.

I heard a hand on the doorknob and wiped my eyes. I don't know who I expected to see. One of my daughters, my grandchildren, Jack maybe. One of the dozens of women who had invaded in the march of the Funeral Fairies. But nothing could have prepared me to stand up and nearly run right smack into a teary-eyed John. When he saw me, he didn't say a word, just engulfed me in his massive hug. He was tall, broad, and strong, and much to the chagrin of Scott and me, the most attractive of the siblings. He had these bright blue eyes and long eyelashes that were balanced out by his masculine features. He was stoic and a giant ass, so it was a tad shocking to be standing in my pantry with this hulk of a man sobbing onto my shoulder.

For just a moment, a beat of a beat, it was as if we were children again. John was my protective big brother. I was his vulnerable little sister. As we stood there in the closet, crying together, I forgot for just a second that we were at odds and he had scarcely talked to me in the past several years.

I was drawn back into the past, into Tammy Hager's grandma's basement in tenth grade. Tammy's grandma was on a cruise, so the beer was flowing, the cigarette and pot smoke was a dense fog, and there were bodies everywhere, some talking, some dancing, some kissing. John was friends with Tammy's older brother Chris, who, much to my delight and John's horror, was the senior boy I had been dating for the last two months.

John and I had arrived at the party together. Even though I had spent the previous four years being his annoying little sister, John and I were getting to be friends again, as if he knew college was looming and he was starting to feel just the smallest bit nostalgic.

"Be good, kid," he had said to me as I made a beeline for Tammy and he made a beeline for the keg. I was a good girl and didn't get into too much trouble. Even still, I never missed one of these parties.

I remember how good my hair looked that night—Mom had ironed it stick straight—how my new wedges made my legs look longer, and how I thought Chris wouldn't be able to take his eyes—or his hands—off me. "Where's Chris?" I had asked Tammy breathlessly.

She rolled her eyes. She wasn't terribly thrilled I was dating her older brother. He was the captain of the football team. He drank too much and smoked too much. He was beautiful and dangerous. And out of all the girls in the world, he wanted me. *Me.* What fifteen-year-old girl in her right mind would have turned that down?

Tammy wasn't going to be much help, so I walked around the perimeter of the room, searching for Chris, a flutter in my heart, a smile on my face. I caught a glimpse of John on the opposite side of the crowded, musty basement with its low ceilings and concrete floors. And I think we must have seen it at the same time. There in the middle of the room was Chris. And

Debbie Larkin. Making out. In retrospect, I should have felt angry. But I wasn't. I was devastated. I thought I was in love with Chris. I would learn that summer, the summer I met Jack, that I hadn't been in love with him. Not even a little bit. But at the time, it was as though all the oxygen had left my body. I didn't want to cry in front of all those people. But my heart was broken. I was humiliated. How could he do that to me? I turned to run, and there was my big brother. He wrapped his arms around me and said, "Let's get you home."

I had relished the knowledge that John was my protector, and that no matter what happened, I would always have him. As we were walking toward the door, I heard Chris calling, "Ansley! Ansley, wait!"

I wouldn't wait. I couldn't. I didn't want him to see me cry. I felt John's hand leave my arm, and through the smoke haze, I watched my brother turn and punch Chris so hard he fell to the ground, clutching his cheek. As he was writhing there, John peered down over him and said in a measured tone, "No one messes with my little sister."

My hand shot to my mouth, and John took my arm again and steered me out of the basement. I felt so safe. No matter what happened, my big brother was going to be there.

In my pantry, I felt that all over again. Despite what had happened between us, despite how much he had hurt me, my brother was here now. And it was all going to be OK.

As he said, "I didn't even get to say good-bye," I came back into the present, where my brother had scarcely talked to me for years over the fact that my grandmother had left me a house, where he had barely called me when my beloved husband was killed in one of our nation's worst tragedies. I needed my big brother to be there for me. I needed him to protect me like he had in Tammy's grandma's basement. I wondered if we could ever get back to that place.

At the same time, a tinge of anger remained, and I wanted to snipe at him, *I sure as hell gave you plenty of chances*, or *Our mother knew exactly what to expect from you at this point, you lazy, selfish moron.*

But he was actually crying. Real tears. It didn't seem like the right time to admonish him for all his failures. I got the feeling he was admonishing himself plenty.

But, let me tell you, I took full comfort in knowing I wasn't the one who had something to be sorry for. I wasn't the one who'd stopped returning his family's phone calls and disappeared off the face of the earth once he was married and settled into his own new family. That wasn't me. That was him. Quite frankly, he should feel sorry.

"What did she say?" John asked, pulling away and sniffling, wiping his eyes. "Was she angry at me?"

I shrugged. "No, John. She wasn't surprised."

He ran his hands through his hair in total distress. "I screwed this up like I screw everything else in my life up. I'm such a failure."

Ah. This was about more than our mother. "Did Sheila leave you?"

He nodded, wiping his eyes. "I didn't even really care, but now she's gone and Mom's gone, and I have no one." He started crying again. "And it was Sheila who turned me against all of you in the first place. She was the one who made me believe you were all against me. She's the one who cared so much about the damn house."

I rolled my eyes. That didn't surprise me in the least. I had always thought Sheila was a vile little yip dog. The minute she and John started dating, something had shifted between us. I remember him telling me she was jealous of how close we were, of how much we talked and depended on each other. I had told him to run. He didn't.

But he was my brother. And I could tell he was sorry. I didn't want to say it. I really didn't. In fact, the words came up like vomit in my mouth, sour and bitter and downright disgusting. "You have Scott and me," I said.

Things weren't as tense between Scott and John, probably because they were men. Probably because Scott didn't feel like he needed his older brother's emotional support and unconditional love. That's why I had made Scott call John to tell him Mom was gone. I couldn't be let down by my big brother's response. Not again.

John hugged me and said, "I promise I'm going to be better, Ansley. I'm going to come home for Christmas and remember my nieces' birthdays. I'm going to make you love me again."

I sat down on my mop bucket and sighed, the pantry suddenly feeling its size with my huge brother crowded into it. Now I was mad. "Yet again," I said, "you have taken something that is supposed to be about someone else and made it about you."

He looked shocked.

"What?" I asked. "You expect to show up here after almost ten years, the prodigal son returning home, and be welcomed with open arms and forgiven for all your sins? This is my time. I get to mourn the loss of my mother in any way I see fit, and I don't need you around to make me feel guilty about that. I'll deal with you when I'm good and damn ready."

I stood and pushed by John and walked with a purpose through the kitchen, feeling guilty already. This was the thing about us. He behaved badly, but the moment I tried to reciprocate that, I just welled up with love for him again.

I heard Mrs. McClasky calling, "Oh, Ansley, dear," as I was walking out the back door, but I pretended not to hear her. I had had it with all of them. Fortunately, Jack's house was only forty steps from mine, so I walked out my back door and into his. I stopped for a moment to admire the finish on the floors. It was one of the most amazing cases of floor salvation I had seen. I'd been certain we would have to replace them all, and it broke my heart. But Hippie Hal had managed to scrape away decades of hideous paint colors that were terrible for hardwoods, reveal a lovely oak underneath, and restore it to a vibrant sheen.

"Jack!" I called. But I didn't run into Jack. I ran into that horrific Georgia. As if my day could possibly get any worse.

"Oh, Ansley," she said, "I'm terribly sorry to hear about your mother." She did seem sorry. She did seem nice. I didn't see any reason why she had to wear those sleeveless turtlenecks that were so tight, but I might have been able to like her. We might have been able to be friends. If it weren't for Jack, of course.

"Thank you, Georgia," I said. "It's a really hard time, but I'm lucky to have so many wonderful people around me. I'm so grateful to live in Peachtree Bluff."

She smiled. "Well, silver linings."

Jack came down the stairs, and much to my delight, walked to me first, gave me a big hug, kissed my cheek, and said, "I hope you're here because you've thought of something I can do for you."

I cut my eyes at Georgia. "No, no," I said. "I just needed a little peace. There are like forty-two Mrs. McClaskys over there."

Jack's eyes widened in mock fear. "Yikes. That is absolutely terrifying." He patted my arm and said, "You may hide out here as long as you like."

"We're going to look at houses," Georgia said.

I didn't like the way she said it, like *they* were going to look for houses—for the two of them. "Like rental property or something?" I asked.

Jack shook his head. "No. I've been toying with the idea of moving back to Atlanta."

"I was in the area," Georgia trilled, "so I thought I'd pick him up."

In the area, my left foot. She was in the area like I was born yesterday.

I could feel my throat go tight. He was actually going to do it. He was toying with the idea of moving away from here.

Away from me. "Hey, G," he said, "would you mind giving us a second?"

She nodded. "'Bye, Ansley. Sorry again. Please let me know if there's anything I can do."

You can get the hell out of my life and away from my Jack, I wanted to say. Instead, I smiled tightly.

Jack squeezed my shoulder. "I'm sorry," he said. "I wasn't going to tell you all this right now. This doesn't change anything. Finish the house. Make it a dream. I just have to look ahead."

I thought I might cry for the fortieth time that day. Instead, I stood there, open mouthed. "You said six months," I whispered.

He smiled. "And I meant it, Ans. This was a convenient day for both of us, and I thought I'd see what Atlanta has to offer."

He didn't add anything like, "We can have a city getaway." Or, "Wouldn't it be so convenient for you to stay there when you go to Market?" Nothing to indicate that he saw me in his future at all. But maybe he saw Georgia in it, which was even worse. She represented the very real idea that he wasn't going to wait for me forever, as he had clearly signaled. I liked to fancy myself the love of his life. I liked to believe he couldn't possibly be with another woman, that what we had was too deep and too consuming. But Jack had waited for me for a long time. And he was serious about being through with all of that.

I walked out the back door, and I could see my brother's big head on the screened-in porch—and my other brother's smaller head beside it. A row of beer bottles were lined up in front of them, ready to be consumed. I sat down in a chair across from my brothers, handed a beer to Scott to open for me, and took a swig. Then I looked at John. "I forgive you," I said. "I still think you're an awful person, but I forgive you. I think I actually did a long time ago."

I smiled at him, and he smiled back. "Thanks," he said. "That means a lot."

"Oh," I added. "No one invited you for Christmas."

We all laughed. I knew even then it couldn't be this easy. It would get infinitely more complicated as the months went on. But, for now, I was sitting on the porch in Peachtree Bluff, drinking a beer with my brothers for what must have been the millionth time. I pretended my mom was right inside the kitchen and I had to be ready to hide my bottle behind my chair if I saw her coming toward the door.

I pretended Georgia was nothing more than Jack's Realtor and nothing was or could be going on with them.

Because, sometimes, the truth, like warm beer, is simply too hard to swallow.

lost

sloane

After Grammy died, I wallowed and harped on the thoughts that I would never eat her particular cheese straws again or hear her tell my kids a bedtime story. I stayed up too late crying and drinking wine and sharing memories with my sisters. But life dealt her a hand. She played it. And that was something to be terribly grateful for.

Caroline and Mom had the funeral preparations under control, and Emerson, ever the cool, fun aunt, had asked if she and Mark could take the kids to the park. I was going to take her up on the offer, even though the boys would come back sugared up and loaded with any toy or trinket they had even looked at. I was going to have to watch her more closely when they got older and started asking her to sign for their tattoos.

I decided to go to the store to get a little bit of peace and quiet and to do the one thing my mother had asked me to: paint a piece for Jack's living room.

I had immediately said, "No."

"But you're painting again," she protested. And I was. I had graduated from blacks and grays to some dark blues and greens, as though my emotions were getting slightly less dark but even more complicated.

"Yes, Mom. But those paintings are just for me. They aren't for the public."

She had crossed her arms. "Jack is not the public."

I smiled when she said it. I thought back to my conversation with my sisters on the boat. Mom definitely had the hots for Jack, no matter what she said. I raised my eyebrows at her, and her face turned beet red. Her blush was one of my favorite things about her. I found it so charming.

"You know what I mean," she said.

When I said no again, she handed me a check. From Jack. For half the money that I wanted to have saved before Adam got home. There was pride. There were standards. And then there was the practical reality that food and clothes and shoes and rent cost money. I snatched the check and said, "It's a pleasure doing business with you. Any color scheme I should be working around?"

She shook her head. "I'll design the room around your painting."

Well, now. That was flattering.

I had told Caroline only weeks earlier that I wasn't going to paint with people looking at me. But the view from Mom's store was so gorgeous that I was at the front, painting my little heart out, while Mom's manager, Leah, waited on a handful of customers. I felt someone looking at me. See? *This* is why I didn't paint in public. I looked up and smiled. Not a scary stalker stranger. Just Jack.

"Hi," he said. "I can't wait to see it all come together."

I was so engrossed in what I was doing that I had, for probably a full twenty minutes, forgotten that Adam was gone. In that moment, it all came flooding back to me so harshly it took my breath away.

"Sorry," Jack said, stepping back as if he had offended me in some way. "I can let you get back to it."

"No, no!" I said. "That wasn't about you. It isn't finished, of course, but I'm kind of liking it."

It was an abstract piece with shades of green and blue and even a little peach thrown in. There was a section of black and one of white, and I hadn't consciously created it at all, but when I looked back at my work, I laughed out loud.

"What?" he asked.

I shook my head. "Nothing. It's just sometimes I get so lost in the work that I don't realize what it is that I'm doing."

"Oh." He looked confused, but he didn't press. I would explain it to him later.

He crouched down on the floor beside me and picked up a sketch Mom had done in black and white of the living room to give me inspiration. "You're a pretty talented mother/daughter duo, aren't you?"

I smiled. "Mom always says I get my artistic ability from

my dad." I paused. "But that's kind of funny because, I don't know if you know this, but Caroline and I both came from a sperm donor."

His expression didn't change at all, like he was bracing himself and trying to keep a perfectly straight face. "Huh," he said. "Yeah, I think I might have heard that." Then he shrugged. "But you never know. The whole nature-versus-nurture thing."

I shook my head. "I think it's pretty well established that artistic ability is a genetic trait. So either my biological dad was an artist or I got it from my mom."

"Definitely your mom," he said, laughing.

I looked up at him and could feel the confusion written on my face. He held up the sketch. "Judging from this, I mean. I obviously don't know your sperm donor."

Then he cleared his throat and said, "That's a nice-looking light thingy."

My turn to laugh. "It's a sconce," I said. I patted his arm.

He sighed. "Is it that obvious that I'm out of my element?"

I tried to look sympathetic. "'Light thingy' kind of gave you away." I paused and added, "But don't worry. I don't know a thing about creating a hot-dog empire like you did."

We both laughed.

Jack stood up, and I thought he would turn to leave, but instead he paused, staring at me for a moment before he said, "Sloane, is there anything I can do for you?" He paused again and stuttered. "I mean, with Adam being in his, um, situation, you know, if you need anything at all, I'm here for you. I know we don't know each other that well and people say these things, but I'm a man, and I don't know what to say so I need to *do* something. And your mom says I can't do anything for her. So I'm useless and lost."

I smiled encouragingly. "You know, Jack, short of bringing my husband home in one piece, I don't think there's anything anyone can do."

"Scott will find him," Jack said confidently.

"I think so," I said. I felt another shot of warmth toward Jack then. I knew everyone else thought I was crazy. They didn't hide their concern and incredulity well. But I knew what I knew. And that was that Adam was coming home.

If only I felt as confident about Emerson's health, everything would be OK. Grammy's death had given her yet another great excuse not to get the tests the doctor recommended.

He nodded and turned, stuffing his hands in his pockets.

"Hey, Jack," I called. He turned and raised his eyebrows. "Thank you. Really. I appreciate it, and I'll let you know if you can do anything."

He smiled, and I think he felt better. I felt better just remembering Scott was getting on an airplane to Iraq that night. I wanted to go with him. I honestly considered it. But when I confessed that to Emerson, who was a tiny bit sweeter than Mom or Caroline, she had said, "Oh, no, that's a great idea, Sloane. Go ahead over to Iraq and get killed. Then *Caroline* will be raising your children."

I loved Caroline. She was a great sister, but she was not the mother I wanted for my children.

We looked at each other and broke out into hysterical

laughter. Like so many things in life, it wasn't funny, but it kind of was.

I was thinking about Emerson and that laughter we had shared as I picked up my brush. I was proud of her and how she had grown. She seemed to be settling into a real relationship with Mark and was even helping take care of my kids.

I was changing too. I had gotten up my nerve to send AJ and Taylor to Mother's Morning Out, which they had come to love so much that I was a little jealous. AJ actually got mad when it was Saturday and he couldn't go. I'm not sure what that said about my mothering, but I was grateful for the time nonetheless. When I was painting or even just doing inventory at the store, my mind was so occupied that I couldn't think about Adam or Grammy. All I could think about was the task at hand, and that was a wonderful feeling. I wondered what people who didn't have a creative outlet did to clear their minds. Maybe those were the people who ran marathons. Like Caroline. Caroline couldn't paint or write or draw or act. But, man, could that girl ever run. So, she ran herself right into that 11 percent body fat she was so obsessed with.

The bell tinkled on the door, and Sandra walked in, breaking me out of my thoughts. I smiled at her, and she smiled sadly back at me, which was when I remembered Grammy was dead, her funeral was this afternoon, and instead of standing here putting paint to canvas, I should have been at home helping my mom and sisters prepare.

"Were you sent here to make sure I hadn't slit my wrists in the bathroom?" I asked.

Sandra laughed. "Something like that."

I stood up, wiped my hands on my pants, and curtsied, making Sandra laugh. "I am all in one piece, blood free and not suicidal."

Sandra nodded and scrunched her nose at me. "But isn't that what suicidal people say?"

I grinned at her. "Scott is leaving after the funeral to go find my husband, so I'm fine. I'm hopeful."

Sandra had been like an aunt to me growing up. She was the closest thing my mother had to a sister—except for maybe Emily—and she had always told me the hard things. She was there when I needed advice, and I felt like she knew me better than most people in my life. So when a concerned look passed across her face and she said, "Sloane . . ." with that air of "you're delusional," I wasn't surprised.

I put my hands up. "Look, I get it. I know it's insane to think my uncle is going to go to a foreign land and track down my missing husband. But you guys don't understand. You don't know what it's like when the love of your life is lost and you are completely powerless to do anything. It's like when kids go missing and their parents roam the forest looking for them. Are they going to find them? Probably not. But you can't just sit there and do *nothing*." I took a deep breath. "He's coming home to me. He is. And this may very well be how."

Sandra nodded and pulled me into her. "I think you're amazing," she said. "You've held up incredibly well in the worst of the worst. I'm not judging you. Just worried."

"Don't worry about me. Worry about Adam."

I was dipping my brush back into the paint when I heard,

"Mommy, Mommy, Mommy!" and my two little monsters tore through the store, Mark and Emerson following closely behind. "Mommy, Mommy!" AJ said, out of breath and sweaty, that little-boy billy goat smell emanating from every part of him. "Mark got me this banana and it had chocolate covering it, and it was so good!"

"Popsicle," Taylor said.

"Yeah, yeah," AJ enthused. "It was frozen like a Popsicle!"

They leaned into either side of me, those babies, so soft and warm. I was so grateful for them. Adam was missing this. I couldn't think about where he might be or what might be happening to him, but he wasn't here. He didn't get to hug these sweaty children who we made so well, and raised well, too. And he might never get to again.

I felt unexpected anger burning in my chest that he had left me here alone. To curb the feeling, I smiled up at my sister. "Seems like you two were a big hit."

Emerson leaned into Mark, and he put his arm around her waist. "This one really knows what to do with kids. It's kind of crazy. Are you sure you don't have one?" she asked him, eyebrow raised.

He leaned over and kissed the top of her head in reply. "Not yet," he said, winking.

They were so adorable it made me want to cry and cheer all at the same time.

I took a deep breath.

"Hey, look," Mark said, "I'm going to run to the church to help set up chairs."

"That's sweet," Emerson said.

"She didn't know that many people here," I said. "Do you think we'll need more seats?"

Mark smiled. "No offense to Grammy, but people won't be there for her. They'll be there for Ansley. And for you girls."

My tears spilled over again because I was so grateful our mother had made our home in a town that loved us so much and would always be there for us.

Emerson and I were hugging, and Adam and Taylor were throwing fabric swatches in the air, when Kyle walked through the door. He put an arm around each of us and hugged us. "I don't like my Murphy girls to be sad," he said.

I wiped my eyes and nose and said, "You always make us feel better."

"Because I'm Super Coffee Man?" Kyle asked, hands on his hips, chest puffed out.

That, of course, made us laugh, and order was restored to the world.

Kyle smiled. "My work here is done. Now I'm off to the church to get set up. Grammy wouldn't want her mourners drinking Folgers."

Everyone we knew and loved in this town was working on this funeral like they didn't have a care in the world, save making my grandmother's final celebration amazing. I sat back down, handed AJ an old wallpaper book and a pair of scissors, and said, "Can you cut some shapes out for Mommy?"

He smiled enthusiastically. "Sure, Mommy. I'll cut you circles."

Then I pushed a huge pile of fabric Taylor's way and said, "Find all the red and put it in a pile for Mommy."

This would buy me at least ten minutes—and be educational—while I put the finishing touches on this piece.

Instead of resuming my painting, though, I found myself staring at my boys. I thought about Grammy and Adam. They didn't get to sit here and marvel at these perfect babies. So I put my brushes down and said, "Never mind, kiddos. Let's go play."

"Yay!" AJ said.

Taylor clapped his hands together. "Play, play, play!"

Like Kyle a few minutes earlier, for a second, I felt like Supermom, like I could raise these kids and have this job and handle anything else that came my way. I'm not sure if it was true. But, either way, it was the best feeling I'd had in quite some time.

THIRTY

eternity

ansley

I don't remember my mother's funeral. I'm told it was beautiful, and I know that was true because I checked the flowers before I took enough of Caroline's in-case-of-plane-flight Valium to get through the church and the handshaking and the stories about my mother with some sense of composure. Caroline informed me I even made a little joke. The mayor had had the hots for my mom for as long as I could remember, so when things got really rough with my former neighbor Mr. Solomon—like the time he said my grass seed had blown into his yard and was now grow- ing there—Bob always took my side. When Mayor Bob came up, blotting his eyes, and hugged me, I evidently said, "Thank God Mr. Solomon went first." I was funny.

My memory kicks in—hazily, more like I'm watching it all play out on video than actually living it—after the funeral, about the time I put on yoga pants and a sweatshirt. It was 75 degrees, but I wanted to feel cozy. I remember my brother Scott knocking on my door. I remember crying on his shoulder and begging him to come home in one piece. I remember John telling me he knew the spreading of our mother's ashes was something he didn't deserve. I remember telling him lightly that I agreed. He laughed, but we both knew I meant it wholeheartedly. And then I said, "You should come, John."

He had looked up at me tentatively, contritely. "I'd like to have this time with you, Ans. I really would."

I smiled. I thought I might like that too.

The girls and I sat around the living room and told stories about my mother. We laughed and cried.

Jack appeared in the living room, and when I saw him, I quit feeling so alone. When he hugged me, I knew I had someone. Though our skiff would have been more appropriate, Jack took our sad and poorly dressed brigade on his boat to Starlite Island. Well, poorly dressed except for Caroline, who looked impeccable in a white shift with a pale blue cardigan draped across her delicate shoulders. "Grammy would roll over in her grave if she saw the motley crew of the four of you," she told us, looking John up and down in his shorts and T-shirt.

"And that," Sloane said, "is why *you* were her favorite." I saw a sadness pass through her eyes with the mere mention of the word *were*. It was a hard pill to swallow.

After he helped each of us out, Jack started to climb back into the boat when Caroline said, "You come too, Jack. You're family."

He looked at me tentatively. I smiled. He was. More than she even knew. Whether we were ever together again, Jack was the father of my two eldest girls. Whether they ever knew that was irrelevant, though I did, as I had for years, intend to tell them. He would always, always be family.

I took comfort in knowing my mother would be here forever, across from the home that had been in our family for generations, and that she could rest peacefully on the island where she had spent her childhood summers, raised her children, and then formed a deep and irreversible bond with her grandchildren. It made me happy that I could always look out my window and know she and my dad were here. Of course, for a little while, it would be too painful to look out the window. But, little by little, the pain would ease until, one day, I would look out, think of my mother resting here, and smile. That day, I would know I was healed.

Each of the girls, John, and I had a jar of ashes. Not a fancy urn or beautiful container, but a plain, glass Ball jar containing what was left of the woman I loved most. Scott had claimed he needed to get to the airport, but I knew it was simply too hard for him to stay. He had said good-bye to Mom in spirit at the church, but to say good-bye to her in the flesh was too much. May as well move on to something where he might be able to help. I thought his Iraqi quest was silly at best, terribly risky at worst. But, as I have known from that moment as a teenager when Jack told me he never wanted children, you cannot change a man. It was fruitless to try.

Sloane opened her jar first and said, "Grammy, we miss

you so much already, but we know you are happy here. You are at peace."

We all wiped our eyes as the ashes blew into the wind, mingling into the sand, being swept out into the water, and catching on the blades of marsh grass. My mother was a part of Starlite Island now, as much as the waves and the wind and the tide. It was just as she had always wanted it to be.

"Mom," John said, his voice catching in his throat. I took his hand and nodded at him to go on. "I know I didn't always make you proud, but I promise you that I'm here now. I will watch over your family. I promise you I will make it right."

I hoped with all my heart that was true. I didn't say it then, but I would tell my brother later that, for me, it wasn't about making anything right. It was what we did now, how we came back together that mattered.

We all took turns saying our piece about how much my mother had meant to us, and even as we were saying our final good-byes, it was incomprehensible to think she was gone. I went last, and when it was my turn, so much that I had wanted to say to my mother had already been said. Jack put his arm around me, squeezing me to his side. "Mom," I started, "I am so happy you get to be here, at our favorite place, with Daddy, for eternity. The two of you together forever was the way it was always meant to be."

Jack looked down at me. I looked up at him. And I wondered if maybe the same couldn't be said for the two of us.

possibly ever

sloane

Adam's return home from his first deployment after we were married was so magical that I felt like it might be worth the time apart if I got to have these golden moments when he came home. He flew into one of our small local airports and when he and his unit arrived, dressed in their Class A's, everyone was clapping and cheering. I felt so proud in that moment. Everything I had sacrificed over the past few months had been worth it. My husband was a national hero. I couldn't help but feel like I was a part of that.

I had made up my mind to finally tell him only one of us had been trying for a baby. But as we fell asleep that first night, and he held me close, I kissed his lips and felt his stubble on my cheek, and I knew I simply couldn't bear it if he left me. I was fine with being alone. I just didn't want to be without Adam.

When we woke up the next morning, Adam rolled over, kissed me, grinned boyishly, and said, "Let's get you pregnant."

I smiled, thinking, *Well, unless I'm that tricky half of a percent, that seems unlikely.*

But I couldn't tell him. Not yet.

As he made love to me with so much feeling, so much intention, I promised myself I would tell him the truth. This had gone on long enough. I was betraying him, and I couldn't do it anymore.

I cleaned up the town house and went to the grocery store to get everything I needed to make my grandmother's chicken divan that Adam loved so much. I bought him his favorite IPA from a local brewery, put my hair up the way he liked, and wore a dress that showed a little more cleavage than usual.

And then I prayed that he would forgive me, that he could understand, that I would be forgiven for treating the man I loved most in the worst way I could imagine. Even in the moment it seemed kind of foolish. Who could possibly understand what I had done?

When we sat down at dinner, candles flickering between us, I took a sip of wine and a deep breath, and said, "Adam, I have to tell you something." I paused and looked down into the plate I knew I wouldn't touch. "It's hard to say, and you aren't going to like it."

He eyed me warily, and I could almost hear what he was thinking. Deployment affairs were not uncommon. I almost felt offended that he would possibly think I would do such a thing—until I remembered that what I had actually done was so much worse.

I took a deep breath and reached for his hand. "Adam," I said. "I wish with everything I had that I had told you a long time ago, when we met." For the briefest of moments I considered telling him I couldn't have children. Then he couldn't be mad at me, right? But I couldn't lie to him anymore. "I don't want to have children now." I paused and said more softly, "Possibly ever."

I felt his hand go limp in mine before he pulled it away. He didn't say anything for a long moment. He took a bite of his chicken, wiped his mouth, put his napkin back in his lap, and stared at me.

I could tell by the look on his face that he was thinking I couldn't possibly have said what he thought I said. "I don't understand."

"I just can't, Adam. After my dad died, I swore up and down I wouldn't put myself in that place again. I wouldn't love with all I had only to be heartbroken." I paused. "I went against everything I had ever told myself by falling in love with you, but I just can't do this, Adam."

The look on his face was something between shock and betrayal. "But we've been trying to have a baby," he said. "We tried for months."

I bit my lip. "Well . . ."

"Well, what?"

"I have an IUD."

Now I wasn't having any trouble reading his look. It was a look that said he didn't know me at all. He stood up calmly and smoothed his napkin, setting it on the table.

"Adam, please," I said. "Let's talk about this. I want you to understand."

"Understand?" he said, emotion filling his voice. "Understand? What I understand is that you have let me think for months and months that we were going to have a baby. I worried myself to death, tiptoeing around your feelings, trying not to make you feel pressured, trying to build you back up after those negative pregnancy tests. And all of it was a lie. How could you, Sloane? What else have you been lying to me about?"

I was crying now, realizing this was even worse than I'd thought. I had never seen him look angry like this.

"Adam, I love you with all my heart. Please don't forget that."

He shook his head. "Sloane, I don't even know who you are right now."

He turned, and I was afraid he was going to walk out the door. I was desperate. "Adam, please!" I said, sobbing now. "Let's talk about this. You have to listen."

He shook his head. "I don't have to do a damn thing." He walked toward the bedroom, which made me feel a little better, and said, "Oh, and while we're being honest, I absolutely hate chicken divan."

It was like he had slapped me across the face. I scolded myself. I had just told the man I had lied to him for our entire marriage, and I was offended he didn't like my chicken divan?

I wanted to go after him, but I didn't. He was too angry, too betrayed. He wouldn't even be able to hear me. So I sat at the table, not daring to move, and watched the wax from the candles melt into a puddle on my antique dining table. I watched them and cried until I couldn't cry anymore, until the flames were gone. When the last light flickered and the room went dark I wondered if my relationship, like my candles, had burnt out.

THIRTY-TWO

safe place

ansley

I was the last one awake that night. I would likely be the last one awake for quite some time, trying to come to grips with the fact that my mother was gone. It was an inexplicably vulnerable feeling. That's the word that describes it best of all. It's a longing of the heart, a fear of the soul, a realization of the mind that your last truly safe place, your last harbor in the storm, is gone. I had felt it excruciatingly when Carter died, been through it maybe even worse when my father died. This death was the last blow, the final straw.

I sat out on the front porch for a long time thinking about her, about what she had meant to me, what she had said to me, the advice she had given me. No matter what, I had always taken Mom's advice to heart.

I thought about Jack and about Caroline saying he would always be our family. I thought about Georgia and the house in

291

Atlanta and how everything I had ever wanted might be right at my fingertips, but also how it was slipping through them at the same time.

My thoughts were punctuated by my eldest daughter bursting through the front door and my scream reverberating through the silent night.

Caroline looked around, shocked. "Sorry," she said, "I didn't mean to scare you."

I patted the cushion beside me, and she sat down. She took the glass of wine right out of my hand, took a sip, and handed it back to me. "I want to talk to you about something," she said.

I felt a knot forming in my stomach. She looked very serious, and I had a feeling this was either about the money her father had promised her that was actually gone or her biological father. Neither was a topic I was prepared to discuss.

So nothing could have surprised me more than when she said, "How would you feel about my doing a little buying for your store?"

Looking into Caroline's dancing eyes, I understood that she needed this. She had mentioned going back to work, and I knew this would suit her well. She had always had an eye for beautiful things.

"I have a friend who has moved to Provence, and she could help us source these gorgeous linens that will take your breath away." She paused. "And wouldn't it be beautiful to have fresh lavender in bundles all around the store?"

I smiled. "It would be perfect, sweetheart. Whatever you think."

There were times to hold on, and there were times to let go. Caroline could absolutely handle a task like this better than anyone I knew. She had perfect taste and was incredibly organized. Now if I could only get her to stay on budget . . .

Reflexively, I looked down to the end of the street, where James was presumably sleeping—alone, I hoped. Caroline had let him keep Preston that night, which was a big step. "You OK?" I asked.

Caroline shrugged. "I will be."

I sighed and could feel the tears coming to my eyes as I said, "When are you going back to New York?"

Caroline waved her hand, insinuating that it would be ages, and I pulled myself back together. Even one leaving would throw off the dynamic.

"Hey, Mom," she said, that conspiratorial twinkle in her eye I knew so well, "I might need your help with one more thing."

When she told me her plan, I said, "No." Flat out. But I was tired and I was sad, and I knew already she would eventually wear me down.

"But Mom, just think how good—"

"No," I interrupted, getting up and heading to the kitchen, where so much needed to be done.

"OK," Caroline said softly. She hugged me in the entrance hall and went out to the guesthouse. She had conceded for now, but I knew this wasn't over.

My thoughts wandered to the house next door, to what Jack might be doing.

Later that night, after the dishes had been washed, the

crystal had been put away, the tears had all been shed, and my children were all sleeping, I walked onto the front porch and sat on my steps. I thought again about what I had to lose if I chose Jack. Then I had another thought. All this time I had been thinking I couldn't be with Jack, but it was certain I could never be with anyone else. I had a secret I could never share with another man, a lie that, if I ever pursued another relationship, would always be between us. I knew I could never, would never, lie to another man like that. I had learned the hard way what a secret of this caliber does to a person, how it wears away at your soul.

All this time I had been thinking that Jack, the man I had always loved, was the only man I couldn't be with. That night, so full of sadness, grief, and angst, it hit me: instead of his being the only man I couldn't be with, I realized that Jack was the only man who knew the whole truth and loved me anyway, the only person who had carried the same weight I had for all these years.

With that, I crossed the yard, retrieved the key from inside the conch shell by the back door, and tiptoed upstairs. I slid into bed beside Jack, and in typical Jack fashion, he didn't say a word, only pulled me closer. He kissed my forehead, and I closed my eyes. In the moments before I fell asleep, I knew that this was it for me. I would never leave his side again.

THIRTY-THREE

coming home

sloane

April 16, 2010

Dear Sloane,

The guys and I were talking tonight about the importance of good-byes. Doing what we do, we become acutely aware of how to do them right, how to live every moment like we might not get the next one. So I promise you, Sloane, every day of my life, I will make sure to tell you how I feel. I will kiss you and savor the moment. Every single day, I will do that good-bye well so you never have to question how much I love you.

All my love,

Adam

EVERY TIME MY PHONE rang when the boys were at Mother's Morning Out, I imagined a million worst-case scenarios: they had fallen off the jungle gym, choked on a Goldfish, gotten pummeled by a kid on the swings, and most horrific of all, an active shooter was in the preschool. I know. But, due to my past, I'm allowed to have these irrational fears.

So, when Emerson, out of breath from sprinting, appeared at the top of the guesthouse stairs where I was sitting with Caroline, my phone in her hand, and eked out, "Scott," I was panicking before it was even time to panic.

"Why didn't you just answer it?" Caroline asked disdainfully, as I said, "Hey Scott!" My tone was supposed to be breezy but ended up sounding forced and high-pitched.

I think he said, "Hey, Sloane. I made it," but the reception on the other end was staticky, so I only got about half of what he was saying. Then I heard, "mumble, to, mumble, civilians."

"What?" I asked, putting my finger in my other ear and running downstairs, as if it were my reception that was bad.

"I've talked to a couple of townspeople about the accident," he said. "I think I might be able to get some—"

"Hello!" I shouted. "Scott! Hello!"

He was gone. I sighed and walked back upstairs, tossing the phone onto the bed, where Emerson was now lying and Caroline was saying, "You're so sweaty. Get off my clean-ish sheets."

Emerson shot up when she saw me. "So?"

I shook my head. "He's there. He's talked to a couple civilians. I think there may be more, but he got cut off."

"He's there, Sloane," Caroline said excitedly. "He's looking."

Emerson took the sweater she was holding and cuddled it

to her chest, saying, "Oh my gosh . . . Scott is going to find Adam and bring him home. Then Scott will win a Pulitzer for the story he writes, I will get to play Sloane in the film adaption, I will win an Oscar . . ." She sighed, dreamy-eyed, and Caroline and I laughed.

"But you're ready to give up acting?" Caroline asked, a note of teasing in her voice.

"Well . . ." Emerson said.

"Now if only my sister would go to the doctor—" I began, but Mom's loud, "Girls!" from downstairs interrupted my sentence.

"Up here, Mom," I called.

Caroline eyed Mom warily as she came up the steps. "Where have you been?"

Emerson raised her eyebrow at me. I had always been so jealous that she could raise one eyebrow, while mine seemed to be attached as though connected by a long string.

Mom crossed her arms. "I was up working out early, you'll be happy to know."

Caroline gave her the up-and-down and said, "Uh-huh. Likely story."

Mom rolled her eyes. "I thought you would be proud."

"Oh, I don't think she doubts you were getting exercise, Mom," Emerson said. "I think she's questioning where you were exercising and with whom."

"Gross, Emerson," I said.

Mom was predictably beet red now. "Emerson!" she scolded as Caroline was simultaneously saying, "Emerson, gross!"

Now it was Emerson's turn to roll her eyes. "You are all such prudes."

Mom was holding a box in her hands, and I noticed she looked very teary. "What's that?" I asked.

"It's a box from Grammy," she said, sniffing. "There's a letter and a piece of jewelry for each of you."

"I miss her so much already," Caroline said, wiping her eyes. "What are we going to do?"

I hugged her and kissed her on the cheek. We all sat down on the floor, in a haphazard circle, and Mom handed us each a letter and a box.

I did a double take because I noticed Mom was wearing an engagement ring. But it was on her right hand, and it was definitely my grandmother's.

Breaking the tension, Caroline pointed to Mom's hand and said, "So what you're saying is I'm not getting Grammy's big diamond?"

We all chuckled through our tears, as the giant diamond James had given her twinkled on her right hand, and Emerson said, "It's a shame, really. You needed a big diamond."

I took a deep breath as I opened my envelope to find a letter in my grandmother's handwriting.

My dearest Sloane,

How I wish I didn't have to leave you now and add to your sadness and turmoil when your life is so up in the air. But life seldom delivers what we wish. What I want you to know, my darling girl, is I see in you a quiet strength that will deliver you through whatever battles life throws your way. You are an incredible talent and a terrific mother, and you possess the kind of loyalty and character not often seen in the world today.

I believe in you, Sloane. I believe in you and the power of your dreams and the strength of your conviction. I want you to know that no matter what happens down there, I am up here fighting for you. I hope you feel that. I want you to feel that. And, in case you can't, I left you something that might help. I miss you already, sweet Sloane, and I'm not even gone yet. I miss you. But I will always be with you.

All my love,

Grammy

I WAS, NEEDLESS TO say, a total mess, as were my sisters and my mom. I could barely see as I opened the box, but I didn't really need to because it was a piece I knew well. Grammy's wide gold bangle with her hand-engraved monogram on the front was in a nest of cotton, waiting for me. She wore that bracelet every day. And now I would. I couldn't have imagined a better gift.

I knew I would do what Grammy said. I knew I would be strong. But I didn't like the feeling—one I had for the first time in months—that it was perhaps possible that someday soon, I could be mourning in this same way, only much deeper, for the man I loved with all my heart.

THIRTY-FOUR

first loves

ansley

Whent I found out I was pregnant with Caroline, it had been difficult to tell Jack good-bye. When I found out I was pregnant with Sloane, it had been inconceivable. Telling him good-bye felt like telling my heart to stop pumping blood. How could I live without him? How could I continue with my life, put one foot in front of the other, make beds, and brush tiny teeth like nothing had ever happened? When I found out I was pregnant with Caroline, I had felt myself slipping back into something with Jack. When I found out I was pregnant with Sloane, I had already fallen.

Our weekends together had become all I could think about, though I feel like I did a good job pretending our life at home was business as usual. And the strange part was that I still loved Carter. I still looked forward to his coming home at night and kissing him good-bye in the morning. I still loved the way he held my hand, the way his arm felt around my shoulder, the way Caroline squealed when he tossed her into the air. I knew with everything inside of me he was the man I was supposed to be with.

I had tossed and turned, my stomach in knots, the nausea more from having to tell Jack good-bye than from the morning sickness. This was a man whose kiss I would lie awake in bed at night craving, a man whose arms around me felt so right and so natural that I couldn't imagine I had ever let them go. But, at the same time, I knew how incomplete my life would have been without children, children Jack didn't want. So I knew I had made the right choice.

When I walked through his front door that morning, Jack knew before I even told him. He swept me up in his arms and kissed me, and when he pulled back to look at me, he said, "Oh no. Please tell me you aren't."

I shrugged. It was a terrible way to feel. As much as I had hoped and pined for another baby to love and as happy as I was about it, being pregnant with Sloane meant saying good-bye to Jack.

He sat down on the couch then and pulled me into his lap, my legs up on the cushion, our faces close together.

"I've thought about it so much, Ansley," he said, a fervor in his voice I knew instinctively was reserved for me. "I know what I said all those years ago, but I want this now. I want you and Caroline and this new baby." He paused and looked me straight in the eye when he said, "I know I said this last time, and I couldn't convince you. But this time I think you feel what

I feel, Ansley. I know you do. I know you love me and you feel like you can't live without me. I want you to come here, with me. I want to marry you. I want to be a family."

I was drawn into his words so completely that I could almost envision myself saying yes—until he said the word *family*, and I remembered what I was really doing here, what this decision would cost me. Carter and I had longed to be a family and, yes, it was because of Jack, but that was what we had become. It was Carter who was there when Caroline had her first fever, who had stayed up all night with me, making sure she was breathing and checking on her every half hour to make sure the Tylenol was working. It was Carter whom I had walked down the aisle to, bought my first house with, and fought over sconces and doorknobs with.

I loved Jack. I would always love him. But I couldn't bear the thought of breaking up my family. And what would happen if I left Carter? He'd never get to see Caroline again? She wasn't biologically his, after all. I couldn't break him like that. He was her father. I wouldn't take that away from him.

I laid my head on Jack's shoulder, my face in his neck. I knew the scent of him so well. I breathed him in, knowing it would be the last time. It had to be the last time. I steeled everything inside of me that felt like it was crumbling. I had to be strong. Strong for Caroline, strong for this new baby, strong for Carter. My husband. The man I had pledged my life to.

Jack pulled me closer to him, and I knew he could feel my tears on his neck. I knew he wanted to protect me and love me. But I would not put my children or my husband through that.

When I made love to Jack that night, I knew it was the last time. I slipped out in the middle of the night, leaving him a note.

It was fitting that it was raining that night as I drove away from Jack's house, away from Jack, away from a man who made me feel like I was perfect, beautiful, and special all at once. I was sobbing so hard I had to pull over. Walking away from him was, without a doubt, the hardest choice I ever made, and I'm almost embarrassed to say it was one of the greatest losses I've ever grieved. He wasn't dead, but he was dead to me. I had to say good-bye. I had to walk away knowing I could never talk to him, see him, feel his lips on mine again. I had to shut the door completely because I knew if I left it open even a crack, I was in danger of sacrificing the wonderful life I had for the longing for one I didn't.

It took a year for me to start to feel like I could breathe again, a year until I could convince myself I had done the right thing in walking away. After that, I still thought of Jack, still longed to tell him something funny, and still wished I could have him in my life. But this was the life I chose, I reminded myself. So I chose to be happy in it. I hoped that, wherever he was, Jack was happy too.

I never would have let myself imagine there would come a day when I would find myself with Jack once again.

On our quiet street in Peachtree Bluff, the morning after my mother's funeral, waking up with him for the first time in decades, I remembered that letter as well as the day I had written it.

Dear Jack,

Please don't hate me for leaving you like this. If you do, it can't be any more than I hate myself. Please don't doubt how indescribably much I love you. Please don't doubt how unfathomably difficult this decision is for me. In losing you, I feel like I am losing a part of myself, one of my very favorite parts, in fact. But to tear life apart for Caroline and this new baby is too big a responsibility for me to bear. I can't put them through that.

I have hoped there was a way I could still have you in my life, that maybe we could talk from time to time or even visit every now and again. But I know where that would lead, and it would only end in heartbreak. For now, I have to close this door or I will not be able to follow through with my decision. And it feels intolerably selfish that I am the one to make it with no agreement from you, but I believe in my heart that you understand.

Thank you, Jack. Thank you for my children. Thank you for loving me enough to let me go. Thank you for loving me enough to let me be the mother I need to be. There will never be a day I don't think of you. There will never be a day when the thought of your lips on mine will not cross my mind.

You will forever remain in my heart and my memory. I wish with all my might that you will find a woman who loves you as much as I do and cherishes you for all you are the way I do. While it is hard for me to imagine

anyone could ever love you as much as I do, I hope that
for you all the same.
    All my love,
    Ansley

I LOOKED UP AT him. He was smiling down on me, and I felt the tears roll down my cheeks.

"Oh, Ans, no. What's the matter?"

"I feel so awful," I said. "I just left you in the middle of the night."

He smiled at me sadly.

"That was one of the worst nights of my entire life," I continued. "I will never be able to describe to you how empty I felt writing that letter, leaving you behind. But I knew it was the only way."

He nodded. "Reading that letter the next morning felt impossible but also, in a way, poignant."

"Were you mad at me?" I snuggled in close to him, for once not longing for my youth but grateful we were here now.

"It's hard to explain," he said, kissing the top of my head. "I was mad at you, but I understood your decision. Even when I was begging you to stay, I knew you had to leave." He shrugged.

He was right. "Plus, the mess we had made was too big to clean up."

He kissed me on the lips this time. "It's a smaller mess now, Ans. It's a mess we can manage."

I gazed up at the stunning canopy bed with the ethereal white curtains I had copied from Phoebe Howard. The walls were a light gray, on the lavender side so they felt warm, not steely. It probably wasn't a color I would have chosen for Jack the bachelor. It was a color I had chosen for me, a color I had chosen for our life together. As I lay there, feeling totally at peace, I finally admitted that, all this time, I had been decorating this house for me.

I could feel Jack's eyes on me, and I smiled at him and rolled over.

"What?" I asked.

"I'm just thinking what a treat it is to wake up beside you."

I smiled back. "The feeling is mutual." I glanced at the alarm clock on his bedside table. I most certainly did not approve that Sony with the radio for the design scheme. I had about a half hour until the girls woke up. I had thought ahead enough to bring my exercise clothes with me so I could come in after they were all awake and act as though I just got back from a walk. I thought I was quite sneaky.

I groaned. "I need to get back over there before the girls get suspicious." Oh, the girls. They were all grown up now. But I still needed to protect them. I still needed to set a good example.

"Speaking of the girls . . ." Jack said, but then he trailed off.

"What?" I asked.

He shook his head. "Nothing. Never mind."

I crossed my arms. "Jack."

"I don't want to mess up this tentative hold I have on you," he said.

I leaned over and kissed him. "It's not tentative, Jack. It's permanent. And that means we tell each other the truth and ask the hard questions."

"OK, if you say so," he said. "So here's what I want to know: Why did you never tell the girls? I mean, it's not like you would have to tell them the whole truth."

Ah, yes. The big question. Might as well go ahead and get it all out there in the open. I had grappled with telling the girls for their entire lives.

"It's tricky," I said. "It's not like an adoption where you're meeting your birth parents, someone who had you and gave you up. In their minds, I don't even know the man. In their minds, their father is Carter. The other half of their genes is a test tube."

He nodded. "I guess I get that. Do you ever want to tell them?"

I laughed. "Oh, Jack. I've wanted to tell them a million times. Of course, for years I never thought it would be possible. Carter didn't want to know who you were, so the girls certainly couldn't. But then once he found out . . ."

Sloane had developed a fascination with her biological father when she was studying genetics. She pushed us to find her father, and Carter and I had agreed. It was incredibly difficult for him, of course, because he had found out that Jack was Sloane and Caroline's father, inadvertently, when we ran into him on the dock in Peachtree Bluff. Jack's shock over my Emerson-pregnant belly told Carter everything he never wanted to know. Carter was terrified Jack would take over a piece of his role in their lives. Carter knew Jack. He knew he was a wonderful man, and in some ways, that made things even harder for him. I had known for years that Jack wanted to know the girls, so I knew he would be thrilled. I still don't know how she did it, but Caroline talked Sloane out of it. To be fair to both of them, they had to agree. They had the same father and they knew it. You couldn't tell one and keep it from the other.

"Then we decided," I said, "we would tell them when Caroline graduated. We didn't want her going out into the world and looking for you. But Carter hadn't been dead a year when she graduated, and that seemed like a terrible time."

For years after Carter's death, I grappled with whether to introduce the girls to Jack and let them know the truth. It felt like a cheap ploy, a Band-Aid for their suffering. You lost your real dad, but here's a replacement one—and only for Sloane and Caroline, not Emerson.

"There were so many times I decided to sit down and tell them, and then something would always happen. Caroline was getting married; Adam was getting deployed. Emerson was feeling low, and I thought this would intensify it and make her feel distant from her sisters, like we had this whole family she wasn't a part of." I sighed. "Now, I can argue it's a bad time because Adam is MIA, but there's always going to be something. It's always going to be a terrible time. So I think I should just tell them. Alone. And then hope they will come to you."

Jack shot up in bed. "Ansley, no."

I was incredulous. "What do you mean, no? I thought this was what you wanted."

He rubbed his head with his hands. "I do want them to know eventually. I really do." He pulled me in close to him. "But I just got you, Ansley. I can't lose you. If they aren't happy with this news, then it will drive you away from me again."

I had spent years grappling with Jack's role in my life. His contribution to it had weighed on me for decades and shaped everything I felt about myself. It had taken me what seemed like a lifetime to get here, but I couldn't see myself walking away from him now, no matter what. I told him that and then said, "I guess I think, what's the worst that can happen? They know they were from a sperm donor. Besides that one time, they've never asked about it."

"What if they don't want to know?" Jack asked.

I answered instantly, as if my mouth was on autopilot. "Then we have to respect that."

He nodded. "Let's wait a little while, OK?"

"OK." I smiled. I thought it was sweet that he was concerned and, really, I'd waited thirty-four years. What was a few more weeks?

Then he leaned over and kissed me. "Let's do this whole morning over again," he whispered. Then he kissed me again. "Let's pretend we are long-lost first loves finding one another again and none of this is even a concern."

As he kissed me again, I wondered who in the world wouldn't be happy to have a man so kind and generous as their father.

It wouldn't be much longer until I found out.

THIRTY-FIVE

moments

sloane

May 1, 2017

Dear Sloane,

There are moments in life to retreat. We have all known, experienced, and felt those inevitable scenarios in which we have no choice but to walk away. As a soldier, I'm faced with them every day, and sometimes I don't walk away, complicating the situation further. But, just as often, more often, I'd like to argue, there are moments to advance, to lunge forward with purpose, with power, but most importantly, with passion. Because any action taken without passion? Well, it's simply a waste of time.

All my love,
Adam

CAROLINE HAD TAKEN A huge step in getting her life back: she had moved into the house James had bought down the street. With him. Emerson had offered us the guesthouse, which I thought was really sweet. I made like I was being selfless, but in reality, I loved being in the main house because Mom got up with the boys almost every morning. That was way better than privacy if you asked me.

Mark was a seemingly permanent fixture in our lives. If we were at dinner, Mark was at dinner. If Emerson left town for an interview to promote her Edie Fitzgerald movie, Mark went with her. They were connected at the hip, and she seemed like a teenager again. Same with Mom, who was trying to deny she was back together with Jack. But it was painfully obvious. The whole world was in love. The whole world had their man. I had a cell phone I kept glued to my hip in case my uncle got enough bandwidth to Skype me or the military called to say they had found my husband.

It was a sleepy morning around Peachtree Bluff. The boys were at Mother's Morning Out. Mom was at the shop. I was taking the day off to get some painting done at the house. I was almost at the point where I thought I might want to sell some of my paintings. And I knew this new series, with its sky blues and soft pinks and yellows, would fly out of her shop. I felt proud, and I couldn't wait to get those commission checks.

As I dipped my brush into the pale pink, the color of many a Peachtree sunset, Emerson walked into the living room. "I need to talk to you," she said.

This was why artists had studios.

"Can it wait?" I asked.

I noticed she had a bag in her hand, and for a split second I was afraid she was eloping. If she was eloping and I didn't tell Mom, Mom would absolutely kill me. It would be almost as bad as if Mom found out Caroline and I knew Emerson was sick and hadn't told her.

She shook her head, and I sighed. "What is it?"

"We're going to New York," she said.

I laughed. "Yeah. Right. Good luck with that one."

She set the bag down on the floor and crossed her arms. "James called me and said this Hamptons party he and Caroline are going to is really a party honoring Caroline."

"For what?" I asked. "Her contributions to Barney's?"

I laughed. I thought I was funny. I was in a pretty good mood this morning.

Emerson smiled. "No, actually. Our sister raised more than two million dollars for a charity that funds arts programs for at-risk schools and physically challenged communities."

My jaw dropped. "Come again? You mean our sister? Caroline Beaumont?"

Emerson nodded.

"That's awesome," I said. "I'm so proud of her. But I can't leave my kids."

"You aren't," Emerson said. "We're all going, and Caroline's nanny is going to keep them at her house in East Hampton."

I could feel my mouth getting dry and my pulse beginning to race. "OK. Then I'm not going because I'm sure as hell not going back to New York."

"Sloane, our sister took care of your children for five weeks without a word of complaint. She was with them all day, every day, helping Mom. She paid all your bills, including your obscene credit card. She would do anything for either of us without a second thought. She is being honored in a big, big way, and we are going to be there for her."

Wow. Emerson was on fire. "Geez," I said. "You've spent way too much time with her this summer."

"I have packed your bag, and I have packed the boys' bags." She paused. "I mean, obviously, Caroline will have what we are supposed to wear to the party sent out to the house, but your other stuff is packed. We need to leave the house at eight forty-five in the morning."

I nodded, but I knew now was the time I could get Emerson to do something for me. I set my paintbrush down and rubbed my hands together. I reached out for Emerson's hand. "Want to go for a walk with me? Get some fresh air?"

She shrugged, and I could tell she was suspicious. "Sure."

As we made our way down the steps she said, "Actually, Sloane, I'm not feeling that great. Can we just go sit on the dock?"

It made my stomach churn. My little sister's arm was wrapped around mine. I pulled up her sleeve and studied a bruise above her wrist. I shook my head. "Emerson," I said breathlessly.

I unhooked the latch on the gate and we crossed the street. We both sat down at the end of the dock, our toes trailing in the water.

"Remember when we used to do this when we were kids?" I asked.

Emerson smiled and nodded. "Yeah. I remember. It was a huge deal when I was tall enough that my feet actually touched."

"I know we're grown up now," I said, looking out across the water, past Starlite Island, out to where our stretch of water met the deep, dark ocean that sometimes felt so pristine and beautiful to me and other times so dark and looming. Today was a dark and looming time. "But you're still my little sister, Em. You always will be. And I'm not going to stand by and let something bad happen to you."

Emerson had canceled her last two doctor's appointments, which was a classic Emerson move. If you don't want to deal with it, avoid it.

Emerson turned.

"I'll go to New York on one condition," I said. "I will go if you go to that hematologist Caroline found while we're there."

She scrunched her nose.

"If I have to face my fear, you have to face yours too."

Emerson rolled her eyes. "Fine," she said.

"Grand," I replied. I noticed she still looked nervous.

I knew how she felt because I felt nervous too. If you didn't have the finality of a diagnosis, in her case or, in my case, a body, you could deny what was happening to you. "It will be OK," I whispered. "Once they figure out what's wrong with you, they can fix it."

She shrugged and bit her lip. "Grammy dying and Adam being MIA has put everything into perspective," she said. "I mean, my whole life."

I leaned back, resting on my hands.

"Everything I've thought was important feels kind of stupid now." She paused. "I mean, I might not be able to have kids. The treatments might not work." She sighed, and I could see her chin quivering. She looked up at me, searching for an answer. "Sloane, I could die."

I couldn't even entertain that thought. "Em, no," I said, sitting up, pulling her into me. I had been the fragile one these past few months. I had been the one who was crumbling and needed someone to give her strength. Now it was Emerson. "We don't even know what's wrong yet." I squeezed her hand and whispered, "You're going to be fine."

I looked out over the water, at a shrimp trawler making its way back home. I didn't want Emerson to see the fear on my face or the tears in my eyes. My sister might be really sick. My sister could die.

The fear of flying and going back to New York was nothing, absolutely nothing, compared to the fear of losing my sister. I thought of Adam and what he would do, and I made it my personal goal to get Emerson any and all treatment and help she needed. I thought of the Army, of its motto, of what Adam always said to me when I was feeling conflicted. I would continue to repeat it to myself over and over again as I faced my fears over those next few days.

Mission First, People Always.

"THIS IS A MOMENT to advance," I said out loud the next morning, reaching my hand into my pocket to feel the corners of the paper with Adam's words that he could never have expected would help me through this anguish. My other hand was holding AJ's. "This is a moment," I said, this time with more certainty in my voice, "to move forward with purpose, power, and most importantly, passion."

I looked seriously at AJ, and he looked seriously back up at me. "Because action without passion is a waste of time, Mommy."

I nodded again and took a deep breath. "Exactly."

I would not be afraid. If I was afraid I certainly would not let my boys see. Fortunately, AJ was too young to be affected by how sweaty my palm was.

"I like that," Mark said from behind me in line, holding his boarding pass anxiously, at the ready. That was how I felt about Mark. He was always at attention, like he was afraid he'd drop the ball and this dream of being with my sister would simply evaporate as if it never happened. "This is a moment to advance."

"But," Emerson chimed in, "there are moments to retreat."

Mark put his arm around her. "Damn," he said. "That man is nothing short of a poet."

"Language," I said, smiling and looking down at AJ, as I tried to put out of my mind that this one flight could wipe out most of our clan. Mom had stayed up half the night reading articles to me about how the likelihood of dying in a commercial plane crash is statistically zero. I don't know when *she* got so brave. Maybe it was because I was her child that she wouldn't let me see she was afraid. Although I couldn't help but notice that Jack was here. She had finally admitted to Emerson, Caroline, and me that she was, in her words, "sort of dating Jack. Taking things slow, seeing how they go."

If they weren't married by the end of the year, I'd be shocked. I loved Jack, but it was still weird to see our mom with someone who wasn't our dad. I couldn't say that out loud to my sisters because they thought I was ridiculous. But I was allowed to have my feelings. That's what Adam would say if he were here. My heart skipped a beat when I thought of him. I had this fantasy that while my phone was off on the plane, they would find him and I would land to a voicemail saying he was OK. Because that's how life works. No matter how vigilant you are, sometimes you miss the moment.

As I put my phone on the boarding pass scanner, I could feel the sweat gathering on my brow. I was doing this. How was this possible? I was getting on an airplane. I was going to New York. Both for the first time since I left, six months after 9/11. If Emerson hadn't pushed me, I'm not sure I would have made it onto the Jetway. And this was with a double dose of Valium. I couldn't imagine what it would have been like without it.

As if this weren't bad enough, I had the dream again last night. Emerson, Caroline, and I were playing on the beach. Caroline's hair was blowing in the salty breeze; Emerson was running back and forth from our castle to the spot where the water lapped the shore. It was a perfect day by all accounts, easy and free, another childhood afternoon full of sunshine and free of worries, until I looked around for Mom and didn't see her. My pulse quickened for a split second until my eyes locked on her. She'd been wearing a mint-green and pink bikini that day. She was so tan, so beautiful. But that day, she had her arms crossed, and her face looked angry and closed off, a way it had never looked before. It scared me to see her like that. There was a man standing with her, and he looked angry too. Angry and sad. He was talking a lot, and she was shaking her head. I remember his hair, how the light shone on it, how it was dark brown but in the sun it practically looked black, like Caroline's. I couldn't hear Mom, but I could tell she was yelling. Not like she did when Caroline and I had been arguing all day. Really yelling, like grown-ups do when they're mad. I'd never seen her do that. It scared me to death. Then Mom was rushing us into the boat, and I could feel her fear. It wasn't until later that I realized we had left our beloved fairy stones, the ones we took with us everywhere.

It had actually happened, long ago. But in my subconscious, it must have been incredibly fresh because, even though nothing particularly terrifying happened, it was still the scariest nightmare I had, seeing my mother like that and wondering who this stranger was and why they were so angry with each other.

I strapped AJ into the window seat so he could see out the window, though who would want to look out I couldn't possibly imagine. I was in the middle, and Emerson was beside me for moral support. Mark had gotten upgraded to First Class. He acted like it broke his heart not to sit with Emerson, but let's face it: Emerson was not as great as First Class.

Mom and Jack had Taylor a couple of rows in front of us. I was glad they had taken him because I was starting to get very, very sleepy, and I knew I couldn't have kept up with him on the flight.

Emerson held my hand and said, "So, what do you think of Mark?"

My eyelids were getting heavy as I said, "I love him, Em. I think he's a prince."

I saw her smile dreamily as my eyes closed. As I started to drift off, I could feel the breeze on my face and the sand underneath my knees. I sat up straighter, willing my eyes open so I didn't have to dream it again. I looked around. Taylor was strapped in his car seat, and I could see his tiny legs kicking. I was at the perfect angle where I could see Mom's face. Her arms were crossed, and she seemed upset. Angry even.

My eyelids were heavy again, and I couldn't tell if the mom who was angry was real, in the plane seat, or in my dream. I opened my eyes again, right before I saw the man she was talking to. I looked forward again to Taylor's kicking feet, to the stream of light that was pouring through the plane window, how it made Jack's dark brown hair almost black. My eyes closed again. I forced them open as Jack turned and I saw his expression. He was always so calm and laid back. This face was anything but. This face was mad.

In that moment I couldn't hold off anymore. I felt my hand

drop out of Emerson's and my head collapse back into the seat. As my subconscious took over and wandered back into my dream, it hit me: The man on the beach that day wasn't a stranger at all. The man was Jack.

CAROLINE'S HOUSE IN EAST Hampton suited her perfectly. It wasn't big, and it wasn't on the water, but every inch of it was elegant and just modern enough. The entire palette was water blues and creams with touches of gold, seagrass, and plenty of natural beauty from resin coral and oyster shells.

I had never been to it, of course. And walking through the front door, I instantly felt calm. I assumed that's what Mom had been going for when she designed it.

I was exhausted but proud, too. I had made it. I had lived through the flight, and we were here. Mom and Jack were staying in a hotel while the rest of us piled into Caroline and James's house. When I walked into the living room with AJ and Taylor, who promptly scampered off to explore, I did a double take and felt my décor-induced calm dissipate as quickly as it had come. As Caroline ran to meet us, I said, "What is that?"

"Well, it's so good to see you too, sweet sister," she said. "Thank you for the warm greeting."

"Caroline," I said, an edge to my voice. "Why is Jack's painting here?"

She looked at me innocently. "Oh, well, we thought it would be so nice to donate it to the cause. We're going to auction it off tonight as I accept my award."

"No," I said. "I told you I'm not ready. I told you I don't want my work out there in the world yet. It's still just for me."

"But Sloane," she said, that crafty calm in her voice, "don't you remember? You owe me."

I felt the color drain from my face then because she had me. I did owe her. She had paid my credit card bill, and I owed her a favor. There was no way out.

To change the subject, Caroline showed me the white linen maxi dress she had bought for me. It was simple, but somehow made me seem taller and made my shoulders seem more sculpted.

As I wore the dress later that night, feeling somewhat confident despite the fact that I was totally out of my element among the coiffed-to-perfection women and men milling about a neighbor's yard, I was so proud of my sister. Her hair was swept up off her face in a simple updo that made her neck seem swan-like, and she was wearing a rose-colored, silk jumpsuit that would have made anyone even slightly less tan look sickly.

As I was admiring her behind her podium, I came back into the moment and it registered with me what Caroline was saying. I felt all the breath leave my body as I heard, "You won't find her on the Internet; you won't see her in the magazines. She's under the radar, but she's one of the hottest up-and-comers in the art world today." She paused. "We're going to start the bidding at five thousand dollars."

I understood now how people felt in those dreams where they're naked in public. I may as well have stripped my dress off. All of my pulse points throbbed. I was a failure, a fraud, a nobody. And five thousand dollars? She was insane. This was humiliating. No one was going to buy this thing, and I was going to be a laughingstock.

Only, people started putting their hands in the air. Caroline left her podium and stood beside me. "See, Sloane? It's beautiful. It really, truly is." She looked at me intently and took my hands in hers. "You're beautiful. And you can do this."

She meant I could paint. She meant I could put myself out there. But she also meant I could raise my two sons and support my family. Hell, I could even get on an airplane and fly to New York.

A few moments later, Caroline hugged me and said, "Did you see that? You just raised eleven thousand dollars for at-risk youth. Aren't you proud? See what good your art can do?"

It was one of the proudest moments of my life so far, a defining one. Because I had faced my biggest fears that day. I had gotten back on an airplane to New York. I had released my art back into the world. I touched the monogrammed cuff on my arm, realizing Grammy was right. I was strong and I was brave.

I knew Adam would come home. I believed it with all my heart and soul. But if the worst happened, if the boys and I were alone forever, we would be OK.

I walked up to my painting, the one that had somehow set me free, one last time. My family was standing all around me. Caroline was yammering on excitedly, "And now I'm going to be your agent, and we're going to get you in galleries—I've already had three requests—and it's going to be amazing." I knew she needed this almost as much as I did.

I took a sip of champagne as I said, sarcastically, "Good one, Caroline."

She stopped in her tracks. "What? What do you mean 'good one'? I'd say this was pretty epic."

I ran my finger down the white blob in the painting, then the black one. "This was supposed to be Jack's painting," I said. "You sold Mom and Jack."

"What?" Mom asked. "Caroline Murphy Beaumont, I knew I shouldn't have let you talk me into this. This is why I said no after Grammy's funeral."

I turned and looked at her. "You're the white streak. Jack is the black one."

Jack put his hand to his heart. "I'm the black one? Is that symbolism?"

"Sort of." I grinned.

"Am I darkness or something?"

"Of course not, Jack!" I smiled sneakily. "You're the groom."

Everyone laughed as Jack said, "From your mouth to God's ears."

"I didn't even realize it until I was finished," I said. That was what I loved most about painting. The surprises. The way a piece could take over if you let it lead you.

Three hours later, I emerged from the marble mosaic-tiled shower, my hair wrapped in a towel, my body swathed in one of Caroline's plush robes, and smelling of her expensive rose cream.

When I walked out of the bathroom and into Caroline's living room, I saw Emerson and Mom crying, and Jack was as white as a ghost. I sensed this was about Adam, but if the military knew something, if they had found him—or realized they weren't going to find him—they would have contacted me first.

My stomach rolled as I sat down on the couch between Emerson and Mom. A YouTube video was playing on Caroline's huge TV over the fireplace. Well, actually, James's huge TV. Caroline hated TVs over the fireplace. I was suddenly freezing.

"What?" I asked. "Please tell me."

But, in a way, I knew already.

Though I tried not to watch often, I'd seen the footage of the soldiers in Iraq, their helmets, their rucksacks, their tanks. I'd heard the ear-splitting gunfire, the missile launches, the yelling, the radio static, the repeating of coordinates over and over again. I'd seen them behind concrete walls, behind little more than sandbags, among the desolate remains of fallen cities. I'd seen armed men fight armed men.

I'd never seen anything like this. But I knew what it was. The grainy, tan picture shot from above. I could make out the tops of the men's heads, the long shadows, and the slow-motion running. The white numbers and letters in the four corners of the screen. This was persistent surveillance footage from a Predator drone. At first, I felt heartened. Maybe this was rescue footage. But even through the grainy picture and the faraway view, I could see these men had no helmets or weapons, and a few of them appeared to be shirtless. It was impossible to get a clear view of them, and the silence was deafening. There was no commentary, no voice-over, just nightmarish quiet. The only clue we had, the only tip, was a simple title below the video frame, "Escaped American POWs."

Common sense told me Adam and his unit were the only soldiers missing. This had to be them. If it was current footage, and if he was still alive, one of these running men was my husband.

"How did you find this?" I managed to eke out. "What is this?"

"Kyle called me," Emerson whispered. "He follows a YouTube channel that posts footage filmed by American soldiers. But the commenters seem to think this footage was leaked."

"So did this just happen?" I asked, my voice shaking. "Are we sure it's even real?"

"I'm sorry, Sloane," Em said. "We just don't know."

I could barely make it out on the camera, but there was a man running, then a man on the ground, still. Even through the faraway picture, I could tell from the way he fell that he had been gunned down. This wasn't a trip or a fall. It was a death. Then the playback ended as abruptly and terrifyingly as it had begun.

"Play it again," I said. "And pause on the fallen man."

"Sloane," Emerson said gently.

"PLAY. IT. AGAIN."

Mom was sobbing horrible, agonized sobs, and Jack said, "Sloane, I'm going to call the post. We're going to get to the bottom of this."

My entire body was covered in chill bumps. My mouth was dry, my insides cold. Was that Adam? Were there more dead men? And if it wasn't Adam it was surely one of our friends. Wasn't it?

My first instinct was to call Major Austin. But I couldn't. If what happened after that man fell was what I could only assume had happened, I didn't want to know the truth. It was as if someone had reached inside me and pulled my heart out of my chest as I screamed, "No! No, no, no!"

I wasn't crying. I was too numb and terrified for that—the exact same way I had felt that day after Major Austin and the chaplain had come to tell me Adam was MIA. That quiet that defied explanation, the intensity of a pain that can't even be expressed.

My sisters were trying to hug me, but I was so far beyond comfort. Jack took my hand, his phone up to his ear. "Is it true, Jack? Tell me it can't be true."

I can't explain why it was Jack I turned to. Maybe it was because he was a man or because he always seemed to take charge. Maybe, I had to admit, it was because he was the closest thing to a father I had left.

He put his finger up, and I could hear him saying, "Then you've seen it too. Yes. Is there any information about the soldiers?"

He walked out into the hall, and the tears finally came.

I picked up my phone and typed to Maryanne, *"Have you heard anything?"*

She responded immediately, *"No. Why?"*

If she didn't know yet, there was no point in worrying her. Oh, God. What if that man was Tom? What if it was Adam? Could any of them possibly have survived? I couldn't breathe. Even still, I managed to type back, *"No reason. Just wondering."*

I leaned over and put my head between my legs. Mom

rubbed my back. "Sloane, it's going to be OK," Caroline said. "We're going to get to the bottom of this."

But it wasn't going to be OK. It could never be OK. Earlier that night, I had felt like I could do it alone, like I could make this work. But now, when I finally feared that the worst had happened and my nightmares had come true, I felt more hopeless, lost, and terrified than I ever had before. And I couldn't begin to imagine how I might face this world without the man who had changed mine completely.

———

IT TOOK MONTHS FOR Adam to forgive me after I told him I didn't want kids. But we had worked through what still remains the biggest test of our marriage. It hadn't been easy, and there had been so many times I thought it might go another way. But, in the end, Adam decided he loved me more than he loved his future, unborn children. He had committed his life to me—and that meant he owed it to me to try to work it out, no matter how badly I had screwed up.

When I look back on it now, I can see that the issue wasn't ever that I didn't want to have children. It was just that after what I had endured, I had so many layers of fear and terror to pull back and so many years of trauma to work through. Marrying Adam and realizing it hadn't been scary, but, instead, had been wholly wonderful, was a huge part of my healing process.

But the pivotal moment of change didn't have anything to do with Adam. Emerson, Caroline, James, Vivi, Adam, and I were in Peachtree visiting Mom. We set aside a full week every summer to be together, and although we certainly saw each other plenty throughout the rest of the year, I always looked forward to it.

Only, this year, I knew things were going to be different. I had received a phone call from James earlier in the week, which was kind of odd. I was scared something was wrong, so I ran out of the gift shop where I was working, saying, "I'm so sorry. I have to take this."

"Sloane," he had said, his Northern accent a bit of a shock after being surrounded by so many Southern voices. "I think I may need your help."

His accent saying *that* was really a shock. "Are you guys OK? Is Caroline OK?"

"Not really," he said, and I felt my stomach clench.

"Sloane, she is obsessed with having another baby. It's all she can think about, and I'm really worried about her."

I knew Caroline was getting ready to try in vitro again, and I knew she was consumed by this quest. But I reasoned that anybody would be.

Two days later, I saw for myself exactly what James had been worried about. Caroline had talked about nothing but babies and pregnancy since we arrived.

Ironically, Caroline was the one who had always been best at talking sense into people. It wasn't my forte, but I was going to try. I waited until the two of us were alone in the kitchen.

"I'm going to have some of my fertility tea," she said, getting up from the island and walking to the stove. Then she turned back to me. "Hey," she said, "do you want some?"

I smiled. She was sneaky.

"You know I don't want children," I said.

She shook her head. "No, Sloane. It's not that you don't want children. You're *scared* to have children."

"And?"

"And there's a huge difference."

She filled up the teapot and turned on the burner. She leaned against the counter and said, "I'm scared too. I'm terrified. I'm terrified every day that Vivi is in the world that something horrible might happen to her."

"So why do you want to do it again?" I asked.

She leaned over the island toward me. "Because, Sloane, one moment of your child being on earth is worth millions of years of worry. There's no way to explain how magical it is to bring another life into the world, how soul-satisfying it is to be someone's mother."

If I was honest, I had started wondering lately if I could do it, if I could put aside my fear and trust enough to give my husband the thing he wanted most in the world, the thing that loomed between us every time we made love.

"It's scary as hell," Caroline said. "In fact, I'd venture to say it's the scariest thing you'll ever do." As the kettle began to sing, Caroline added, "But I swear to you, Sloane, once you have a child, you'll feel like your life before was black and white. And now everything is in color."

I realized that night I hadn't done a thing to convince my sister to give up her fertility project. In fact, quite the opposite. She had convinced me to take up a fertility project of my own. I woke Adam up. He smiled at me sleepily. "What's shaking, sugar?"

I had had my IUD removed years before, and I was holding my birth control pills in my hand. Adam closed one eye and looked at me. "What are you doing with that?"

"I'm throwing it away."

"Is it bad or something?" he asked.

I shook my head. "It's not bad," I said. "It's just that I think we should have a baby."

Adam shot up in bed and looked around. "Is this real? Am I dreaming?"

I kissed him softly and laughed. "You're not dreaming. I've been thinking about it for a few months now. I don't think I was ready before."

He nodded and pulled me to him. "You are going to be the best mother in the world. And I promise you I will do everything I can to ease your fear."

"You already have," I said.

And I knew, as he pulled me on top of him, that it was true. It might have been Caroline who pushed me over the edge. But it was Adam, with his patience, love, and care every single day, who had made me trust again. And nothing in this world, nothing in my entire life, made me happier than to repay him for that gift.

our truth

ansley

It seemed fitting that Carter would find out the truth about Caroline and Sloane's father in Peachtree Bluff, on that boardwalk where we shared our first kiss, against the backdrop of a pink-and-blue, cotton-candy sky. I never really expected, in my heart of hearts, that I could go a lifetime without Carter finding out who Caroline and Sloane's biological father was. But I assumed, eventually, he would insist I tell him.

It never occurred to me that we would pass Jack on the dock in Peachtree Bluff, that he would be completely shocked by my Emerson-pregnant belly, and that, in that look he gave me, in the simplicity and nothingness of that moment, the secret we had kept for years and years would be revealed.

When Carter ran away from me that afternoon, I didn't run after him. I knew better. Instead, I took the time to truly thank the man who had given me my family. Things were different between Jack and me that day. The heat between us had cooled some, as it tends to when separated by time and distance and a good dose of grown-up rationality. But I still felt nervous standing beside him, my face flushed and my heart beating a little too fast.

It was only as I walked away from Jack, as I felt that familiar piercing pain around my heart, that it occurred to me how long I had had that feeling. Part of me wanted to go back to him, but I had finally gotten to a place where I knew I had done the right thing. I had finally begun to feel like my life was playing out as it should. Sure, I would be happy for that moment with Jack, but that moment would only lead to months of heartache.

There was no question I had done the right thing. No question, that is, until I got back to the house two hours later.

When I found Carter, he was pacing the length of our bedroom. "Glad you two had time for a quick tryst for old times' sake," he said.

I rolled my eyes. "Carter, come on. Don't be ridiculous."

If I had thought I was nervous with Jack on the dock, it was nothing compared to now. It wasn't that I thought Carter would leave me, but it was one of the first times in our relationship that I was truly at a loss for what to do. I didn't know how to make him feel better or how to make this right. The indignant part of me wanted to yell, "You did this! It was your idea! You created this situation to begin with." It made me realize I still carried anger at him for placing this huge burden onto me.

I sat down on the edge of the bed, placing my hands protectively over Emerson in my belly. Carter took a deep breath and said, "I have never felt so stupid in my entire life. Jack? Really, Ansley? The guy was Jack?"

I sighed. "So would it be better if it were our yard man, Carter? Maybe the plumber? Maybe one of my friends' husbands? If it were someone you saw every week, would that make you feel better?" I crossed my arms, resting them on my barely protruding belly. "This was going to be terrible no matter what, Carter. Any way we did this, it was going to be awful. So, I'm sorry, but I thought Jack was the best choice. I trust him. He doesn't want kids. It made sense."

"You trust him?" Carter practically spat, still pacing.

I felt anger well in me. "So what did you think, Carter? What was your best-case scenario here? How was this ever going to be anything but awful?"

What he said next knocked the wind out of me. It is a moment I will never forget, one of those moments where a new truth washed over me so completely it was as if I'd been immersed in water. But, instead of feeling cleansed, I felt tainted and dirty. Carter stopped pacing, looked directly at me, and said, "I never thought you would do it."

I sat there for a long moment, my mouth hanging open in shock. "*You* were adamant that we wouldn't adopt. *You* didn't want me to do IUI again. What choice did you leave me?"

He shrugged. "I figured we wouldn't have kids." He sighed. "I knew you weren't with Jack because he didn't want kids, so I knew I couldn't say I didn't want them. I figured you would realize there were no good options, and we would go along just the two of us, no harm, no foul." It was like being punched in the gut. He started pacing again. "I swear, Ansley, for a long time, I actually thought Caroline might really be mine. I honestly did. Because I couldn't imagine you would have had it in you to get pregnant by anyone else." He laughed incredulously then.

I felt sick. It was one of those moments, one that I think most people have at least once during the course of a long marriage, where I realized I didn't know this man at all. Or maybe it was myself I didn't know. Because beneath my anger and shock at what he was saying was the question of what my motivation had been. I had ascribed the blame for this situation to Carter for all these years, and now I had to wonder if maybe all that blame should really be put on me. I was the one who went to Jack. I was the one who fell back in love with him. I was the one who risked my marriage for children. It was the first time I wondered if Carter and I could possibly make it through this. After all we had done to hurt each other, did we even stand a chance?

I put my head in my hands, trying to come to grips with what Carter had just said to me. Then I looked up. "So why did you ask me to do it again? A second time?"

He shrugged. "At that point I figured Caroline needed a sibling. We'd made it through once. We'd make it through again."

"And now?" I asked, my throat thick with tears.

That was when I finally felt him soften. He sat down beside me. "And now we have another baby, one who is finally ours. I hate that Caroline and Sloane aren't mine, Ansley. I really do. But I don't love them any less because of it."

"So it's just me you love less," I said, tears streaming down my cheeks.

He didn't answer, which was not exactly the response I was looking for. Seeing the pained expression on his face broke something inside me. I knelt down in front of him and took his face in my hands. "I want you to hear me when I say this, Carter. You are the one. You have always been the one. Our lives may not have unraveled as perfectly as we had imagined, but I have never, not for one day, lost sight of the fact that you are the man I was meant to be with. There is no one—and I do mean no one—I would rather share this life with. You are my home, Carter. I never want to live without you."

He took my hands and said, "Get up off the floor, Ansley. You're too beautiful for the floor." When he held me to him, I knew it was going to be OK.

I was still hugging him, resting my head on his shoulder, when Carter sighed and said, "Do you love him?" I could tell by the way he asked it, so quickly and breathily, that he was terrified to learn the answer.

I could have said, "A part of me will always love Jack. He gave us our girls." The truth was that I had loved him all day, every day for most of my life, and I knew that would never end, no matter how much I wished it would. But, despite that fact, I loved Carter more. I loved my family more. I didn't like lying to Carter. I never had. In some ways, I felt relieved that I didn't have this huge secret weighing on me anymore. But I knew better than to push it. So I said, looking out over my husband's shoulder, "Of course not, Carter. I only love you."

It was another lie, maybe only the third one I had ever told my husband.

I pulled away from him then, and he said, "I'm so sorry, Ansley. I shouldn't have said that to you. I never wanted to say that to you."

"So it's true then? You weren't just angry? You really never expected me to get pregnant?"

I saw the pause in his expression, the way he took a moment to think before he answered, like I had only seconds before. He hugged me to him again and said, "Of course that's not true. I was upset, so I took it out on you. This was the plan. You followed through. End of story." But he couldn't look me in the eye when he said it.

It was the second lie we had told each other in as many minutes. But even though I knew he wasn't telling the truth, his little lie appeased me, just like I'm sure mine had him. Maybe it should have worried me, but it made me feel better. We were both willing to put aside a piece of our truth, a piece of ourselves, to make the other one feel better. And, every now and then, I believe, that's what real love—the down-and-dirty-in-the-trenches kind—is all about.

I HAD NEVER BEEN so grateful for James. He was going to let us use his NetJet hours to take Sloane home the next day.

I remembered going to visit Sloane on post when Adam

was first stationed in North Carolina, decorating her little blue town house and trying to make it feel as comfortable and restful as possible. She had scolded me when we passed the row of stately historic officers' homes because I had said, "When do I get to decorate one of those for you?"

Adam had laughed, but later, Sloane had said, "I don't ever want to make him feel like what he does or where we are isn't good enough."

I had only been joking, but I felt badly and hoped I hadn't hurt Adam's feelings. I truly hadn't meant to. I admired how he was working his way up with patience and determination.

As a mea culpa, I had a set of antique linen hand towels embroidered for Sloane. *Home is Where the Army Sends Us,* they read. Where would home be for Sloane now?

Emerson, Caroline, and I packed her bags. We all knew it would be a sleepless night.

This was the moment we had all dreaded over the past months. It was the moment we had wanted to prepare Sloane for, the moment she simply would not accept as a possibility. I realized now it didn't matter whether she had prepared herself. It would have been impossible to face no matter what.

Jack was making phone calls, sending emails, getting in touch with every politician, military figure, reporter, or investigator he had ever met. But there wasn't anything he could do. There wasn't anything anyone could do. Still, the fact that he was trying told me everything I would ever need to know.

I was leaning against the kitchen counter, and Caroline,

Emerson, and I were all looking at each other, numb. "What do I do?" I asked.

"We take her home," Caroline said. "We'll get through this."

In that moment, my phone rang. "Oh my God," I said, my voice catching in my throat. "It's Scott."

I looked at the phone, frozen. "Well, for God's sake, answer it," Caroline said.

But it was Emerson who grabbed it. "Scott!" she said.

"Uh-huh. No! You're kidding me. Uh-huh."

We were looking at her, gesturing for her to fill us in, but she put her finger in her ear and waved us away. "Oh my God, Scott. I can't believe it."

Was it a good "I can't believe it" or a bad one? There was no way to tell.

It felt like hours, but I'm sure the phone call was less than two minutes. Then I heard Sloane's phone ring. Then Jack's.

And before Emerson could relay to us what Scott had said, Sloane flew out, wide-eyed, holding her phone. "They found him!" she screamed in a state that could only be described as manic.

At first, I thought she meant his body. We all stood motionless, afraid of what was going to happen next. "They found him. They found Adam. He's alive." She crouched down on the floor and started sobbing into her knees. "He's coming home. Adam is coming home!"

I wasn't sure I believed her. But I looked at Emerson, and her nod through her own tears confirmed what Sloane had said.

It was as if a thousand pounds I had carried around for

months was lifted off me. I felt myself slide down the wall until I was sitting on the floor, face in my hands, crying.

"Look at my texts," she said. "I have a picture."

"Oh my God!" Caroline screamed. "It's him. It's Adam!" She turned the phone to the side. "He's so damn thin."

"Of course he's thin," Sloane said. "He's a freaking prisoner of war."

She stood up with purpose. "Oh my God. Scott is my favorite family member!"

"Scott is my favorite family member too!" I exclaimed.

Sloane looked around. She started sobbing with pure, utter relief. "I have to get to DC right now," she said. "They're bringing him to Walter Reed, and I have to be there."

"Back up," Caroline said. "When will he be there?"

Sloane crossed her arms. "Well, they're taking him to Landstuhl for triage and then—"

"What on earth is Landstuhl?" Emerson asked.

"The hospital in Germany," Sloane said impatiently, raising her voice.

"Do you want to go there?" I asked, trying to be helpful.

Sloane sighed. "They offered to fly me there, but by the time I get there, he'll probably be leaving. This makes the most sense."

We all stood there, silent and processing. Was this actually happening?

No one moved. Sloane clapped her hands and said, "Now!"

Three hours later, Sloane was kissing the boys good-bye inside the jet, with her bag slung over her shoulder. "Be so good for Gransley," she said. Then she grinned. "I'm going to get Daddy."

There was a part of me that was worried she was meeting Adam at the hospital and a part of me that wondered what that meant for him, for my daughter, and for their future. Even still, those might have been the sweetest words I had ever heard.

THIRTY-SEVEN

the meaning of life

sloane

July 18, 2017

Dear Sloane:

I am coming home to you!!!! Wow, I didn't think I would ever see your face again. Or kiss my boys, throw a ball with them, feel your soft body snuggled up next to mine at night.

I am weak and exhausted. My leg and a few of my ribs were badly broken in the crash, and my shoulder was dislocated. Of course, I've had no medical care, so there is work to do. But I can't comprehend how lucky I am to be alive. We lost one of our men here, and I'm not sure I will ever be able to come to terms with the fact that I made it while he did not. How can that be?

I am rambling now when all I want to say is this: Sloane, you got me through these months. The thought of you, the memory of you, the warmth and the love of you is what pushed me forward when it would have been so much easier to succumb to the death that was so close I could almost feel it. I live for you, Sloane. I would die for you. And everything in between. And now, I get to see you again. Words do not exist to describe how much I have missed you, how I have longed for you in the darkest, deepest parts of me. I should warn you that once I come home to you, I may never leave your side again.

Counting down the moments, my beautiful wife, until I am in your arms again. Until then, I am, faithfully, lovingly, eternally . . .

Always and forever yours,
Adam

HOLDING TAYLOR IN MY arms for the first time was the last time I'd had this feeling that everything in my life had changed, like everything I had believed to be true was insignificant compared to this moment. To think I had lost my true love only to find him again . . . It was nothing short of rebirth.

I had looked at my watch every three minutes for the past few days, willing the time forward. I had gotten to Skype Adam and hear his voice, proving to myself he was alive.

And now, every ounce of me was buzzing with the pure thrill and unbridled joy that I would get to touch him, kiss him, and hold him close to me once again.

I was standing on the runway at Joint Base Andrews. Normally, I might have been excited to see Air Force One or been making small talk with Major Austin, the rear detachment commander who had kept me abreast of everything for the past few months. But I couldn't. I had never felt this level of anxious excitement. A C-17 Nightingale flight would be bringing my husband from Landstuhl and landing right here in a matter of moments. I would get to ride in the ambulance with him to Walter Reed, where he would be having surgery and receiving treatment before I could take him home for good. This was the moment I had envisioned for all those long, painful weeks. And now it was here.

As the jet came into view, I had the sickening feeling it was coming in too quickly. But I should have known better. As it landed, blowing everything in its path including my hair and the cream sundress Caroline had let me borrow, I squinted to keep the debris out of my eyes, but wouldn't dare close them all the way. I would get the first glimpse of Adam. When I saw the door open, I started running. There he was. My husband, my world, everything I wanted and needed.

He was in his combat uniform and boots, his arm in a sling and a cane in his hand. I ran to him, my tears nearly blinding me. I threw my arms around him, he threw his one good arm around me, and I kissed him like I'd never stop. He might have been pick thin and badly wounded, but he was still Adam. He was still that strong, confident man I had fallen in love with in line at the post office.

I could feel my tears and his tears mingling together like ingredients in a saucepan, could taste them between our kisses. I wrapped my arms around his middle so tightly he groaned, which is when I remembered his broken ribs. Poor guy. "Sorry," I said.

But he smiled at me. "I don't care," he whispered into my ear. "You're here, Sloane. I'm here. We're together."

I barely remember the ambulance ride or entering Walter Reed. I know there was paperwork and rustling and doctors and nurses, and then Adam was in a bed and a doctor was talking about taking him into surgery in the morning. I couldn't process any of it, because he was home and we were going to spend the rest of our lives together just like we had planned. I had never felt a glee this pure. It was a high I didn't know a human could experience.

At last, when we were alone, I finally noticed how gaunt and gray Adam looked, the exhaustion in his eyes, the new lines in his face.

I ran my hand along his sunken cheek. "Honey," I said, "what happened to you?"

He shook his head. "Sloane, I'm alive. One of my men lost his life. An innocent kid lost his." I had never, in all his deployments, seen my husband this raw, this vulnerable.

I felt myself bristle when he said "innocent kid."

"What do you mean?" I whispered, my stomach already turning, not truly wanting to know the answer.

"A seventeen-year-old kid, one of the sons . . ." He trailed off, and I waited patiently. "He helped us escape," he said, his eyes filling with tears.

"What?" I asked, truly stunned. "I thought it was a Delta Force operation."

Adam bit his lip. "Well, it was, technically. And thank God. If they hadn't been on their way, we'd all be dead. No question." He swallowed hard, and I took his hand, rubbing it. He teared up and said, "I'm sorry."

I kissed his forehead. "Don't be sorry. There's nothing to be sorry about."

"If we'd just waited ten more minutes . . ."

I wasn't surprised by his emotion necessarily, but it unnerved me all the same. I had never seen him like this.

"This brave little kid got us out." He looked around and continued. "If we had just waited, if we had just been patient, that kid would still be alive. His father wouldn't have killed him for being a traitor."

I put my hand to my mouth. I felt sick. Sicker than sick. But my job here was to soothe my husband. "You don't know that, Adam."

He nodded, tears in his eyes. "I saw him fall. And it will haunt me forever. I can't help but feel like it was my fault."

I remembered the drone footage, the man running and falling. That wasn't a man at all. He was a child. A teenager. A son. I wondered if his mother was grieving, if she was alone in her grief. "It's not your fault, Adam," I said. "It was God's plan. We can't control it."

"It was a sucky plan," he said under his breath.

"Adam!" I scolded.

"I thought we were all dead, Sloane. I swear I did. And I wanted to stay alive and be there for you and the boys, but I knew I'd rather be dead than spend another second in that hell-hole." He cleared his throat. "I felt the vibration even before I heard it. I thought I was hallucinating. But then I started to hear it and I knew it was real." He paused. "I looked up, and there it was, a Black Hawk. We were being shot at and running for our lives, but when I saw it, I knew we were saved."

My heart was pounding in my chest now, torn between the terror that my husband had nearly died and the swelling pride that God had saved him. I knew there had to be a great purpose behind that moment. Adam was here for a reason.

"They saved me, Sloane. They saved us all. I wouldn't be here." He rubbed his chin and kind of half smiled. "Those guys from the 160th and Delta Force are such badasses."

I laughed. "They have great hair, too." Members of Delta Force needed to blend in with their surroundings and, as such, generally had longer hair and beards. They stuck out like sore thumbs when compared to the clean-shaven faces and clipped heads on post. "I should make them cookies."

He looked up at me and really smiled now, and it was as if the filter of those negative memories was washed away and he was seeing me with fresh eyes. I leaned down and kissed him, remembering how he used to sweep me up in his arms and carry me up the stairs. I considered that that was a thing of the past. But life is one big series of surprises, inconveniences, and things not working out like you thought they would. And so, we press on. We choose to fight into another day. That's what Adam and I would do.

"I love you," he said. "Have I said that? I love you so much. You kept me alive, Sloane. I fought through every day for you."

I nodded. "I love you too. I can't believe you're here." I paused, and I could feel the tears in my throat. "But you're going to leave again. You're going to be deployed again and leave me."

He tucked my hair behind my ears and shook his head. "Babe, this leg healed enough on its own that I can hobble on it. But even after the surgery, I will never be able to be back out in the field."

"I shouldn't be happy about that," I said, feeling terribly guilty. I didn't want my husband to have a terrible injury that would never heal just to have him stay home with me. But, truthfully, I'd take it. "I'm really sorry."

Then there was silence.

I was used to this; I remembered it well. After a deployment, it took a few weeks for Adam and me to get back in our groove. He didn't want to talk about where he'd been or what had happened. I didn't want to talk about anything else, because nothing would possibly compare to what he was dealing with. I understood he was trying to protect me, and in some ways, was grateful for what he didn't say. I couldn't imagine how I would feel if I knew what he had been through when he was gone. But there was no doubt that his other life I knew nothing about created a bit of distance between us.

Eventually, as the days wore on, we would fall back into our rhythm. He would wake up early and work out before the kids got up. We would all have breakfast together. These small moments would weave themselves together in the way of a beautiful yet simple tapestry.

Today I said, "Caroline and James bought a house in

Peachtree while you were away. She said we can live there as long as we'd like."

Adam smiled and shook his head. "Sloane, we can't live in their house."

I understood where he was coming from. But, in my eyes, it wasn't even a question. Caroline was my sister. I had always thought of what was mine as ours. Emerson's, Caroline's, and mine. We were as good as the same person. Granted, Caroline had a lot more to give than I did. But that didn't mean that, in her heart, she felt any differently.

"She's going to move over with the kids and Emerson into Mom's guesthouse. James has to go back to the city, but she wants to stay in Peachtree a little longer."

Adam nodded. Then he wrapped his arms around me and held me there for a long time.

I finally got the nerve to whisper, "Tom?"

"He made it," Adam whispered back. "I don't know if they will be able to save his left arm, but he made it."

I was dually sad and relieved. I couldn't wait to call Mary-anne.

Adam cleared his throat. "So fill me in," he said. "What's been happening since I've been gone?"

"Oh, nothing much," I said, fluffing his pillow. "Just the usual. James had an affair and was on TV with his girlfriend, who Emmy then played in a movie. She is back together with her high school boyfriend and may have aplastic anemia or something equally as horrible, but Mom doesn't know. Mom is back together with her first love. Grammy died . . ."

With a very straight face, Adam nodded and said, "You're right. Nothing out of the ordinary."

Then we both laughed with everything we had inside of us, with the happiness that Adam was home, the knowledge that our little world was coming back together, and the elation that we were us again.

I thought about all I had to catch Adam up on. It was time to come clean about the credit cards, brag a little about my paintings, and tell him about Mother's Morning Out. But there would be time for that. Thankfully, joyfully, there would be time.

———

TEN DAYS LATER, WE were settling into a routine. Caroline and James's house had been the perfect place to come home to. Adam was undergoing physical therapy and struggling, not just physically, but mentally. But I had been prepared for this.

Even so, it terrified me when Adam woke up in the middle of the night ranting that he had to go back there and get his men. He cried almost daily for the friend he'd lost, lamented that he was the leader, that he should have been the one that died. There were times when I noticed the dullness in his eyes, the pain behind them, the haunted look.

It scared me, but it made me strong, too. As they had always been, Adam's problems were my problems. We were married. After what I had been through over the past few months, I could handle being in charge now. I could take care of Adam. And, amidst the pain and suffering, there were still moments of normalcy between us, and better yet, glimpses of the great love we had always shared.

As I served breakfast that morning, Adam already sitting at the head of the table, he scooped me into his lap and kissed me. "It's strange," he said, "how one minute I can feel like everything is completely meaningless, how all that matters is what's over there, and how this life we lead is so trite and so insignificant. And then, the next moment, I see you and think everything that matters is these small things, these eggs and strawberries, the stories we read to the boys."

I smiled at him. I didn't understand. I never would. But I tried and would continue to.

It wasn't the perfectly choreographed moment I had planned, but it somehow felt right.

"Adam," I said, "speaking of the meaning of life . . ." I paused, kissed him, and added, "What would you think about my going back to work, showing my art, and continuing to help Mom at the store?" He didn't say anything, so I kept going. "I mean, I know I'm an Army wife and my role is to take care of my family—"

Adam cut me off. He pulled me closer. "Sloane. You're not just an Army wife. You are *my* wife. You are the most perfect woman in the world. Your role is what makes you happy. Nothing more, nothing less."

"Yeah?" I asked, swallowing hard.

He looked at me almost sadly, as though I had underestimated him in some way. "Babe, yes. Of course. I miss your art. Nothing would make me happier than to see you go back to it."

"Really?" I could feel the tears in my eyes, and it wasn't until I felt them that I realized how much this truly meant to me.

Adam wiped my tears and laughed. "Sloane, are you serious?" He shifted. "I want you to be you. I fell in love with you and all your complexity. My favorite thing about you is how you keep surprising me."

As the boys ran to the table, I thought my heart would burst. "Bacon!" AJ practically sang. The boys were beside themselves to have their daddy home. I stood up just in time for Taylor and AJ to crash into Adam, and there was no other way to describe it: life was as it should be. Life was perfect.

Well, perfect except we were still waiting for test results from Emerson's New York doctor's visit. We were still waiting to find out what exactly was wrong with her. The fact that Mom still didn't know anything about her illness gnawed at me, perhaps more than it should have. But I couldn't imagine something being wrong with one of my children and having everyone keep that from me.

Later that morning, Mom came to get the boys for a little Gransley time, and Adam's physical therapist arrived. I was attempting to fold laundry and trying to ignore my husband's pained groans and muffled screams.

Afterward, Adam lay down for a nap—he was still regaining his strength slowly, day by day. I sat down to open the mail and pay the bills, but the way the sun was glinting off the water inspired me so much that I couldn't concentrate. I had to paint. It felt more satisfying than it had in some time. This was a piece that would make someone else happy. This was a painting I would sell.

Two hours later, I walked back into Mom's house, which was buzzing with activity. Mom was in the kitchen making snacks, Vivi, who was home from camp, was helping AJ with a particularly intensive car-building project, and Taylor was napping upstairs in his old room. It was a calm yet electric time.

I hugged Caroline, who was flipping through product photos on her computer, shopping for Mom's store. "It is beyond sweet of you to let us stay at your house. We can never repay you."

Caroline and I both looked at Mom. She rolled her eyes. "Yes, yes," she said. "What a gift that someone would just take you in off the street." We all laughed.

Caroline put her arm around Mom. "I missed Mommy Dearest's guesthouse. It's quite fabulous. I'm happy to be living there again." She paused and whispered, so Vivi couldn't hear, "And you won't believe it, but I kind of miss James."

Mom whispered, "So do I."

We all laughed.

Jack walked through the door and kissed Mom on the cheek. We all made gagging noises, but really, it was sweet. She was so starry-eyed over him that she could hardly put one foot in front of the other.

"I'm glad you're here, Jack," I said. "The painters finished, and Caroline and I volunteered to put your house back together for our darling mother."

"You two are peaches," she said, grinning. "Have I told you what they are making me pay them per hour?" she asked Jack, eyebrow raised.

"I'll help you move the furniture," Jack said.

I put my hand up to stop him. I needed Caroline to myself to talk about the thing that had been gnawing at me for almost two weeks. "No, no. It's all on sliders." I paused and said, "Plus, that hourly rate thing."

As we closed the back door, Caroline said, "What's going on?"

I bit my lip. "I've been thinking about some things, and I want your opinion."

She nodded, and I realized she was wearing six-inch wedges. She might not have been the best choice for furniture moving. "You know the man on the beach that day? Who was fighting with Mom?" I asked.

"You mean when we were kids?"

I nodded.

"Yeah," she said. "What about it?"

"It was Jack."

Caroline stopped cold between the two houses. "Keep walking," I scolded. "You'll look suspicious."

I opened the back door and Caroline said, "How do you know that?"

I shrugged. "I have such a clear memory of it. When Mom and Jack were on the plane, the light hit his hair a certain way. Then it dawned on me it was him."

Caroline nodded. I was shocked that she didn't argue with

me, but she probably knew I wouldn't bring this up unless I was sure. "OK. So what does that mean? What would Mom and Jack possibly have been fighting about on a beach when we were little girls?" She gasped. "You don't think they were having an affair or something, do you?"

I shook my head. "Don't be ridiculous. Mom would never do something like that."

Caroline scrunched up her face. "Yeah. She's pretty vanilla. So what, then?"

"That's what I've been trying to figure out," I said. "So, a few weeks ago, I was in the store, and I said something about getting my artistic talent from my father and Jack said, 'No. You definitely got that from your mother.'"

Caroline opened Jack's refrigerator, removing a Smart-Water and handing me one too. "So what? He was complimenting Mom."

"We just eat out of Jack's fridge now too?" I asked.

"Why not?" Caroline said. "At the rate things are moving between them, I think it's safe to say he's our almost-daddy." Then she dropped her water on the floor, her hand frozen in midair. "You think Jack said that because he's our sperm donor and he knows he doesn't have any artistic talent?"

She leaned over and picked up the bottle, not even the slightest bend in her knees. I was so envious. I could barely touch my shins.

"I mean, it's kind of a stretch." I shrugged. "I don't know. I'm just wondering."

"And she didn't want to date him." Caroline nodded her

head furiously. Then she swallowed and said, "And you over-heard her telling him she had so much to lose if they were to-gether?"

"We are a lot to lose," I said. My head was spinning now. I felt totally sure Caroline was going to talk me out of this and tell me I was insane. Then I could put this out of my mind as a series of odd coincidences. But now that Caroline thought what I thought . . . My mind was racing. What did this mean?

"Do you honestly think he's our father?"

She walked into the living room, where all the furniture was covered with sheets and pushed to the center of the room. "Let's get this moved."

"Oh, right," I said. Then I added, "How would we feel about it?"

"I feel kind of weird," Caroline said. "Although strangely better than if my father was a random test tube, which is how I've always imagined it. How do you feel?"

"I don't know. Maybe we're just trying to come to terms with Mom dating again, a new man being in her life, so we're projecting all these feelings onto him?"

I nodded, gesturing to a large secretary that had to be moved, thankful it was on sliders. Caroline obviously didn't know that because as I started sliding, she started lifting. Three drawers rushed out of their slots and crashed onto the floor, their contents dispersing wildly throughout the room. "Nice," I said. "One priceless antique, totally ruined."

Caroline pulled the sheet off and said, "This thing made it

over on a ship from England like two hundred years ago. Surely it can take a little bump."

I knelt down to pick up the drawers and stopped cold. Heat rose through my body. Caroline wasn't moving either. She was flipping through a stack of pictures in her hand.

But when she looked up at me and what I had in my hands, she gasped.

She handed me the pictures, and I handed her the bag. Tears sprung to my eyes, but I wasn't sure why. The pictures were of us. Caroline and me and then Caroline, Emerson, and me. Each had the date on the back in Mom's handwriting.

"They could be Christmas card pictures?" I said hesitantly, knowing they weren't Christmas card pictures. "Maybe he's really organized about them?"

She opened the pink bag that had our monograms on it and handed me a fairy stone. I looked up at my sister and I thought of Grandpop and his words of encouragement to us that day. "I guess he needed them more than we did," I whispered.

The door slammed shut, and Caroline and I got the photos and stones put away just as Jack appeared in the doorway. As if he were reading our energy, Jack seemed flustered. "Everything OK?" he asked.

I looked at Caroline, and she looked at me, but neither of us said a word. I could feel the heat in my face and my racing heart. Could Jack be our father? I couldn't ask. The look on Caroline's face told me she couldn't either.

I looked at her again, helplessly, urging her without words

to take control like she always did. I could sense Jack was about to say something when I heard, from the backyard, "Sloane! Caroline! Come quick!"

I wasn't sure I could make my feet move, but when Caroline grabbed my hand, I did.

"Do you think?" I asked her when we were back outside in the yard.

She shrugged. "I mean, I don't know. Let's not read too much into this, OK?"

All these years I had wondered who my biological father was, but now that the truth was potentially right in front of me, I wasn't sure I was ready for it.

As we reached the front porch, I looked out over the sparkling water, the sun setting hot and vibrant, warming our little patch of earth.

Emerson looked as if she were about to burst wide open as she called, "Mom! Hurry up! Get out here."

I looked at Caroline again, and I wondered if we had done the wrong thing in walking away, if we should have stayed and learned the truth.

But maybe it didn't matter. What would it change, really?

I wondered again if we should have asked Jack about our suspicions. I felt in my heart that he wouldn't lie to us. I felt in my heart that we were connected more deeply than our brief encounters would allow. And I had to admit that connection, that voice in my head that recognized that I relied on and trusted Jack far more than was reasonable, was something I had been ignoring for a long time.

Caroline squeezed my hand, and I wondered if she felt that with Jack too. I squeezed back, but I didn't say a thing.

And I realized when it comes to matters of the heart, when it comes to love, no matter what form that takes, sometimes there really are no words. Sometimes, the right answer, the only answer—the truth—is something you have to feel.

THIRTY-EIGHT

the beauty of the silence

ansley

For one of the first times in months, I was blessedly, silently all alone. Emerson had gone out with Mark, Caroline and Sloane were next door moving Jack's furniture, and he had gone over to see if he could help. I sat down in one of the Louis ghost chairs around the antique wood dining room table in front of the "orchard," as we had affectionately nicknamed the spot where all our Macs generally ended up every day.

I sat down to check my email, and Biscuit jumped in my lap. "Hi there, little girl," I said, scratching behind her ears. "I think we made it. I think we're all going to be OK."

I'm not sure if dogs can smile, but I'm pretty sure she did.

I clicked on my in-box, absentmindedly deleting emails from Moda Operandi, Vogue.com, Jetsetter. *How did I get signed up for all these email lists?* I paused my cursor over one labeled "test results." I almost deleted it, assuming it was spam. But I clicked instead.

> *Dear Emerson:*
>
> *I have received your test results, and I'd like to set up a phone call to discuss. If you would prefer, I can see you in the office, but I believe you were flying back to Georgia when I saw you last. Please call the office to schedule.*
>
> *My best,*
>
> *Dr. Douglas Thomas*
>
> *Park Avenue Hematology & Oncology*

I WAS PARALYZED BY panic. This was not, in fact, my MacBook Pro. It was Emerson's. And something was seriously wrong with my child. Oncology? Dear Lord, did she have cancer?

I was about to begin a full spiral when I realized I could just ask her, which was what I was about to do when I heard Emerson calling Sloane and Caroline. And then I heard her calling me. I stormed outside, about to give her a piece of my mind, but when I opened the door, Biscuit under my arm, I sensed this wasn't the right moment. Emerson was standing to the right of the doorway, Mark's arm around her. They were both grinning like they used to when they found out they were getting a hurricane day off from school. Caroline and Sloane were across from me, close enough to the steps that I wanted to pull them back so they didn't fall. Emerson squealed, "We're engaged!" holding her hand out to me, before I could launch into my interrogation.

My eyes widened. I knew she liked Mark, but engaged? Now I had an entirely new set of questions. I grabbed her hand, and said, "Oh my gosh, Emerson."

Caroline was jumping up and down, hugging Mark, and Sloane was smiling at me, her face mirroring the shock I felt. But, I reasoned, Mark and Emerson had known each other their entire lives. If they wanted to marry each other, then nothing could thrill me more. A tingle of glee that maybe Emerson would move to Peachtree Bluff with Mark started in the tips of my toes.

Jack walked out his front door, and I smiled, realizing that I might get to have this moment with him. I smiled because I could finally admit I might like to have this moment with him.

There were so many questions, but I couldn't ask them. I gazed at Emerson's jubilant face; she didn't look sick. She couldn't be sick. There had to be a simple explanation for her doctor visit. I had struggled with low iron in my twenties. It was probably nothing more than that.

I looked out at Starlite Island, as if I could will my late parents to help me and give us all a moment of calm.

As the water rushed by, making its way to another part of the world, I suddenly realized what a tiny part I was in the grand scheme of a greater whole. And I had a thought that soothed me: we are all destined to be forgotten. Maybe not the one percent of the one percent who do something earth-shaking like discovering electricity or becoming queen. But the rest of us will be gone and, by the time our children are gone and most certainly our grandchildren, no one will remember we even existed.

I looked over at Starlite Island again, and I didn't feel that pang in my gut, that devastation around my heart, with the remembrance that my parents were gone. Instead, I looked across into the dusky night, where the moon was beginning to rise on my favorite fragment of the world. And, despite the turmoil swirling in my mind, I felt at peace.

The girls, who were chattering and squealing, ran inside as Jack walked out the front door and, wordlessly, squeezed my shoulders. He pulled me closer to him, protectively. I was grateful for a man who understood my quiet, who knew when all I needed was his presence beside me.

As I watched the wild horses graze, I realized maybe it didn't matter that we were all destined to be forgotten. Maybe all that mattered was what we did while we were here, how well we lived, how much we loved, how hard we tried with all our might to care for the ones around us. I turned to kiss Jack. Instead of living for tomorrow and worrying what the future would hold, I had to live for today.

I would never discover the telephone, create a masterpiece that would change the world, or write a piece of legislation that would be remembered for years to come. But I would love my family and fight for them until the day I died. I may not be put in some hall of great women, but that was my purpose in life. And tonight, with the man I had loved for a lifetime beside me and the breeze in my favorite place in the world rustling in the trees, that was good enough for me.

As he held me close, my heart beating in time to his, I knew that whenever we decided to tell the girls Jack was their father, they might not understand. It would probably take time for them to adjust to this new reality. I wasn't even sure what I would say. But sometimes the words don't matter, I realized as I stood with Jack, as he stood with me, saying nothing but telling me everything I would ever need to know.

I thought of my parents again, finally resting across the water from me, of the seeds on Kimmy's farm sprouting in the darkness, of my grandchildren sleeping upstairs.

And I knew for sure that, sometimes, the truest things in life, the ones that mean the most, can't be explained in words.

It reassured me to remember that, oh so often, the truth is found in the beauty of the silence.

acknowledgments

I have always been in awe of the sacrifices soldiers make and of the ways in which those left behind carry on while they are away. Writing this book, envisioning what it must be like for a military wife to continue on with her life during the worst of the worst, and hearing stories from actual military wives along the way, was one of the most gratifying parts of writing this novel. I want to thank all the members of our armed forces and their spouses, first and foremost, for the sacrifices you make for our safety. This story is out of my imagination and any mistakes are mine and mine alone, but I have to thank my friend Army Brigadier General and author A.J. Tata for talking me through some of the finer points of military life.

Lauren McKenna, I think you are perhaps the finest editor

in all the world. Thank you for your time and attention to this novel and for your help in making my first series as strong as it could possibly be. Sara Quaranta, Marla Daniels, Abby Zidle, Jen Long, Jen Bergstrom, Diana Velasquez, Theresa Dooley, Michelle Podberezniak, and everyone at Gallery Books, thank you for all you have done to make this novel come to life. I've never been more convinced that launching a book is like raising a child: It takes a village.

Kathie Bennett, thank you for your vision for my career and your determination to make it happen. You have made me believe in myself. Susie Zerenda, thank you for sharing the gift of your words and for tirelessly touting my novels.

Bob Diforio, thank you for shepherding this book into the world and for your advice, support, and guidance.

I am eternally grateful to the bloggers, reporters, reviewers, and book angels in my life. There are too many to name here, but Jenny O'Regan, I wanted to give you a special thank-you. You were the very first person to email me to ask to help when news of my first novel broke, and that did and still does mean everything to me. Deirdre Parker Smith, not only did you guide me through my very first newspaper internship, but you have been such a cheerleader for me and have gone above and beyond at every turn. Stephanie Gray, Jessica Sorentino, and Stacey Armand, it is new bookish friends like you that keep this journey fresh and fun. Nicole McManus, from My Sister's Books to Aries Girl to *Sasee*, you have given my books so much love wherever you go, and I am grateful. Andrea Katz, thanks for your listening ear, your good advice, and for generally being a rock star. Kristy Barrett, you are always a ray of sunshine right when I need one. And Susan Roberts, Susan Walters Peterson, and Jenny Belk, you were my first early readers and remain some of my most supportive. I wouldn't be here without you.

My design blogger girls, there are too many of you to name here, but, literally, you launched my career. Hands down. Thank you for your enthusiasm, your support, and for sharing your readers and your corners of the internet with me year after year. I love you all so much and am in awe of your generosity!

From the time I was a little girl, independent bookstores have been some of my favorite places on earth, and I have to thank all of them around the country, especially the SIBA stores, for being such cheerleaders for me. South Main Book Co., The Country Bookshop, Litchfield Books, Buxton Books, Fiction Addiction, Dee Gees, Park Road Books, The Bookshelf, BookTowne, FoxTale, Books Unlimited, Downtown Books, Duck's Cottage, and Avid Book Shop, thank you for making the Southern Charm tour such a huge success. The Pat Conroy Center and East Carolina University, thanks for launching this one. It is such an honor for me to be a part of all the good you do!

Beaufort Linen Company and Neuse Sports Shop, thank you for being the most amazing booksellers in towns where we, sadly, don't have a bookstore. You guys rock!

acknowledgments

Sabina Hitchen, I've said it before and I'll say it again: You're a big handful of brilliant glitter and your enthusiasm and wonderful ideas are always just what I need!

Macie Flynn, thank you for all your help this year with a million different things. I can't wait to see what you do next!

Tamara Welch, you are one of those book angels I was talking about, and I don't know what I would do without you! Thank you for sharing your gifts and talents with me.

It isn't often that we get to meet our heroes in real-life and even less often that they become our friends. Mary Alice Monroe, I am so honored to count you among mine, and I can't thank you enough for your beautiful endorsement of this book.

My Tall Poppy Writer friends, I hope you know this, but each and every one of you makes this experience so much fun. I am so blessed to have you!

I absolutely could not do what I do without my family. Thank you to my parents, Beth and Paul Woodson, for always believing in me and for making my life easy and picking up the slack so I can do what I love, especially during my tour. Big, huge thank-you to my husband, Will, and my son, Will, for being so supportive of my very big dreams and for being with me from the first word to the final edit on each and every novel. I love you all so much.

It is beginning to sink in that this is my fourth novel, that only four years ago I was hoping and praying that I would get to see just one book in print. I have to thank you, the reader acknowledgments

who holds this book, for helping to make my dreams come true, for telling your friends and writing reviews, for hosting and coming to my events . . . I am here today because of you, and, even though we may not have ever met, I count you as one of the people I am most grateful for every day.

the secret *to* southern charm

THE PEACHTREE BLUFF SERIES #2

Kristy Woodson Harvey

This readers group guide for *The Secret to Southern Charm* includes an introduction, discussion questions, and ideas for enhancing your book club. The suggested questions are intended to help your reading group find new and interesting angles and topics for your discussion. We hope that these ideas will enrich your conversation and increase your enjoyment of the book.

introduction

When Sloane Murphy hears that her husband, Adam, is MIA, she breaks down. Thankfully, she finds herself in the care of her sisters, mother, and grandmother in her family's home in Peachtree Bluff, Georgia, where the sky is blue, the breeze is fresh, but naturally—nothing is ever as simple as it seems. Sloane must learn how to pick herself up and out of bed, be the mother she needs to be for her two sons, and prepare to pick up the pieces in case Adam never returns. Meanwhile, her mother Ansley's affections with her teenage sweetheart grow more complicated when he forces himself into her life in an unexpected way. There's never a dull moment in the Murphy household, and book two in the Peachtree Bluff series proves it!

topics & questions
for discussion

1. There are three generations of mothers, and likewise, many styles of parenting in this novel. Discuss the different relationships that exist and consider the relationship between Sloane and Ansley or Sloane and her grandmother, and how Sloane and Caroline view parenting.

2. Discuss the title *The Secret to Southern Charm*. Secrets abound in the novel: Sloane neglects to tell Adam she uses an IUD and doesn't truly want kids; Jack is Sloane and Caroline's father, yet Ansley won't tell them; Ansley's early financial woes that her daughters know nothing about; and Grammy's decision to hide her illness from the family. Discuss what other secrets exist and how they impact the characters in their own ways.

3. "Grammy had said earlier that the accent was the secret to Southern charm. But she was wrong. This putting on a brave face, carrying on, helping others, being kind and humble and giving, believing with all your heart that the world could be a better place and that you could make it that way . . . that was Southern charm. Looking around at these women who embodied those qualities so well, I had to think that maybe Grammy was wrong. Maybe it wasn't a secret at all" (page 240). How do you interpret the title and Grammy's thoughts on what the secret of Southern charm is? After reading the book, do you think this is what Southern charm is about? Why, or why not?

4. Ansley mentions her longstanding desire to decorate the home next to hers. When her new neighbor ends up being her former lover, Jack, she offers her service to him. How does this decision play out for Ansley? Do you think it was wise for her to pitch to Jack? Why, or why not?

5. Sloane describes her marriage to Adam as love at first sight. Do you agree with Ansley that their engagement moved quickly? Do you think this intensity so early on in their relationship creates any sort of bond for their future? Why, or why not?

6. Take a moment to think about the different women in the novel. What does it mean to be a mother, a daughter, a

sister, or a wife in the book? Discuss how the relationships are different or similar. Is Ansley the same type of mother her own mother was? Is Sloane like Ansley? How would you describe Sloane and Caroline's relationship versus Sloane and Emerson's? Lastly, discuss the difference in marriages that exist: Sloane and Adam versus Caroline and James. Recall Caroline's story from *Slightly South of Simple* to help with this discussion.

7. "Sometimes being a mother isn't about having to fix it. Sometimes, the best thing a mother can be is there at all" (page 13). Discuss this quote in the context of Ansley's treatment of Sloane in the first half of the book versus her own mother's "help" in her own time of need. Do you agree with their behaviors and decisions? Do you relate to either relationship?

8. The concept of a home versus a house is an underlying theme in the book. Discuss how the family home in Peachtree Bluff is a home rather than a house.

9. On page 181, Grammy says to Sloane, "I'm going to say this. I love you, Sloane. You're a beautiful, talented, artistic bright light. It has bothered me for years that once you married Adam, you became this . . . 'Stepford wife.' " Based on what you've read about Sloane's marriage and her life after it, do you agree with her grandmother? Why, or why not?

10. "I've always been very good at being numb. I'm the doer, the fixer, the one to take charge. It keeps my mind off of what is actually happening so I don't have to face the sadness" (page 199). What does Ansley mean by this thought? Do you think she hides from her feelings in the book? If so, in what ways? In which circumstances?

11. Take a moment to reflect on the events in *Slightly South of Simple*, the first book set in Peachtree Bluff. Although it is focused on Caroline's experience, would you say the characters have changed at all in *The Secret to Southern Charm*? How so?

12. There are a lot of thoughts on memories in the book, either in creating new ones (Grammy's desire to take a trip to Starlite Island) or reminiscing on the past (Ansley's early years with Jack). How do the characters preserve memories or describe important moments? What would you hope your family would remember about you on your last day?

13. Which of the characters do you relate to the most? Is it helpful to read new points of view in each Peachtree Bluff novel to understand the Murphy family? Can you make any predictions for what comes for the Murphys or Emerson?

14. Sloane describes their life on the army base in a few chapters. Do you have any familiarity with living on an

army base or have you had friends/family who have done so? What do you imagine it would be like? Have you had friends or family who have married military personnel? In what ways do you think their lives are similar to Sloane's?

enhance your book club

1. For your next book, consider reading a memoir about being an army wife such as *Unremarried Widow* by Artis Henderson. Do you see similarities in Sloane's and Artis's stories?

2. If you live near a lake or a waterfront, consider taking a tour of the area on a sailboat as the sisters do to drop Vivi off at camp.

3. As a group, go to your local painting party shop. Try your hand at some conceptual art as Sloane does or try a paint by numbers-style class.

4. Connect with Kristy Woodson Harvey on Facebook, Twitter, and visit her official website at: KristyWoodson Harvey.com. Consider inviting her to Skype in with your book club.